The Curse of
Snow Falls

You've heard the story in *People, Rolling Stone,* and the *New York Daily News....* Now read the book!

> *"Author Stephen King is giving back by donating thousands of dollars to ... Farwell Elementary School ... so the students in its Author Studies Program can publish two books. [The students] mapped out character development, plot, and overall story line with the help of another Maine author. The result is two books — an original and a sequel." — CNN*

You are about the read the sequel. Be sure not to miss the original, *Fletcher McKenzie and the Passage to Whole.*

FLETCHER McKENZIE
AND
The Curse of Snow Falls

GARY SAVAGE

**and students in the Farwell Elementary School
Author Studies Program**

KINGSLEY BOOKS
NASHVILLE, TENNESSEE

Fletcher McKenzie

And the Curse of Snow Falls

Copyright © 2021 by Gary Savage

Fletcher McKenzie and the Curse of Snow Falls is the second book in
the adventures of Fletcher McKenzie, a boy living in Maine. The
first book is *Fletcher McKenzie and the Passage to Whole.*

Contributing authors: Wyatt Tarr, Rebecca Jacques, Audrey Bilodeau, Annora Johnson,
and Miriam LeMay. All these students participated in the Author Studies Program at
Farwell Elementary School in Lewiston, Maine. These students wonderfully created
Lalia and her cat, Humeante. Both are important and vibrant characters in this book.

Published in Nashville, Tennessee, by Kingsley Books,
Inc., P.O. Box 121584, Nashville, TN 37212

ISBN: 978-0-9888923-6-1 (paperback)
ISBN: 978-0-9888923-7-8 (ebook)

Cover painting by Frank Victoria

Cover design and typesetting by Bill Kersey, KerseyGraphics, Nashville, Tennessee

Printed in the United States of America

AUTHOR'S NOTE

FLETCHER MCKENZIE AND THE CURSE OF SNOW FALLS IS A WORK OF FICTION. The author has combined historical nonfictional events and people with fictional ones. Mollyockett, Tomhegan and Pidianiski are all historical Maine figures.

Mollyockett did place a curse on the small village of Snow Falls, Maine, after being turned away during a violent blizzard. She traveled to Paris Hill where Dr. Hamlin gave her shelter even though his infant son was near death. Mollyockett helped nurse the baby back to health and blessed him before she departed the home several days later. The baby's name was Hannibal Hamlin, and he went on to become a member of the U.S. House of Representatives, a United States Senator, governor of Maine, and the first vice president of the United States under President Abraham Lincoln.

The legend has it that Captain Jonathan Snow was massacred by the Saint Frances Indians of Quebec at Snow Falls in 1755. The falls were named after Captain Snow, and there is a plaque at the side of Route 26 honoring him. A retaliation raid on their mission by the English killed most of the ladies, babies and elderly Native American Indians living there.

Tomhegan actually traveled from Lake Umbegog in Oxford County, Maine, and attempted to raid Bethel (Sudbury Canada back then) and kill Colonel Clark from Boston who was currently living there in 1781. His plans were thwarted after Mollyockett warned them of his plan.

Bethel, Maine, holds a Mollyockett Day celebration every third Saturday in July.

Ollantaytambo is an actual village in the Sacred Valley of South Peru, located on the edge of the Urabamba River below snow-capped mountains. It is known for the Ollantaytambo ruins, a massive Inca fortress with large stone terraces on a steep hillside. Major sites within the complex include the huge Sun Temple and the Princess Baths Fountain. The village's old town is an Inca-era grid of cobblestones streets high in the South American mountains. Elevation: 9,160'

CHAPTER 1

TEMPEST OF NUKPANA

Two men stepped outside the barn and walked in step on the cold, moonlit path. For a few minutes they said nothing. Their rusty gas lanterns swung in their hands as they strode towards the sound of moving water. They stepped over a huge granite block that had been part of an old lumber mill, which had been shuttered more than two centuries ago. Suddenly, they stopped and listened intently to the sound of a small animal scurrying from the thick underbrush adjacent to the path. Content they weren't being followed they quietly turned the metal dials on their lanterns to turn off the flames. Secrecy was paramount. The moon illuminated their faces as they faced each other.

"I can't believe it's actually time. From what you told me—"

"I know. Seems like a lifetime," replied Chesley Snow, the older of the two. Holding his lantern up, he pointed towards a small narrow path that was slightly hidden by a thick clump of bushes.

A swift stream of water flowed over the granite lip of the river and crashed angrily into a pool of dark water. The moonlight illuminated white bubbles swirling on top of the famous watering spot in western Maine. The men's canvas coats rubbed on an old log rail as they bent over and searched with their eyes.

"I thought you said we'd be able to see a change," said Croft, his muscular features moving in and out of the dim light as clouds blocked the moon's glow. "I mean, it looks just like it did earlier today."

"Have faith," Chesley replied. "I was told it'd be tonight."

"By whom?"

"That's not important. Just be glad I asked you to join me."

"I'm still confused."

Chesley nodded but did not respond. He pulled on the arm of his heavy canvas coat and quickly pushed a small button on his watch. "We're still a few minutes early," he said lowly.

"Maybe we should walk down to the bottom of the falls if it's *under* like you said," said Croft. "Nothing about this feels right. Are you positive?"

"I said stop," Chesley snapped. "They just said to go to the falls."

"Well I say we go to the bottom."

Again, Chesley, said nothing. His gaze had wandered over the precipice and towards a large boulder sitting in the middle of the small river. He heard a muffled sound of movement in the bushes to his right. Instinctively both men reached for sharp knives tucked into their leather belts.

"Shhhh," Croft whispered, pointing towards where he thought the movement had emanated from. Just before they made a move a startled squirrel scampered quickly towards some old railroad tracks at the base of a small wooded hill.

"Maybe you're right. It's got to be the bottom of the falls," conceded Chesley as he tucked his knife back into his waist. "It only makes sense." Few a few seconds they stood still and looked at the falling water. "Just be quiet and follow me. The frost on those wet leaves is nothing to fool with," Chesley whispered. "The last thing we need right now is an accident. And trust me. If that happens, I'm leaving you behind. There's too much at stake."

"Okay, Chesley," Croft whispered in a low, unsteady voice. "I'm starting to wonder if I should've come."

"Trust me, you'll be glad I brought you," said Chesley, pointing towards the opening of a precipitous downward path. He carefully stepped onto a granite footing covered with brown leaves. Croft watched him closely then waited for his shadow to disappear before following his steps. Neither man said a word as they navigated the slippery trail to the bottom of the falls. Chesley looked around at the misty darkness when he reached the pebbly beach, as if hoping there would be someone waiting for them to arrive.

"You're sure it's tonight?" Croft mumbled as he stood beside Chesley.
"Positive. Don't ask me again."

The spray from the waterfall made the already cold night even colder. The steep granite walls of the canyon also blocked most of the light the moon had to offer.

Everything that was happening was like reliving an old reoccurring nightmare. For a brief second, Chesley stared at the base of the falls trying to decipher if there was anything behind the misty cloud as an eerie feeling of *déjà vu* swallowed his mind.

"I think I heard something," whispered Croft, jerking Chesley back to reality. "Listen."

The elder man closed his eyes for a moment or two and quietly focused on the sound of the water directly in front of him. He had grown up a Snow and was extremely proud to represent his family who had suffered for generations under the curse. The story had been passed down with the knowledge that one day there would be a moment that would belong to them. Little did they know *that moment* would take nearly two hundred years. Two centuries of suffering at the hands of an Indian doctress who had no business interfering with their little community. Now, the moment of revenge had arrived.

The very thought this was happening was mind boggling to Chesley, as though he were actually living a dream at that very moment.

"You're right, I hear something too," he whispered back. "I hope—"

His words were cut off by the loud scraping of rocks slowly moving. Croft stepped backward and fell behind Chesley.

Chesley closed his eyes again and considered the origin of the curse. The moment had arrived, and he needed to be brave. He was now the protector of all the Snow ancestors who had waited anxiously for this very moment. He sensed he was being watched as he stepped closer to the water and towards the grinding sound.

"You're not going to—?"

Croft stopped mid-sentence as Chesley bent over and put his hand into the swift moving current. Croft looked around in the darkness, hoping this all was just a bad dream. He now deeply regretted accepting Chesley's offer to join him. *There's no way this is real,* he thought.

Barely five seconds passed, when a huge boulder crashed out from under the falling water and into the deep pool. Immediately, it sank to the bottom, sending a two foot high wave of water outwards and soaking their leather boots. An aged oak tree that hung precipitously on the edge of the water creaked as it slowly toppled forward into the swirling water.

"What's happening?" Croft stammered. "Is that part if it?"

Chesley stepped backwards towards higher ground. "Just as predicted. Gloriousness is now with the—"

He stopped mid-thought as the Earth suddenly shook and the slow grinding sound of rocks intensified as boulders, leaves, trees, and even fence posts fell into the water. It felt as though the entire canyon was falling down around them. Croft thrust his hand under his coat and found his hunting knife as he fell backwards onto the wet rocks A flash of white light illuminated every square inch of the river. Chesley immediately fell head first into the frigid pool of water. Quickly, he grabbed onto a large log and kicked violently towards the rocky shore.

"Run," he screamed as he pulled himself back on shore and crawled towards Croft. The cold water still hadn't stiffened his muscles.

Croft was bleeding. He felt the warm liquid moving downward and into his boots, but he had no idea where the injury was or how bad it was. Clutching his knife in his left hand, he quickly stood up and raced towards where the trail to the top of the waterfall had been. He looked around; the path was no longer there.

"Where is it?" he screamed as he turned to see where Chesley was.

"Right in front of you," yelled Chesley, limping towards him. He came to an abrupt halt. The entire hill they had just descended had completely changed. The massive boulders that had formed the sides of the canyon for thousands of years were no longer there. The moon now illuminated sharp and jagged rocks and roots jutting outward and caused the water to veer over the western side of the canyon. The entire shape of the falls was dramatically altered.

"What the?" Chesley gasped as he fell to his knees. The injury to his right leg now registered with his nerves.

"How do we get out of here?" yelled Croft over the sound of the roaring water that was cutting a new path through the newly carved canyon. He looked up and around just as the log fence they had leaned on earlier crashed over the rocks and into the dirty, roiling water beside them.

Slowly, Chesley stood and stared directly at him. "There's no way this is a coincidence," he said calmly, attempting to overcome the pain advancing through his body. *I've waited too long for this to run,* he thought. Methodically, he moved past Croft. He needed to understand exactly what had just happened. *He was a Snow, and this was his destiny,* he thought as he fixated on a large cave-like opening where the water had fallen for millennium. *That has to be it.*

"Over here," he yelled, looking back.

Croft looked at him warily. "I, um, are you sure?" he replied unsteadily.

Chesley ignored him. He couldn't blame him, but he was here for a reason. "Fine, stay here if you want to, but I'm going in. I've waited too long." To his right, he noticed one of the badly dented lanterns wedged between two large boulders. Quickly he crawled over several massive rocks, grabbed onto it and then scurried back over the boulders as quickly as possible. When he was back down where Croft stood, he reached into right pocket and grabbed the watertight container holding matches.

"Are you coming or not?" he yelled as he scraped one of the thin sticks on a dry piece of slate like rock jutting out towards the water. Quickly the lantern illuminated the entire canyon with warm light.

"You've got to be kidding me. What on earth did you get me into?" Croft responded as he slowly walked towards him. Subconsciously he hoped the canyon's collapse was just a coincidence.

"Listen, from what I've been told, it's not going to be dangerous," Chesley grunted as he grabbed onto some jagged rocks to pull himself up."

"Told by who?"

"Doesn't matter. Just be glad you're here. I know of many people who would love to be in your shoes right now."

"Well they can have it," Croft said. "I've been visiting this waterfall since I was a kid and what are the chances of *that* happening while we're here. I mean, we almost died."

"Listen, if there's an exit out of that opening up there," Chesley said, "We'll take it, okay?"

"You sure you—?"

"WHERE HAVE YOU BEEN?" a loud voice from the dark opening shouted.

Chesley and Croft froze.

Croft turned and started to run with surprising speed back over the rocks blocking his escape route.

"STOP RIGHT NOW!" boomed the voice as another flash of white light suddenly illuminated the entire crevasse.

Croft fell between two large boulders as a jet of brilliant light shot past Chelsey and directly towards him.

Still stunned, Chesley set the lantern down and held his hands in the air as a sign of surrender. "We give up," he yelled unsteadily. "We bring no trouble. Just tell us want you want."

Sensing a diversion, Croft jumped down between a large branch from a fallen oak tree and one of the boulders that had landed at the edge of the water. *All I need to do is make it to the water, and I'll swim the rapids. I'd rather drown,* he thought as he quickly plotted his escape route.

Chesley turned his head towards Croft.

A low roaring began to rise behind Chesley. Then in an instant the air was filled with a beam of scarlet light that arched over Chesley and towards the swirling water.

Croft wheeled around and screamed, "Please, I didn't—"

The light pierced his abdomen before he could finish.

"AARRGH!" he screeched as he was violently thrown into the air high over the still raging pool of water.

Chesley watched in horror as his friend jerked into a somersault just as a second beam of light shot out from the cave at warp speed.

"Croft watch out!" he boomed. He dove onto the flat rock to his right just as an eerie *pffff* sound reverberated in his ears. He kept his head down and covered his ears.

When he looked up, the air over the pool of water was filled with thousands of red embers slowly falling towards the earth and Croft was gone. He rolled over and listened to the water cutting its way through the debris. He slowly sat up. Chesley wondered for a moment if the embers were his unfortunate friend. His body appeared unscathed for the most part. He touched his face. He didn't feel any blood. He slowly stood up and then faced the cave. It was a wide, dark, and deep opening, much greater that what had been there earlier.

For fear of facing the same demise as his friend, he cautiously stepped over the rocks and debris as he approached the cave opening.

As he moved forward he recoiled when he spotted the source of the bright light that had just evaporated his friend. Standing at the edge of the hole stood a man with long dark hair that had been woven into a complex braid. His angry, black eyes bore into Chesley. Wrapped around his forehead was a leather strap decorated with dozens of tiny blue and red gems that sparkled in the moonlight and the remaining tiny red embers. Dangling from his ears were blue gems with small white feathers attached. They swayed in the slight breeze although the man's head remained motionless. He was wearing a crude leather coat and matching pants that had two rows of black-and-white porcupine quills arranged in linear patterns. In his hand, he was holding what looked like a gold staff that could have belonged to an ancient Egyptian King. Chesley fixated on his black painted fingernails.

Motionless they faced each other for what seemed like an eternity. Chesley felt as though the man's black eyes were penetrating his very thoughts. Then he spoke. "You know, the story your family passes down is wrong." Chesley stood slowly, so as not to anger him. "The curse is *not* only impacting your family, Mr. Snow." Chesley recoiled at the mention of his name from the strange man's mouth. "Do you honestly think Mollyockett was wandering through here that snowy night by chance?" the man asked. His voice was getting louder and louder as he spoke. "Let me tell you. As of tonight, things are going to be different. Finally, it's our turn."

"I want . . . I . . . um . . . I mean . . . what is it you want?" Chesley muttered, still unable to move.

"Come closer," the man commanded.

Without hesitation, Chesley picked up the lantern and walked forward, plotting his path over an army of strewn boulders and rocks. As he approached the cave's opening he did all he could to mask the fear coursing throughout his entire body. On the ground, he noticed the skeletons of dozens of individuals. Most, still clothed in old military attire. He swallowed hard and carefully stepped over one that had a gaping hole in it's skull.

"Chesley, Chesley Snow," he said holding out his right hand. The stranger remained motionless.

"What does it matter what your name is?" the man barked. "We're all made of the same thing aren't we? Or are *your* people made of something different? Something better perhaps?"

I wonder if this is Tomhegan, Chesley thought. *Nimsy's description matches him to a tee.*

"No, I'm not Tomhegan," the man yelled. He grinned as his eyes honed in on the lantern.

Chesley could not speak. He took a small step backwards. The Indian's expression did not change. His black eyes were transfixed on the rays of the lantern. "If we're giving names," he said. "They call me Nukpana. Has been long before your family *invaded* this area." He paused. "Obviously you got the timing right or you wouldn't be here right now, would you?"

"We were told that when Venus and Earth line up, the eldest Snow was to come to the falls."

"Until now, no one alive has viewed the rarest of eclipses," Nukpana said casually. "On Earth, you can rarely see Venus when it passes in front of the sun because of its orbit. Fortunately, the sun, Venus and Earth lined up today. Just as important, it coincided with the Moon of Falling Leaves *and* on the first frost of the winter. A very rare collision indeed. Seems like destiny to me . . . hmmm? We've waited for this day for a very long time and a good many of *your* ancestors would love to be where you are right now." He grinned devilishly.

Chesley wasn't quite following him, but he relaxed slightly. "Which means? I mean, how am I involved now?" He turned and looked at the spot where Croft had last stood.

"Which means there is work to be done. Follow me," Nukpana commanded. "I won't be lighting up anyone else tonight if that's what you're thinking. That is, if you do what your told."

He turned and stared directly into Chesley's eyes. "You've no idea how disposable you are."

CHAPTER 2

GRAVE CIRCUMSTANCES

FLETCHER OPENED HIS EYES AND TOOK IN THE BRIGHT SUN'S RAYS invading his room. The autumn leaves had peaked last weekend, but the view of the mountains from his bedroom was still spectacular. He'd spent the evening with his mother in her garden removing bean stakes, tomato cages, and trellises. Muriel had buried the fruits of her labor in the root cellar in the basement weeks earlier. She valued self-sufficiency and noted the importance of each vegetable to Fletcher before she covered it up with the clay-like soil. Opting to not rain on her parade, he decided not to tell her that he'd learned all she was doing in the book *Whole Abounds* he read two years earlier while in Whole. He was just thrilled she was home and safe. She'd suffered severe post-traumatic stress disorder in the months following the experience she'd endured at the hands of Tomhegan and Nimsy Cortland. He'd heard her screams at night as she suffered nightmares and flashbacks of the physical and mental trauma. She made the decision the day she was rescued by Fletcher, however, that she'd never talk about the events ever again. Everyone, including Aldous, honored her decision and supported her fully. She privately struggled through the fame she and Alek Von Piddle experienced with their *discovery* of the lost temple in the Quechuan Valley in Peru. The stunning temple and its village was immediately declared a World Heritage site. The world never learned of Fletcher's heart-pounding visit where he'd sealed the mysterious entrance to Whole that was secretly located directly under the ruins. Aldous did his best to keep the press away from Muriel and convinced Von Piddle to handle all the interviews with the international press, which he whole heartedly accepted. He relished telling stories and this topped them all by far. Muriel begrudgingly agreed to give Nimsy's eulogy at the packed memorial service where everyone in town mourned her deeply. *If only they knew the real story,* Muriel thought as she sobbed during the memorial. The tears were genuine but not for Nimsy. The fact that she had become best friends with that monster shook her to her very core. But for the sake of Fletcher, she put on her best face and strived to move forward. Her daily struggle was very real and very severe.

"Fletch, if you're going with me, you need to get up," Aldous yelled from the bottom of the stairs.

"I'm coming dad. I'll be down in a sec."

He was tired. Strangely, the brown marking on the back of his right hand felt as if it were still burning as severe as it did the night before. For over an hour, he'd lain in his bed with his eyes closed, rubbing his hand trying to sooth the pain. He hadn't fallen back asleep until after five in the morning.

Today was the annual fall festival in Mahoosuc, and the entire family was joining in the celebration on the town common after apple picking on River Road in Bethel.

"Well if you ask me, texting is just a lazy way of avoiding the time to pick up the phone and call someone," Fletcher heard his grandmother say as he entered the kitchen. "And write a letter? Land sakes, I'm convinced I'm the last person on the planet who does that."

"Mornin', Fletch."

"Hey, Grans, I'll write you a letter if you'd like. Just promise you'll not correct my spelling like you always do, okay?" He laughed as he sat down at the table. "No spell check with a pen."

"Well, if you're not going to spell it right, don't put it down on paper. Leaves a trail you know," she said laughing. "Who knows, it might end up on one of those talk shows Winola and Serena are always chirping about. She bent down and kissed the top of his head.

Fletcher laughed.

"Where's dad?"

"He said he'd be right back. He's helping your mother set up the artist tent on the common."

"I thought that went up the other day?"

"Did. It blew over during that storm two nights ago." She paused and wiped her white apron with her hand. "That's what you get when you bring out-of-staters to help you do something."

"What's that mean?"

"You know, all those Boston people coming up to see the leaves. Think they know—"

Fletcher suddenly got up and hugged her. He pulled hard to put a lot of unsaid things into his grip.

She stepped backed and looked at him closely.

"My, my, you're growing up, Fletch," she said. "And too fast if you ask me."

"Cam is on his way over so you may want to add a few more eggs to that pan," he said, ignoring her.

"Already expecting him," she said with a laugh. "I saw his father this morning at Kemos'."

The kitchen was immaculate as usual. Every surface sparkled. Copper pots and huge iron skillets hung over the granite island in the center of the kitchen. As usual, the kitchen smelled of bread baking in the oven. Lucille and Edmond, Fletcher's maternal grandparents stayed on after the *miraculous* recovery of Aldous and the *shocking* discovery of Muriel after being lost in the Quetzal rain forest with her *former* best friend Nimsy Cortland while on a Cygnus business trip. The dual events shocked the entire family to its very core and was the lead story in the local, state, and national press for weeks. The attention was unwanted by many in the peaceful Maine town. Fletcher was glad his grandparents agreed to stay on. The worst of everything was behind them, including the Coronavirus pandemic that had swept the globe at the exact time. The vaccines hadn't come soon enough for the traumatized nation.

"Can't wait to get those apples," she said while polishing the bottom of a copper pan. "Been a few months since I've baked my award-winning pie you all love."

"I was thinking of inviting Camway and Quinn over for dinner, Grans."

"Ah, more flat-landers in town," she said with a laugh. "Well just be sure you pick more of—"

Slam! The front door slammed shut followed by the sound of rapid footsteps approaching the kitchen.

"Must be your—"

"Fletch," Uncle Woodrow bellowed as he entered the kitchen. "You won't believe what happened two nights ago!"

"Ever heard of knocking," Lucille said while putting the pan down on the counter. "Everything okay, Woody?" she then asked. The seriousness on Woodrow's face spoke volumes.

"What's happened?" Fletcher asked apprehensively. It was the first time he'd seen his uncle without his periwinkle blue sweater.

"Mollyockett's grave," Woodrow replied as he opened the rolled up *Newry Tribune* and pushed it in front of him. "Here, take a look."

Fletcher immediately dropped his fork and swallowed hard. He couldn't believe his uncle had even brought up the topic of Mollyockett in front of his grandmother, who was now sitting beside him. Quickly she pulled the crumpled paper towards her to share with her grandson.

A photo of an unearthed grave with a fallen gray headstone was prominently displayed in the top section of the front page. Adjacent to the large photo was a smaller historical sketch of the very familiar Mollyockett. Fletcher immediately recognized her by the top hat on top of her head and the feathers jangling from her loopy earrings. Beneath both photos a headline read:

MOLLYOCKETT'S GRAVE VANDALIZED!
OXFORD COUNTY AUTHORITIES BAFFLED BY CRIMINAL ACT THAT EXPOSED HER FINAL RESTING PLACE!

Lucille gasped and pulled the paper closer to her. "Who on earth would—"

"No!" said Fletcher loudly.

Lucille reached into her apron and pulled out her glasses. She snatched the newspaper and began to read the two page article aloud.

"*The famous Native American doctress, who's final resting place is at Andover's Woodlawn Cemetery, is now the victim of an unthinkable crime. Immediately after arriving at work yesterday, a long-time caretaker of the cemetery knew something was wrong. Knowing that there were no funerals scheduled for the day, the mound of fresh dirt in the middle of the graveyard was deeply suspicious. He quickly discovered that the grave belonging to Mollyockett had been unearthed. Her headstone had been overturned and desecrated. Careful not to disturb anything, the caretaker immediately backed away and notified local authorities who discovered that not only had the actual grave been unearthed and disturbed but the vandals had carved two crude mysterious symbols on the back of her stone. The sheriff's office were now working with experts from the State of Maine in the hopes that the markings would help lead them to the criminals who committed this despicable act. Authorities are asking that anyone who may have been traveling down Swift River Road to—*'

"Land sakes," exclaimed Lucille. "Might as well make the poor woman die all over again," she cried. Fletcher and Woodrow looked at each other.

Woodrow immediately regretted making his serious concern known to Lucille. She was still unaware of his and Fletcher's adventure a little over two years ago which led them right to this *actual* gravesite then on to the passage that swallowed Fletcher and lead him to Whole where Mollyockett was actually waiting for him. He'd learned everything from his nephew after he shockingly returned from his adventure with his presumed-dead mother who had been missing in the Quetzal. Although Lucille found the story they'd spoon-fed her hard to believe, she didn't ask any questions. She was completely overwhelmed to have her missing daughter safely back.

"What do you think happened?" Fletcher asked, staring directly at his uncle. He glanced back at the familiar grave marker now laying on the brown grass. Yellow tape surrounded the upper half of the weathered stone.

Marie Agathe
Molly Ockett
Born 1740 – Died 1816
Last of the Pigwackets

"Dunno," replied Woodrow. Deep concern was etched on his aged face. He knew too much to know that this wasn't just the act of local vandals. It was too brazen. "What do you say we take a quick drive to the inn, Fletch. I need your help putting all that lawn furniture into the basement. You know those old bones."

"But Camway is on his way over," Lucille said, looking at both of them suspiciously. The very fact that Woodrow was not wearing his blue vest spoke volumes. "Plus, he's going apple picking with all of us. And what are you doing putting lawn furniture away during the fall festival? You've had weeks to get this done?"

"We can meet you on the common, Lucy. I really need to get that furniture tucked away safely. Never know when the first flakes will fly. Fletch can text his friend."

"Heavens to Betsy, Woody!" Lucille said, shaking her finger in his face. "I know you two are up to something, and yes, I'll cover for you." The start of a smile curled up slightly on her lips as she glared at the both of them. "We'll meet you on the common at one. Sharp, you hear me."

"You're a saint as usual, Luce."

"Let me put on my boots," Fletcher said, running towards the stairs to his bedroom.

Lucille raised a large mixing spoon up and in front of Woodrow's face. "I don't want you two traipsing all over the place like you did last time, you hear me?" She said curtly.

Woodrow didn't respond. He was just relieved that he was able to get Fletcher into his Land Rover before they'd all left for the apple orchards.

"Mind if we take two of those muffins with us," he said. "I'm famished."

"Help yourself. They're made with whole wheat. And will you do me one favor? Just keep him away from Woodlawn Cemetery with all those law enforcement people there," she whispered. "Don't want the two of you committing perjury if asked if you've been there before."

"I swear you should've worked for the Central Intelligence Agency, Luce," Woodrow said softly as he walked to the bottom of the stairs leading to the second floor.

"You never know. I just may have," she replied laughing quietly. Woodrow smiled and gave her a thumbs-up showing he'd overheard her.

On the drive to Mollyockett's final resting place Woodrow mused, I've no idea what's going on, but it's not good Fletcher."

"I know. Who would rob a grave, especially hers."

"Fletch, that's just the half of it," Woodrow replied gravely while gazing at Fletcher out the side of his eye.

"Meaning what?" Fletcher asked as they drove through the small town of Hanover.

"Snow Falls," said Woodrow. "Snow Falls."

Fletcher turned and stared directly at his uncle. "Exactly what does that mean?"

"Remember when we promised to share everything with each other, Fletch?"

"How could I forget? But what's Snow Falls got to do with what's just happened to Mollyockett's grave being robbed?"

"It may not be robbery," he said and then paused. "Hopefully we can get some clues from Mr. Walton when we see him at the cemetery. I'm sure he remembers us." They both chuckled at the thought of their last visit to the gravesite. After finding the elusive marker on the bottom of Mollyockett's grave, they honored her by chanting an ancient Native American prayer for the departed while banging on a crude drum. Simple Mr. Walton didn't know if he should run for his life or alert the Andover police.

"There's something else I need to tell you Fletch."

Fletcher clicked off the low jazz music playing on the old radio.

"So what's Snow Falls got to do with all of this?" Fletcher asked flatly.

"Well, I saw Officer Webster at Kemo's this morning while I was gassing up. Apparently, there's been a drowning at Snow Falls."

"Drowning? How's that possible with all the fences?"

"I'm with you on that, but this may be a little different," Uncle Woodrow said. He paused and turned the radio back on while keeping the volume on low. Jazz music calmed him. "Apparently, Croft Snow has gone missing and is presumed to have drowned at the base of Snow Falls on the same night Mollyockett's grave was dug up."

They both knew the importance of both locations.

"Officer Webster said that?"

"He's not connected the two events Fletch, but the timing is obvious."

Fletcher swallowed hard.

"Is he a member of *the* Snow family?"

"He's a distant cousin," Woodrow said, glancing over to gauge Fletcher's demeanor. "And get this. Apparently, it happened right about the time Mollyockett's grave was vandalized."

"Didn't you say her grave was robbed during the night?"

"I did. From what they could ascertain, sometime after midnight."

Perplexed, Fletcher looked at his uncle hoping for more information, but there was none. "What was he doing swimming *there* in the middle of the night?"

"No idea. He may not have been swimming. Doesn't sound too smart if you ask me," said Woodrow while turning onto Swift River Road. "Especially given the storm that blew through. I'd heard that West Paris and Snow Falls bore the brunt of the winds."

"You said *presumed to have drowned,* what's that mean?"

"Well, get this," Woodrow said, swallowing hard. "He was reported missing by Chesley Snow at five in the morning yesterday."

"You're kidding! *The* Chesley Snow!" Fletcher gasped, totally caught off guard. The image of the patriarch of the Snow family raising the first place trophy for the Mollyockett day parade over his head flashed into his mind.

"I know. Of all people. It's hard to believe. From what Officer Web—"

"It's definitely related to Mollyockett's grave if it happened at the same time," Fletcher said, cutting him off. "How'd they know he's not lying. *He* could've killed him and said he drowned."

Woodrow pondered Fletcher's words.

"Could've Fletch, but I don't think he'd have called the authorities if that was the case. You know how private *that* family is." He paused before continuing, "My bet is he was afraid of his body washing up downstream."

"Hmmm, you may be right."

"As of a few hours ago, they've still not located him. They found one of his boots downstream." Woodrow stopped talking and looked directly at Fletcher. "It was badly charred."

"As in burned?" gasped Fletcher. "How could that happen while being in the water?"

"Dunno, but it was enough for them to bring Chesley down to the Sheriff's station in South Paris for more questioning. Apparently, given his past, the police found it difficult to believe his story. He said they were out walking when Croft fell into the stream."

Fletcher laughed sarcastically. "I'd say. Didn't you say there was a huge storm going on?"

Woodrow didn't respond.

Perplexed, Fletcher turned the radio back off and looked directly at his uncle.

"What do you think exactly is going on? Everything *has* to be related. Has to be."

Woodrow did not want to admit what he was thinking about the two events, but he owed it to his nephew. They'd been through too much together.

Woodrow could feel Fletcher looking at him and was relieved he was driving. He didn't want to look him in the eye.

"I'll be honest with you. I don't know Fletch," he replied. "I almost fainted when I found out everything. I was *actually* reading the article in the paper when I ran into Officer Webster. I almost fell out of my truck when he told me about Croft Snow."

Silence filled the Land Rover as they contemplated everything and took in the leafy colors of the stunning northern New England autumn.

"Here, let's see what we can find," Woodrow said as he pulled over to the right side of road in front of the large cemetery.

Immediately, they both noticed the yellow police tape surrounding a fresh mound of dirt in the old section of the graveyard. A police vehicle was still parked on the small dirt road next to it.

"Good, it's Bill Tobins," Woodrow said as they drove under the old wrought iron arch that said *Woodlawn Cemetery.* "He'll be able to help us. Just don't act suspicious, ok?"

"Well, what *exactly* are we doing here Uncle Woodrow? Just passing through?" Fletcher said sarcastically.

"Good point," Uncle Woodrow conceded, "We need a plan."

Suddenly, a strange burning sensation began in Fletcher's left foot and shot up throughout his body and into his fingers. He closed his eyes and grimaced but said nothing.

"What's wrong Fletch?" Uncle Woodrow said loudly. "You okay?"

Just as quickly as it came, the pain subsided.

"I'm okay, I think it was something I ate," Fletcher conceded. He didn't want to alarm his uncle. It was as though something had crawled inside him and had found a home. His fingers continued to tingle just slightly.

"We can leave if you want."

"I'm positive I'm okay Uncle Woodrow." The pain in his body was gone, but it no longer felt like *his* body. "I've been through worse, remember?"

"You're definitely a McKenzie, Fletch," his uncle said. "Hmm, why don't we tell them that we want to make sure the headstone is okay and that I'm here on behalf of the historical society. That'll keep the suspicion to a minimum."

"That sounds good. Let's just get it over with. I mean, everyone is waiting for us at the orchard, remember?" said Fletcher with a slight wince. He averted his uncles concerned eyes.

They both remained silent as they walked towards the large pine tree looming over Mollyockett's open grave.

"Afternoon Bill," Woodrow said, extending his hand. "Unbelievable someone would do something like this."

"Hey Woody, Fletch. What brings you all the way out here?" Officer

Tobins replied, holding a large Sunday River Brew Pub thermal mug. "Don't get too close. She's not a pretty sight."

Fletcher gasped. "You're telling me you can see her?" He hadn't expected the grave to *actually* be disturbed.

"Two centuries will take its toll on anyone." He paused. "Whoever did this will be caught. Mark my word," said Tobins with dead seriousness. "They ought to throw the key away too."

Woodrow held out his left arm and pressed against Fletcher's chest just as they neared the dirt pile. "Not too close, you hear. We're just here to take a look at the gravestone, Bill. The historical society is concerned that it may have been damaged," said Woodrow with sincerity. He'd had eighty-odd years to perfect his words. "Gotta respect the departed."

"It's right over there behind that tree, Woody," said Bill. "We moved it there so the tractor wouldn't run over it when they filled in the hole."

"What do you think happened," asked Woodrow, pushing back his white hair. "This is so bizarre that someone would do this."

As Fletcher walked behind his uncle, he felt strangely lopsided as if someone was pushing the right side of his body downwards. Slowly, the tingling sensation in his left fingers and arm intensified. *Something is pushing me towards the grave,* he thought. It was though the open grave was a magnet, and he was made of metal. Fighting back the pulling sensation, he stayed on his uncle's heels.

"Well at least it's in one piece." said Woodrow with relief.

Laying on the brown grass and propped up slightly on an exposed root of the pine tree was the familiar stone they'd explored a little over two years ago.

Fletcher walked over and bent down to get a closer look. "Uncle Woodrow, I don't know how to tell you this. Take a look?" he said, aghast.

"I can't believe it," Woodrow replied, openmouthed. He was in absolute horror. The bottom of the stone was totally immaculate as though it had just been extracted from the quarry. Someone had chiseled off the entire soil stained bottom. More importantly, the symbol of the crescent moon surrounded by six stars was missing. The exact symbol they'd taken a rubbing of on their last visit.

"What should we do?" asked Fletcher with desperation in his voice.

"It's gone." His uncle knelt onto the grass beside him. He watched as Woodrow slowly ran his hand along the base of the grave marker.

"Fletch, who on earth would do this? And Why?" They were both stunned.

Woodrow gazed desperately around the moss-covered stones surrounding them. He recognized the surnames of a few families from the Mahoosuc valley.

"Here, help me turn it over. The paper said something about a mysterious symbol on the back."

Fletcher slid his finders under the rough marker and pulled upwards. Respectfully, they turned it over and lowered it on the grass. Etched in the very center of the back of the stone was what looked like the letter T that was the middle and starting point of a complex maze. Next to it was a second drawing of a majestic bird with square shaped wings.

"What do you think they mean?" Fletcher asked. The sensation in his head intensified. It felt like his brain had its own pulse.

Woodrow took out his camera and snapped a series of photos.

"Beats me. I'm sure Alek Von Piddle can help us."

"You think?" asked Fletcher with a chuckle as he imagined Von Piddle's eye glasses bouncing on his nose while blinking rapidly.

"Let's go see if Mr. Walton can give us some information," Woodrow said as he stood. "He was here first. I noticed his truck in the back when we arrived."

Fletcher was thinking fast as he followed his uncle back towards the open grave.

"It's got to be *him*, Uncle Woodrow," said Fletcher, "I've no doubt in my mind. Wouldn't you—"

Fletcher's body suddenly jerked so violently he knocked into his uncle who tripped and fell hard onto a grave marker that was laid flat into the ground. He immediately tasted blood. Fletcher looked down and saw his uncle lying face down at the base of a black gravestone near Mollyockett's grave. Feeling out of control, Fletcher fought the overwhelming sensation to jerk toward the deep grave. The tingling sensation in his left arm increased to the point where his fingers splayed open and stiffened as though carved of wood.

"Uncle Woodrow, help me!" he gasped as his chest jerked forward. "I don't know what's happening."

Woodrow rolled over and jumped up.

"Fletch, what's happening?' he asked just as Fletcher's hand twitched uncontrollably. The veins in his neck pulsated blue as they bowed outwards.

"We're going, Fletch!"

He pulled Fletcher by his armpits towards the Defender 90. They could hear Tobins running towards them.

"Good God, what's happened?"

"He's just not feeling that well," Woodrow said. "Must be the flu that's going around."

Tobins grabbed onto Fletcher's arm and helped Woodrow move him away from the grave. Fletcher's eyes were glazed over, and his body was immobile. His feet dragged on the ground as the men carried him by his arms. Searing hot pain moved slowly upwards from his abdomen and into his head. Tingly black spots swirled inside his eyes, causing him to become horribly dizzy. Everything around him seemed to be spinning uncontrollably.

"Just hang on Fletcher. We're almost at the truck," said Woodrow, "I'll get you home."

"I'll open the door," Tobins offered sympathetically. "Can't believe how quickly this came on. I mean, he looked fine when you arrived."

Fletcher fell into the seat and closed his eyes. He could hear the two men talking after they buckled him in. Slowly, the pain and twitching subsided. Whatever had invaded his body was slowly ebbing out of his head and towards the bottom of his feet. It felt like his very soul was being drained of an invading foreign substance. As it flowed southward, a slight hissing sound filled his ears. Then, as fast as it came, it was over. Fletcher pulled the sleeve of his shirt over his hand and wiped the sweat off his forehead. He was drenched in perspiration.

"I'll get him home," said Woodrow. "By the way, would you mind giving Mr. Walton my phone number? There's something I need to ask him."

"Well if you can find him, let *me* know," replied Officer Tobins. "We've been looking for him ever since it happened."

"Isn't that his truck over there?"

"It is, but no one has seen him since he called it in," he replied, spitting onto the ground. "Some weird stuff going on."

"Not to intrude on your investigation, but do you mind if I ask, *like what?*"

"Just some strange things which is why we've not filled the grave in yet," Tobins offered up. "Well, first, when I first arrived his truck was running, and the driver-side door was wide open. Next, I found his cell phone lying in the grass beside the open door."

"No sight of him?" asked Woodrow. "Maybe someone picked him up."

"Well, if they did, he left in a hurry."

"Meaning what?"

"Strangest thing," said Tobins, raising his eyebrows at Woodrow. "I found his boots, or I think they're his boots, a short distance from his phone." He stopped to analyze Woodrow's reaction. "And get this, they looked like he'd been walking through a firepit or something. Soles are completely burned through as well as most of the leather on the sides. Even the steel toes are slightly melted."

Woodrow opened his mouth, but no words came out. He was stunned.

"What?" he said after a few seconds.

"I know, as soon as I saw them I notified his wife and she was positive that—"

"If you don't mind, I need to get Fletcher back home," said Woodrow, cutting him off. If any doubt lingered in his mind about the two events being connected, it was now quickly erased. Confused, Tobins stepped back as Woodrow started the truck and raced out of the cemetery. He unknowingly scraped the side of the black metal arch marking the entrance to the graveyard causing it to bend slightly. He looked over at Fletcher sitting with his eyes closed. He could clearly read his thoughts. They both knew who was responsible.

CHAPTER 3

SLAUGHTER MAKERS

WOODROW APPEARED IN THE FRONT DOORWAY BEFORE ALDOUS AND Muriel had even reached the granite steps. Lucille and Edmond were quick on their heels.

"He's upstairs," he said, starting to feel guilt ridden.

What was I thinking bringing him there? he thought as he quickly moved to the right to let them enter the house.

"What happened," snapped Lucille. She glared at Woodrow who averted her eyes. She knew something was amiss.

"You sure it's the flu?" Muriel asked as she swiftly climbed the stairs behind Aldous. "He's had his shot and everything."

Quickly everyone assembled in Fletcher's room only to find him sitting in front of his computer. Woodrow immediately recognized the logo of the Andover Historical Society in the upper right of the computer screen. Everyone else was too focused on Fletcher to notice. He quickly minimized the page.

"Fletch, what happened?" said Muriel, feeling his forehead. "Your father heard your name over the police scanner. Something about you fainting out in Andover. What were you—"

"How dare you," Lucille hissed at Woodrow. Muriel stopped talking and looked at Woodrow.

"I'm fine. I knew I shouldn't have eaten it," Fletcher exclaimed, stealing a slight wink at his uncle.

"Eaten what!" protested Lucille. "When you left here, you'd just eaten breakfast." She was deeply proud and protective of her cooking.

"Not that Grans. I'm talking about *Aunt Riffy's Whoopie Pie.*"

"You what!?" Lucille and Aldous said in unison.

"I'm sorry, Uncle Woodrow told me not to buy it, but I just wanted to try one." Fletcher feigned innocence without looking at his uncle.

"Er, um," said Woodrow, caught off guard. He quickly fell in line with Fletcher's concocted story. "Those things are heart clogging missiles firing right at your aorta. Still my fault, I should've put my foot down and—"

"Having a *Whoopie Pie* picnic at the cemetery in Andover were we?" asked Lucille, scolding them. "Perfect day to sit on a blanket and look into an open grave isn't it?"

Edmond remained silent. He'd learned years ago not to interfere with his wife when she was speaking her mind. He twirled the ends of his handlebar mustache and stood back.

"What on earth?" whispered Muriel to Aldous. She hadn't heard the news of the desecration of Mollyockett's grave. "Open grave?"

Lucille immediately regretted her words. Her daughter had been through a lot in the past three years. The last thing she wanted to do was reopen the past. Muriel's wounds were still raw and very deep.

"He looks okay, if you ask me," Aldous said, changing the subject. "Serves you right, Fletch, eating one of Aunt Riffy's Whoopie Pies. He smiled at Woodrow to ease the man's guilt. "I've bought a few myself. Did a lot of injustice to my stomach."

"Aldous," Muriel croaked. "Have you noticed what's in those things?"

"Just trying to size up the competition, you know. Need to know what *they're* doing."

"Competition, my foot!" Lucille huffed. She quickly glared at Woodrow.

Fletcher laughed. Immediately everyone relaxed. "I'm ready to go to the fall festival," he said. "Quinn and Camway are waiting for me."

"You sure, honey?"

"Mom, I'm positive. I threw the Whoopie Pie up, so I feel a lot better," he lied.

Woodrow stepped forward and analyzed Fletcher.

"My goodness, those three sisters are criminals with what they're doing with their *nutritional* creations these days. Absolute unforgiving barbarians," huffed Lucille, glaring at Woodrow once again.

Woodrow smiled feebly. Deliberately going against the wishes of Lucille was cause for concern. When it came to her grandson, she always had the final word.

"Um, hello?" Fletcher asked, struggling to raise himself on his bed. He'd been sleeping for several hours after enjoying the fall festival and dinner with his family, Quinn, Camway, and Cicely, with whom he'd secretly had a crush on for several years. Breathing fast and hard, he stared at the entrance to his bedroom. The door was open. He slowly reached for the light switch beside his bed and clicked it upwards. Nothing. *I swore I heard something,* he thought as he contemplated his next move. Closing his eyes, he patted his lips with his fingers in an effort to calm his nerves. A sudden draft pushed the tiny hairs on his arms back and forth. Something was amiss.

Something lightly brushed the side of his bed. Then he heard an eerie whisper: *"It's time."*

Barely had the words registered in his mind when a cold breeze enveloped the entire room. A light fog rolled out from under his bed and over his blankets. Fletcher closed his eyes and tried to convince himself that it was only his imagination. The fog encased him, quickly moving upwards then encircling his head. It was so thick he gasped for breath.

"Camazotz and Uktena will kill you Fletcher," a low raspy voice called out.

Fletcher swallowed hard and closed his eyes tighter to consider what he'd just heard. Small beads of sweat rolled down his forehead.

"Er, who's there?" Fletch whispered back shakily. The thick fog continued to hold his head hostage.

Silence filled the room.

Fletch lay there as his heart beat rapidly while waiting for a response.

"Do as you're told, or they all die," the voice whispered, and the stench of rotten flesh filled his nostrils. *"You've seen the power behind Whole. Don't even think to question us, Fletcher."*

He was aghast. It knew of Whole and its mysterious secrets. He glanced around the dark room. A low hum was emanating from the top of his dresser. He quickly zeroed in on the stone star he'd removed from the symbol at the entrance to the southern passage in Whole more than two years ago. While at Christmas Cove he'd learned from Machias and Pidianiski that the symbol was exactly like the one in the root cellar in his basement and the one that had been on the bottom of Mollyockett's desecrated grave stone. Pidianiski and Machias, who both called Whole home, were very familiar with its secrets and had instructed Fletcher on how to unlock Whole's powers to defeat Tomhegan. Additionally, in order to save Whole's southern passage from being discovered, he'd removed the star as instructed and carried it home with him. He was now the sole protector of Whole.

Through the thick fog, Fletch could see the star begin to glow a light green and pulsate. He turned back and looked in the direction of the voice. His heart was beating so wildly that it actually hurt. He began to ask, "What do—"

"Pick up the star and go to the root cellar," the voice commanded coldly. *"Or everyone else in this house dies. Now!"*

Adrenaline quickened his pulse and strange electricity made his skin tingle. He knew he needed to react. He had no choice.

"Okay," he said and stood up. He bent down and felt for his navy blue Balston Prep shorts. He quickly slid them on. Without hesitating, he moved towards the glowing star and picked it up. It was warm and felt like it was actually alive. The yellow agate rock now glowed dull green.

"To the root cellar," the voice hissed quietly as the fog balled up and moved towards the door.

Fletcher looked directly at it and thought he saw the outline of eyes and tall horns directly above them. He didn't respond but quietly walked in the direction of the hallway. His mother was a light sleeper and the last thing he wanted was her innocently stumbling into anything that involved Whole.

The walk down the stairs, through the kitchen and down into the basement seemed lengthy, but because of the threat against his family, he kept going. As he quietly crept, he stole a glance behind him and noticed the foggy ball was quick on his heels. The warm star in his hand felt slightly comforting. Oddly, it lighted his way.

"Open it slowly," the voice said. It was now right next to his left ear.

Fletcher looked around in the darkness, as if hoping Mollyockett would be there to save him.

He moved the stone into his left hand and grabbed onto the door handle. It too was warmer than usual. The hinge's recognizable creaking sound reverberated throughout the basement. He stopped pushing and lifted slightly. He was very familiar with the Bacchus Den and how to quietly enter it. After his mother had disappeared in the Quetzal, Fletcher, along with Quinn and Camway, moved three old chairs into the root cellar and sat them on an old Persian rug. From that point on, it was their private den and the perfect spot to form a secret society. At the suggestion of Woodrow, it was named after Bacchus, the Roman god of wine and revelry.

Fletcher had learned that a huge barn had been built on the property over two hundred years ago only to be destroyed by fire roughly fifty years later. For over one hundred and fifty years, the rock wall in the root cellar belonged to the Maine elements. Huge trees sprung upwards and claimed what remained of the abandoned hole. Aldous, who later inherited the property, decided to build a house as a wedding present for Muriel on the exact foundation. Much to the vehement objections of the architects, he decided to clear the trees and use the rocks as the foundation for the massive house.

He and Uncle Woodrow later learned from Alek Von Piddle that the foundation had been dug by Fletcher's ancestors centuries ago for a reason. It was the exact spot where an ancient eagle's nest had been for generations.. The *very* site where Mollyockett had noted was the *actual* location of the passage to Whole which she'd passed on to Fletcher's ancestors hundreds of years ago.

Later, and more importantly, with the trusted help of Squire Susup, Fletcher and Uncle Woodrow learned that the *actual* entrance to Whole was in the root cellar. It was now the most important place in his life. It was the starting point for his annual visit to the amazing world of Whole. His mother gladly let them share her space after she healed from her misadventure.

"Take the star and place it on its twin in the symbol," the voice hissed impatiently.

Fletcher quickly moved towards the corner of the damp room and bent down. He sat the stone star down and started to push the clay dirt towards the rock wall. The star hummed and continued to illuminate his surroundings. He was gentle with his mother's vegetables that she'd buried a few weeks earlier. After a minute of digging, his hands scraped a large circular stone beneath the cool soil. There on the stone were the crescent moon surrounded by six stars, exactly like the symbol that had been removed from the base of Mollyockett's grave marker. He quickly brushed the dirt off the top star. Swallowing hard, he picked up its twin he'd brought with him.

"Place it exactly on the top star. Now! This will buy you some time, Fletcher, but trust me, your entire family will die ... in due time," the foggy voice said firmly.

Fletcher's spirits plummeted. He wanted to take the pointed rock and throw it in the direction of the voice but knew deep inside it would be fruitless and would only exasperate the already dire situation.

"Don't even think about it."

He tilted the stone in his hand then placed it directly on the top star.

"Keep your right hand on them both and press hard," commanded the voice coldly as the fog quickly enveloped the star and hole he'd dug.

He did as instructed and closed his eyes. He'd been in this exact spot three times. He anxiously waited for the symbol to turn into a thick gray liquid to be followed by a whirling sensation, all signs that announced the arrival of Whole and preceded his tumbling and spiraling downwards.

Nothing.

He turned to see if the ball of fog was still behind him and wondered if Mollyockett would be waiting for him as she had on every one of his annual visits to Whole.

Suddenly, a ray of blinding light flew through the air. It seemed as though the house had been struck by lightning. A crisp burnt smell filled the room. The door to the cellar creaked and then slammed shut. A cold breeze stirred up the dirt by Fletcher.

He silently counted down from ten. Painfully, he jerked his right hand to his side. The brown mark was severely burning. Again, he closed his eyes and waited for the passage to swallow him. The ritual was a lot different this time but he somehow expected the same result. Instead, the dirt floor started to rumble. Then there was a loud explosion and the sound of wood splintering somewhere behind the six enormous boulders that formed most of the north wall of the basement.

Fletcher opened his eyes wide to find the boulders slowly rolling backwards into what looked like a dark cave of sorts. A loud thud reverberated towards him as the top three rocks crashed onto a solid granite floor causing two of them to split in half. Immediately, the fog coiled back into a ball and slowly swept the floor from the hole he'd dug and towards the newly created opening. Fletcher stood frozen. He wondered if his family had heard the commotion.

"Bring the star and follow me," the raspy voice commanded. There was clear pleasure now in the words.

Fletcher blinked, then rubbed the dust out of his eyes. He wanted to run but knew better of it. The lives of his entire family were at stake.

"Now!" the voice commanded, catching him off guard.

Quickly he bent down and picked up the yellow rock made of agate and moved towards the hole in the wall.

Through the darkness, he could make out a large tunnel. He lowered his head and entered the musty cavern. He cautiously walked forward, hoping there were no surprises. He said nothing, following the fog, which was spiraling forward with a purpose.

As he rounded a bend, he came to a large room. He stopped dead in his tracks. The room was dimly lit. On the granite walls were magnificent carvings created by master artisans. Faces of evil-looking people glared directly at him. They resembled portraits of Native American Indians he'd seen in history books. Interspersed amongst the carvings were dozens of unrecognizable symbols. His gut told him to memorize as many as he could.

The fog moved forward, saying nothing.

As he neared the last of the carved faces, the light slowly grew brighter and brighter.

"So, we finally meet!" roared a voice in front of him.

Fletcher's eyes quickly adjusted. Stunned, he came to an abrupt halt. Behind a white film-like curtain that appeared to be made of billowy clouds stood four beautifully carved chairs with square backs. He estimated they were over eight feet tall. Four men with angular features were staring directly at him. Symbols that resembled the ones he'd seen carved on the chambers walls a few seconds ago were expertly carved on the wood headrests above their heads. His heart skipped a beat then raced uncontrollably. Tomhegan was seated among them. He was glaring hatefully at Fletcher with his black eyes.

So he did survive Whole, he thought silently. *I wonder what happened to Nimsy.*

Just then Fletcher noticed standing to the right of the men two enormous moose-like creatures that stood reared on their hind legs. Their hairy bodies were powerful. Both had long limbs with four digits on each foot and hands that morphed into razor-like claws. Rows of pointed teeth gleamed along the side of their long mouths, which took up most of their block-shaped heads. Tall antlers rested on top of their skulls. The first creature's antlers had seven points, the other nine points. Two bat-like ears sprouted from each side of their heads, which framed almond-shaped eyes that glowed bright red. Fletcher could feel and taste their putrid smelling breath. It was clear he was their target.

"Push it over to them!" Commanded the voice. He refocused his attention on the four Native American Indians.

Confused, he hunched his shoulders as he rubbed the back of his right hand. The burning was so severe he almost wished they'd cut his hand off.

"The star, push it towards the two Slaughter Makers," demanded the man seated next to Tomhegan. He had long black hair that was woven into a complex braid. His eyes were just as dark and empty as the others. A leather strap was wrapped around his forehead and decorated with dozens of tiny blue and red gem stones. The blue stones were adorned with small white feathers and also hung from his tanned and wrinkly ears. A crude leather coat and matching pants were decorated with three rows of black-and-white porcupine quills. In his hand, he was holding an ornate staff. Fletcher immediately recognized it as being similar to his own staff he'd acquired from Squire Susup. He gasped at his black fingernails. *Very familiar.*

"I said push it!" he commanded.

Fletcher immediately laid the agate star on the floor and pushed it hard towards the two moose-like creatures.

Immediately one stepped forward then bent down and brushed it towards the men while the other beast's eyes stayed fixated on Fletcher, ready to pounce with the slightest command.

"Thank you, Croft," said the man laughing.

Fletcher immediately wheeled around and looked toward the man speaking.

Did he say Croft? He thought to himself. *He said Croft.*

The filmy curtain caused the four men to appear like they were a mirage of sorts as they bent and moved slightly in the light.

Tomhegan looked Fletcher in the eye and sneered.

"I'd turn them loose if it were me, Nukpana," Tomhegan went on, "Are you sure we need—"

Nukpana held up his hand, and Tomhegan backed down at once, watching resentfully as Nukpana stared at Fletcher.

The two other men stayed silent.

"History, Mr. McKenzie." He paused and pointed at the two creatures who were clearly waiting for the word to pounce and devour their prey. Reluctantly they cowered and backed towards the granite wall. "History is what brings us here."

Fletcher breathed a sigh of relief and refocused on Nukpana.

The two silent men sniggered and smiled, enjoying the scene unfolding before them.

"It appears we have a slight misunderstanding. You see, there's a piece of property that belongs to us, which *your* family has *stolen,* unwittingly perhaps." He said condescendingly, tilting his head a little to one side as he considered Fletcher. "I think you know what I'm talking about."

"Let's just have them kill him and get it over with," said Tomhegan eagerly. He stood up and moved closer to the white cloudy curtain in front of him, stopping abruptly as if fenced in by an invisible barrier.

"Enough," shouted Nukpana, who was deeply annoyed at the interruption.

The other men watched Nukpana apprehensively, clearly afraid they'd be the next target of his growing anger.

Tomhegan backed into his chair and stayed focused on Fletcher. Images of their violent encounter in Whole was still raw in his mind.

Fletcher closed his eyes reliving the horrific scene which had claimed the life of Nimsy Cortland, the traitor responsible for his mother's disappearance.

"Whole," said Nukpana coldly.

"Can I ask what it is you need from me?" Fletcher asked boldly, considering what he faced.

"Three important possessions of yours. You see, the rules of Whole are changing, much like nature itself. Thankfully." He paused. "You McKenzie's may think you've won the war, but *that* was *only* the first battle." He turned and shamefully analyzed Tomhegan.

There was silence in the room. No one dared to utter a word.

"Luck was on your side, murderer," said the man sitting on the other side of Nukpana, "Don't expect the same results again."

"Thank you, Tygorge, obviously your prediction of the fourth age of man is presenting itself," Nukpana replied, sounding pleased.

He continued, "The days of your family controlling Whole and it's secret powers are over." There was venom in his words. "I'm giving you until when the Moon of Popping Trees comes to Snow Falls to give me what is rightfully mine."

Fletcher was perplexed. *What on earth?* he thought.

"That staff you've absconded with, *Whole Abounds,* its release code, and finally, the patera. I'm positive you're familiar with these objects."

"Release code?" asked Fletcher, confused. He immediately regretted his words knowing he'd showed his hand.

"Let me be deadly serious with you. Your entire family will have an *unfortunate* and *unpleasant* meeting with my little Slaughter Maker friends over there: Walton and Croft," he said, pointing to the two cowering animals.

They killed 'em. Fletcher thought. *Uncle Woodrow was right. Croft and*

Mr. Walton are connected. He glanced to his right and analyzed the facial features of the wild beasts.

"*Whole Abounds* and the patera are in Whole," he said flatly. He now knew they needed his help and likely weren't going to kill him.

"Since you're the protector of the passage and you value the lives of your family, you have a little work to do I'd say," Nukpana said condescendingly while staring at the brown marking on Fletcher's right hand—the sign he still held the power of the passage.

"Tygorge,"

"Yes, chief."

"Show our little friend what his family is in for, will you? Hm."

Immediately Tygorge stood up and pulled out what looked like a foot-long brown stick with a large tan-and-white feather tied to the bottom. Laser quartz and amethyst stones decorated the tip of the whittled wand. Deep in thought, he aimed it at a small opening behind the Slaughter Makers. A large boar weighing roughly three hundred pounds suddenly bolted out and into the open arena. Two razor sharp tusks protruded outwards from its fleshy snout. Asserting its dominance, it pivoted and faced the Slaughter Makers. All eyes focused on what was about to happen. Fletcher turned and looked at Tygorge who was still aiming his wand. There was no mistaking the contempt and deep anger in his eyes. The one Nukpana had called Croft immediately pounced on the swine as the other beast circled and crouched as if stalking its prey. The boar squealed so loud that it actually hurt Fletcher's ears.

Nukpana laughed and casually folded his hands on his lap as if watching a Broadway play.

The sounds of tearing flesh and crunching bones reverberated throughout the cavern and bounced off its granite walls.

Fletcher closed his eyes and covered his ears. He'd witnessed enough.

The mark on his right hand was so searing, it was hard to focus.

The slaughter was over in an instant.

Silence filled the room.

"Look. At. Me." Nukpana said with absolute authority.

Fletcher recoiled then opened his eyes. Blood was everywhere and pieces of flesh and bone were strewn throughout the entire room. Croft and McGovern were both crouched down and gnawing on snapped bones that were dripping red. A broken tusk lay at Fletcher's feet. The frenzied and savage attack had left not a piece of the boar larger than the size of his hand.

"You're boring me," said Nukpana casually. "Do not underestimate my request, Fletcher. I'll announce my next arrival the same way I did with respect to tonight's little party." Everyone but Fletcher chuckled.

Nukpana nodded towards Tygorge who stood and raised his wand-like stick once again.

"Manaba," he called out.

A flash of brilliant white light filled the room and illuminated every corner. Fletcher was thrown backwards towards the bend in the cave and smashed hard into a granite wall. He crumpled to the floor and laid silent, hoping they'd think he were dead. The smell of burnt flesh wafted to his nose just as a burning sensation emanated from the brown spot on his right hand. The Slaughter Makers screeched viciously out of fear caused by the lightning bolt that missed them by mere inches. Before Fletcher could fully grasp what was happening, a second and brighter bolt of light hit his back, lifting him off the floor and causing a searing pain to course throughout his body. Thoughts faded into tiny bits of memory then ebbed into unconsciousness.

CHAPTER 4

PUZZLING CLUES

FLETCHER WAS DAZED BUT AMAZINGLY UNINJURED WITH THE EXCEPTION of his right hand, which was badly singed around the brown spot. He opened his eyes only to find himself laying on the Persian rug and under one of the stuffed leather chairs that was overturned. Clearly, everything he'd been through with respect to Whole had hardened him. He glanced at his clay-covered shirt and immediately righted himself then looked towards the back wall. The opening was gone. It appeared exactly like it had looked for centuries. He glanced at the small clock on the wall. Five ten.

Grans will be getting up any minute. If she sees my shirt like this, she'll freak, he thought as he moved towards the hole he'd dug earlier. *I need to rebury the symbol and get back to my room.*

Overwhelmed with thoughts of what had just happened, he began to pull scoops of the clay soil back towards him. The burnt mark on his hand made the task painful and difficult. Then he abruptly halted. Sitting at the base of the rocky wall was *Whole Abounds,* the book from Whole that had taught him its secret powers, enabling him to over-power Tomhegan and save his mother. He quickly finished filling in the hole and scrambled over to the ancient book.

A piece of paper was sticking out. Without opening it, he walked silently out of the root cellar and towards his room.

Quietly, he crept upstairs and into his room.

Uncle Woodrow was aghast. He picked up the note left in *Whole Abounds* and read it out loud:

Fletcher,

So, our paths will cross twice in one year. Shocking.
As you've figured out by now, dark times are ahead.
Resist at any cost!! Mollyockett will be waiting for you
in Whole earlier than you've planned. She's asked me to
leave this for you. Know it well. She also gave me a quick
lesson on vitamins and minerals, specifically calcium and
vitamin D along with an elixir she'd personally concocted.
Amazingly, it healed all of your broken bones within
seconds. I'll be in touch shortly with further instructions.

Remember,
RESIST!
Squire Susup

"And you're positive no one in the house heard anything?" Woodrow asked. He was desperate given that his entire family has been threatened.

"Nothing. I'd have known at breakfast," said Fletcher, totally exhausted. He'd been dropped off at the Double Moose by Muriel under the guise that he was meeting Quinn and Camway for a school project. Instead, Uncle Woodrow was waiting for him. They needed a rouse so as not to upset Muriel and Lucille. Their latest adventure to Mollyockett's grave was an absolute disaster. *Over her dead body,* would Lucille let Fletcher visit with Woodrow for quite some time. She did, however, notice the bags under his eyes and was deeply concerned. It was Columbus Day weekend. Monday was a holiday at Balston Prep.

I wonder if that has anything to do with the timing of everything, Woodrow thought. He'd heard on the news yesterday that several states and cities had changed the holiday by proclamation to Indigenous People's Day in honor of the sacrifice and contributions of the "First Nation people of this land, including the Abenaki, their ancestors, and allies" as stated by the governor of Vermont. He was positive the McKenzie family fell into the allies category to some of the First Nation people but not to those who were enraged by the transfer of control of the passage from Mollyockett's line of ancestry to the McKenzie bloodline. The desire for revenge was absolute.

"And you're absolutely positive these two, um, monsters were named Croft and Walton?"

"How could I forget. They were about to tear me to shreds like that poor pig thing," said Fletcher emphatically.

"And Croft was definitely more violent than Walton?" Woodrow asked, remembering the scorched footwear left behind at Snow Falls and Woodlawn Cemetery. He shook his head in disbelief. Clearly, these two *men* were now pawns in a very dangerous game. "I'm getting Alek Von Piddle involved," he said. "I trust him, and we desperately need his help at this very moment. Time is not on our side. Just like ergot doubling two years ago at the very places Mollyockett lived at during the final years of her life. They are, once again, desecrating locations that are part of her history."

Fletcher smiled weakly thinking back to the time he, Camway, and Quinn discovered the riddle on the back of Mollyockett's portrait in his parent's bedroom. It seemed like decades ago. He yearned for those wonderful days. His entire world was spinning out of control once again.

"In fact, I called him right after you phoned me this morning, Fletch," said Woodrow with dead seriousness. "He's on his way over to the inn right now. Let's go."

"Now!?" Fletcher asked in shock. He hadn't expected the pace at which things were moving.

"We've no idea what the Moon of Popping Trees is Fletch. For all we know, it could be this week."

Fletcher froze. *How can I be so stupid?* he thought. *I hadn't even thought of that.*

Outside, he paced the side of the Defender 90 while Uncle Woodrow quickly paid the check. His backpack containing *Whole Abounds* and staff literally felt like a ton of bricks.

"So this guy named Nukpana called poor ol' Walton and Croft Slaughter Makers?" Woodrow asked, looking at Fletcher nervously.

"Several times," Fletcher said. He grabbed the leather strap over his head as Woodrow rounded a sharp corner on Sunday River Road a little too fast. "I mean, how could—"

"You're *really* trying to use common sense right now?" Woodrow asked, cutting him off. "I think we both know when it comes to Whole, rationality is thrown out the window."

Fletcher nodded in agreement while continuing to stare out the front window.

"I want you to write everything down as soon as we arrive at the inn while it's fresh in your mind. Would you be able to recreate those symbols you saw on the walls?"

Fletcher closed his eyes and rested his head on the neck rest. "I think so."

"Well, do the best you can. Von Piddle will want you to come as close as possible. Even the slightest deviation could have life threatening consequences."

Fletcher gaped at him. It was implausible that the two of them were, once again, in a race against time to save his family. Silence filled the rig as they sped towards the inn. Fletcher looked towards the Mahoosuc Mountains and took in the autumn beauty. Suddenly, the death of Summer's bountiful offerings oddly mirrored what was happening to the McKenzie family.

"What on earth!" said Woodrow. Aldous' car was parked in front of the inn. "Did you know he was coming here?"

"I didn't even know *I* was coming here," replied Fletcher. He'd told his family he was going to meet Quinn and Camway when his mother dropped him off. It was the first time he'd lied to them.

The driver's side door flew open as soon as they parked behind it.

"Uncle Woody, Fletch," Aldous called out as they exited the Defender 90. "I want to know everything that's going on."

"How'd you—"

"You're forgetting that Fletcher isn't the *only* one who's familiar with Whole," he said. Fletcher took two steps backwards. He'd never seen his father so tense. "Besides, when the door slammed to the root cellar last night, it woke me out of a dead sleep. I went to investigate. First, Fletcher was nowhere to be found. Second, as hard as I pulled, I couldn't open the entrance to the root cellar. I was just about to call the police when I heard Fletcher sneaking back upstairs. Thank God I didn't wake Muriel." He paused and glared at Uncle Woodrow.

"You need to remember that I too have had my own personal experiences with *that* passage. I decided to give Fletcher his space out of respect for the power that he now holds," he nodded at Fletcher proudly. "I've gotten no sleep since that door woke me up. I made the decision to ask him in the morning as not to alarm his grandmother. It was right around the time she always woke up and knowing her, if she found the both of us up, she'd know that something was amiss." He stopped and turned towards Woodrow.

"I was just surprised and a little hurt when he called you instead of—" Aldous paused. Fletcher lowered his head. "Remember," Aldous continued, "I *was* filled in on *everything* after you returned from Whole with your Mother, Fletch."

"Aldous, I'm sorry, we—"

"It's water under the bridge," he replied, cutting him off. "Obviously, it's serious. I know the two of you and your faces speak volumes."

"It is. Deadly serious." Woodrow looked at Aldous and held the stare.

"Meaning?"

"Meaning that we've all been threatened by forces that may be well outside our league, Aldous."

"That true, Fletcher?"

Before Fletcher could answer, Alek Von Piddle's car pulled into the circular drive. He was driving a tiny red convertible and wearing old, black aviator glasses over his thin, wire-framed glassed. A bright yellow scarf was wrapped thickly around his neck. The dark glasses contrasted with his snowy white hair, which was so heavy with gel that it stayed firmly in place even with the car's top down. He quickly exited the convertible. True to form, he was wearing bright red pants and L.L. Bean duck boots, and in his right hand, he was holding a black computer tablet.

"Snappy day to be driving with all these glorious leaves," he said jovially while striding towards them. "Must say, Maine has to be the best place on earth this time of year. Does remind me of—"

"Aldous, Aleksandr Von Piddle. Alek, Aldous McKenzie," said Woodrow, cutting him off. Fletcher rolled his eyes quickly. He was surprised they'd never formally met.

"Ah, fine genes you have, Mr. McKenzie. Esteemed pleasure to finally meet you fine sir." He held his hand out to greet Aldous.

"Ive heard great things. Pleasure to meet you too, Mr. Von—"

"Alek, just Alek."

"Pleasure to see you again Mr. Von Piddle," said Fletcher, firmly shaking his hand.

"You too, young man." He stood back and sized him up. "Sprouting up just like the son of that Bulgarian soldier who's in charge of the Plovdiv Amphitheater. Impressive site, impressive. Hard to believe the Romans *actually* built it." Aldous stood silent and took in the eccentric man. *We'll need to somehow get him to leave,* he thought, not knowing that Woodrow had invited him.

Woodrow was impatient but dreaded telling Aldous they'd invited Alek and not him.

"Alek, if you don't mind we—"

"Reminds me of the time I first visited Bulgaria. Timing was absolutely dreadful. You see, the Cold War had just hit rock bottom. Quite literally had to *sneak* photos of Nicopolis ad Istrum out in my undershorts. Would have led to a nasty international incident if I . . . but, that's a story for another time."

Wait for it, Fletcher thought humorously. *Three, two, one. . .*

As if on cue Aleksandr started blinking rapidly, causing his small wire-framed bifocals to bounce on the tip of his nose.

Aldous was now seriously studying the new arrival. *Who on earth?* he thought. *How is it that this squirrelly man actually helped save my wife?*

"Speaking of monumental matters, Fletcher," Alek continued. "What grade did you get on your summer project we worked on? You know, where the ancient eagles nest? Must say, even I was—"

"Aldous," Woodrow interrupted, taking control of the situation. "Alek has been a very close friend of mine ever since I attended Balston. He's the one I told you about who was so instrumental in helping us find the passage to Whole." There, he'd laid it out in the open.

Alek turned towards Woodrow and furrowed his brow. "Passage to where, Woody?" he asked. "Never heard of that odd sounding destination. Around here is it?"

It was all coming together for Aldous. He now knew Mr. Von Piddle had been invited here. Why Alek was now confused needed explanation.

"I say we head into the private dining room and have a lengthy discussion," Woodrow said, ignoring Von Piddle. A man and woman were heading towards them.

"You may want to remove your camouflaged coats," Woodrow advised as they strode towards a worn trail near the entrance to the inn. "Lots of hunters out in those woods. You never know."

The guests turned towards them, mouths gaping. Immediately, the female sprinted towards the inn as if it were the finish line at a marathon. Her companion was quick on her heals. Clearly, the Maine woods were foreign to them.

"Boston," Woodrow muttered and lead them inside.

"You're absolutely positive we can trust him with all of this? Whatever *all of this* is," whispered Aldous as they climbed the stone steps.

"Positive," said Woodrow. "Plus, when you hear what's going on, you'll definitely agree that we'll need all the help we can get. As quick as possible."

There was grave concern in his voice.

Aldous stopped mid stride and turned towards him, analyzing his demeanor.

"Ah, young man, couldn't believe all the coincidences when it came to that paper you were writing two years ago," Von Piddle said, placing his hand on Fletcher's shoulder as they walked through the comfortable lobby. A warm fire was blazing in the center of a handsome fireplace. "Bet it knocked the wooly socks off your teacher's feet when she found out *you actually* live on the exact spot that was central to your thesis. Reminded me of the time when I was sailing to Cape Town and our mast literally broke right in half during a raging storm in the Atlantic. There we were, at the equator, just sitting. . ."

Fletcher had drowned Alek's words out and was deep in thought memorizing all he'd seen last night.

Woodrow quickly herded everyone past the guests and staff in the fully booked inn and towards a small room adjacent to a stately dining room that was humming with activity in preparation of a wedding reception due to start in less than four hours. "Jessica, make sure we're not disturbed, okay?" he said firmly, grabbing a full coffee pot from a small table next to the fireplace. "Can you make another one for the guests, please? Oh, and would you mind bringing some bottled water and orange juice?"

Woodrow spent the next twenty minutes filling in Aleksandr and Aldous on all that had happened. Aleksandr was so stunned, he couldn't move. His eyes scanned the dining room looking for hidden cameras. Aimlessly, he bit down on one of Woodrow's popular Paw-Paw Bars, a healthy, whole grain, energy bar sold throughout New England. *I've got to be on one of those television shows,* he thought after listening to Woodrow's riveting words. Aldous, however, was completely horror stricken. The lives of his entire family were being threatened by unknown violent killers. He had to take the lead this time.

For a few minutes, mayhem broke out as they both pelted Woodrow and Fletcher with a cascade of questions.

"Calm down everyone," Woodrow finally said, attempting to bring order to the meeting.

Von Piddle responded with a full minute of rapidly blinking eyes. His wire-framed glassed bounced on tip of his nose then onto the floor. His mind was in a fog. He'd traveled the entire world and experienced everything that even the most seasoned adventurer would drool over. Little did he expect that in the final years of his life would fate offer up the biggest adventure one could ever imagine and right in his very own back yard. It was absolutely mind-boggling and incomprehensible..

"Fletcher, would you mind writing down what you saw last night including those symbols you mentioned?" Woodrow said after restoring order and convincing Alek he was not an unknowing actor in a hidden camera show.

Aldous remained silent, still contemplating his next move. The fact that Fletcher had collapsed at Mollyockett's grave and had almost been killed by two savage beasts last night was deeply disturbing, not to mention that they'd just learned Fletcher was fully convinced that an unknown force had attempted to pull him into the open grave.

Woodrow quickly distributed pens and notebooks to everyone after exacting a vow from Alek that secrecy was paramount. They needed to be methodical and have a solid plan. And they knew time was not on their side.

Alek clumsily cleaned his glasses then wiped small beads of sweat gathering on his aged forehead. His heart beat wildly as he analyzed the photo taken from the back of Mollyockett's headstone. Everyone watched as he opened his tablet and clicked open the World Wide Web.

Quickly, he found what he was looking for and focused on the screen.

"Woodrow, you don't reckon that we talk privately, do you?" He discreetly nodded towards Fletcher, concerned that he'd not be able to handle what he just discovered.

"He's fine," said Aldous quickly and with deep authority. "We need to agree right now that *all* information found is to be shared immediately with every one of us. Including Fletcher. He's old enough to handle it."

Woodrow winked at Fletcher.

"Well," Alek hesitated, "as long as you're sure, Aldous." The old wood floors creaked as he repositioned himself in his chair. *How on earth did I end up here,* he thought as he prepared himself to share what he'd just found.

Fletcher moved his chair to the other side of the table next to Aldous.

Alek stole a quick glance towards Fletcher and swallowed hard.

"Get on with it. What did you find?" asked Woodrow impatiently.

"Well, hmm," he paused and looked back at the screen. "First, with respect to the Moon of Popping Trees, it's in reference to the full moon in the month of December, which is on the seventeenth this year. It's been named that by Native Americans for thousands of years. I now remember learning that many years ago."

Woodrow glanced towards Aldous and Fletcher, both of whom were looking directly at Alek with disbelief. They had a little more than two months.

"Go on," said Woodrow flatly while jotting down the findings.

Alek gazed at each of them for several long moments then looked down at his research.

"That maze symbol with a letter T in the middle is actually the Hopi maze, otherwise known as the Mother Earth symbol. He adjusted his head to accommodate his bifocals and read:

> *The maze represents the maze of life, that is, the obstacles*
> *and challenges that one has to overcome to evolve spiritually*
> *and become one with the divine power. The center line*
> *symbolizes the child, a metaphor for the beginning of*
> *our philosophical journey, and the surrounding maze*
> *represents the Mother Earth's or Nature's support that*
> *is always available to guide the child through life. The*
> *Mother Earth/Maze symbol identifies all that is sacred in*
> *nature and reminds man to revere and be thankful to it.*

"Now, that doesn't sound too bad to me," announced Woodrow, slightly relieved.

Alek looked at him impatiently. "Well, there's more."

With that Woodrow's demeanor changed.

"That *majestic* bird with those square shaped wings may shine a little more light on the situation when added to the maze," said Alek, picking up a second Paw-Paw Bar. "These things are delicious. How come I've never had one before? Kind of reminds me of the time—"

"For goodness sake, get on with it!" yelled Woodrow. "You were at the bird with square wings."

"Well," huffed Von Piddle, slightly offended. "I didn't ask to be part of—"

"I apologize for getting you into this, Alek," Aldous said. "I need your help, please. Obviously, the lives of my entire family depends on it."

Von Piddle patted the beads of sweat on his forehead and then blew his nose. He avoided looking at Fletcher. With fumbling hands, he hit the button to light his tablet.

"Well, I'll be glad to give you any help you need," he said, nodding at Woodrow and Aldous. "Now the square-winged bird is the Thunderbird, a mythical Native American creature that dominates all natural activities. He held up the tablet and moved it closer to his face and read:

The Thunderbird symbolizes divine dominion, protection, provision, strength, authority, and Indomitable spirit. This cross-cultural symbol is found among the plains Indians as well as tribes in the Pacific Northwest and Northeast, though it's meaning may vary across different groups. Some tribes considered the Thunderbird to be a sign of war and the sound of thunder in the clouds was believed to be a prophecy of victory in wars if dances and ceremonies were performed.

"Any idea what the two symbols mean when they're combined like on the back of Mollyockett's stone?" asked Aldous. "There's got to be a reason why those two were chosen."

"Well if you ask me, the maze clearly indicates a journey of sorts in nature is about to begin by someone."

"Nature, as in Whole," Fletcher said sharply. "It's obvious that's what it references.

"Well, young man, I'll have to trust you on that one," replied Alek quickly. "I'd have given my right leg to have joined you on that little jaunt."

"It's an amazing place," Aldous said, reinforcing what had been described to a breathless Von Piddle at the start of the meeting.

"Absolutely mind-boggling," Alek said. "Now back to the Thunderbird. Again, I may be wrong, but I'd say whoever is about to take this journey is literally declaring war on those who may not approve."

"Tomhegan," said Fletcher. "It's obvious what he's trying to do."

Woodrow stood up and filled his coffee cup. "From what you've described, Fletch, " he said. "Tomhegan clearly is not the leader of whatever is going on right now. What'd you say were the names of those two other guys?"

"Nukpana and Tygorge. At least it sounded that way."

Von Piddle quickly clicked away at his keyboard, carefully navigating his way through years of research. After graduating from Balston Prep, he'd obtained a doctorate in both survey engineering and Native

American studies at MIT and was considered an expert at locating ancient burial sites long lost to the elements throughout the world. Woodrow considered it a stroke of luck that Alek returned home to Mahoosuc, Maine, to live out his final years.

"My, my, what do we have here," Alek said, sitting up quickly and ready to feed the hungry listeners with more information. "According to this, Nukpana is a Native American name meaning evil," He stayed focused on the screen and clicked away. "Hmm, strange. Nothing regarding Tygorge. I don't know if it's *actually* spelled the way you said they pronounced it, Fletcher."

"He's the one with the wand, isn't he?" asked Aldous. Fletcher nodded.

"Any idea what Slaughter Makers means?" Woodrow asked, jotting down Alek's every word.

"Zippo. Unfortunately, nothing comes up, which is unusual. But sounds like those *pretty little darlings* are appropriately named," he said, holding onto the tablet while dropping two lumps of sugar into the coffee Aldous had just poured for him.

"You know what I find interesting," Woodrow chimed in. "If you actually listen to what Fletcher said happened to him last night, it's obvious that the four men sitting in those chairs were unable to cross over into *our* world because of some type of thin barrier."

"What do you mean?" Aldous and Von Piddle said simultaneously.

Woodrow stood. "First, that foggy thing visits Fletcher's room and instructs him to carry the stone star to the root cellar. Then they threatened death by two monsters named Camazotz and Uktena. Next, the man called Nukpana instructs Fletcher to push the star to the Slaughter Makers who were standing beside the thin white curtain thing. Wouldn't it make more sense for them to actually take possession of the star rather than to have Fletch slide it over to the Slaughter Makers? And didn't you say that they were moving and bending like some sort of mirage, Fletcher?"

"It looked that way. They all swayed in unison like an old television reel."

"What do you know about old televisions?" Von Piddle asked.

Woodrow continued, "Finally, Fletcher said Tomhegan made an

attempt to attack him but ran into an invisible window that blocked his way. Didn't you say you heard a bang?"

Fletcher nodded. "They do have that star, though. I wonder if it gets them into Whole?"

Silence filled the room.

Von Piddle sat down and closed his eyes, contemplating Woodrow's thoughts.

"It's like they need Croft and McGovern to do the dirty work for them," said Fletcher aimlessly. Nothing made sense.

Everyone stopped and looked at him.

"Brilliant," said Alek. "The Slaughter Makers are actually the pawns for whoever *they* are. It's like they're building their own little army to do the dirty work for them."

"Unbelievable," shrieked Aldous. "How many more innocent souls will suffer the same fate."

"I really feel bad for what happened to Croft and Walton," sighed Fletcher sympathetically. "You should see what they look like now."

Again silence filled the room.

"Well what else do we have," Alek murmured. He didn't even know what to do next. "I think I need to ponder all this at Ye Old Boot."

"I was waiting for that," Woodrow muttered. Happy hour was calling, and Von Piddle was known to answer.

"*Whole Abounds,*" Fletcher gasped, remembering the backpack he'd brought. "It's in the truck." He quickly sped off to the truck.

"I thought that was in Whole?" Aldous asked confused. "How'd it—"

"Err, we forgot to tell you about that," Woodrow confessed. He turned slightly red and averted Aldous' eyes. "Squire Susup left it for Fletcher last night after he healed all his broken bones."

"Broken what?" gasped Aldous, jumping up. "What on earth are you talking about?"

Alek flashed a confused glance at Woodrow, then went over to examine the inventory of the small bar.

"Aldous, there is so much going on right now. It slipped my mind," replied Woodrow in an attempt to disarm the situation. "I had no idea where to start. Honest."

Fletcher's father sat back down and closed his eyes. "What broken bones?" he whispered in an attempt to calm his nerves.

"I've no idea. I never asked," Woodrow murmured.

The tension was immediately lowered when Fletcher ran into the room carrying *Whole Abounds.*

Alek immediately put down the green bottle that he'd been holding and ran over to him. He recognized the book as being extremely old and very rare. "My stars, where'd you get that? You had *that* in your backpack?" He was aghast. "May I?"

"Help yourself," Fletcher invited.

Alek quickly pulled two white linen napkins off a side table next to the small bar. Everyone remained silent as they watched him take the two napkins, wrap them around *Whole Abounds,* then carry it to the table as though it was the original *Mona Lisa.*

"Where'd you get this?" he asked.

"Pidianiski translated it from Kozart's writings two centuries ago while in Whole," said Fletcher, moving closer to look at the writings. "It's meant to teach us what's in Whole and the importance of everything there."

"Ah, two new characters. Are these good or bad people?" Alek stood up and went back to the bar. "Or do I dare ask?"

"Your uncle mentioned something about broken bones, Fletch. Mind if I ask what happened?" said Aldous with genuine concern as Alek poured a small drink from the green bottle and downed it before returning to the ancient book. "No idea, Dad. After the white light hit me the second time, I've no idea what happened. When I came to, the wall completely closed and *Whole Abounds* was lying next to it." He reached into his left pocket and pulled out the note left by Squire Susup. "This was inside."

As Aldous read the note out loud, a loud commotion was heard in the dining room.

Must be the wedding party, Woodrow thought, at first looking at his watch. *But there's no way they'd arrive this early."*

Everyone's attention was turned towards the door.

"I told you, Mr. Whoever you are, they are not to be disturbed, plus you really need to get your dog out of the dining area. Maine law allows only service dogs," Jessica stammered as the doorknob rattled loosely.

"Woodrow was insistent that you . . . You can't go in there!"

The stranger was clearly determined.

"Who on earth?" Woodrow said, moving towards the disturbance just as the uninvited visitor stepped into the room.

Alek quickly moved back to the green bottle and poured a larger portion and gulped it down in an instant.

"Ah, Fletcher, Aldous, great to see you again," said the new arrival, brushing a flabbergasted Jessica aside.

He had intelligent brown eyes and long, jet-black hair that was woven into an intricately complex braid. Beside him stood a girl with long black hair. She was petting a totally black cat. Fletcher and Aldous remembered seeing her with Squire Susup at the last Mollyockett Day festival on the Bethel Common.

Alek immediately recognized him as being a member of the Wabanaki tribe. "People of the Dawnland," he whispered to himself. He focused on the stovepipe top hat that had three blue feathers sticking out the top. They bent slightly as they brushed the ceiling. His eyes moved down to the black bow tie and yellow sweater, which was covered by a long-tail tuxedo jacket. All ten of his fingernails were painted black. He was casually leaning on an ornate cane. Beside him stood a muscular, short-haired white dog that was panting and drooling slightly. The young girl was obviously Wabanaki. She had long black hair that was held together by a single braid down her back. Her deer hide headband matched her dress as did her moccasins. Her black eyes were soft and deeply pene-trating. As she took in the onlookers, she continued to pet her cat.

"Mr. McKenzie, I'm so sorry. I told them that they couldn't come in here and that his dog needed—"

"It's okay, Jessica," Woodrow said raising his hand. "You've done nothing wrong." He paused and looked towards Aldous who was clearly relieved. "Would you mind having the kitchen prepare some sandwiches for us?"

The calvary was there. Its name was Squire Susup.

CHAPTER 5

FRENCHMAN'S HOLE

ON THE MAP, HIS DESTINATION HAD BEEN A SMALL ROAD WITH A GRASSY strip in the middle. It ended at the base of the Mahoosuc Range of the Appalachian Mountains in Western Maine. No busy highways nearby, or anything, really. They'd been left far behind. Harrison Sweet had put a photo of Frenchman's Hole on his small refrigerator in July. It'd be the ideal place to find the *perfect* shot for the article assigned to him by the publisher of *New England Magazine*.

Given how many tourists were in the area, he was surprised that the small parking lot was empty as he parked his rental at the top of Frenchman's Hole. *Nothing like Beacon Hill, thankfully,* he thought as he carefully navigated the hazardous path towards upper Sunday River. Freshly fallen leaves crunched under his new leather boots he'd purchased in Freeport on the way towards Bethel.

The thick woods had not been expecting him. If anything, it tried to throw him out, over and over again with the combination of wet leaves, slippery rocks, and thick mud. Both he and his camera were jostled as he slowly navigated his way towards the swirling water. The imagery was stunning even though the foliage had peaked a few days ago. He stood on a large smooth rock at the edge of the water and looked towards the falls. He'd read that Frenchman's Hole was a popular swimming spot for locals and adventurous out-of-staters who braved the cold clear water and dangerous currents. He stopped and listened to a small squirrel scampering up the hill and towards the dirt road. *There's no way my photo won't make the cover,* he thought even though he had made the decision not to attempt to cross the river after carefully analyzing the pattern of slippery boulders protruding above the fast flowing river. Still, he carefully jumped forward onto a larger rock.

His expensive camera was heavy. Although it was a short walk to the top of the waterfall, it was a treacherous one. Slowly, the sound of falling water intensified as the popular swimming hole came into view. Not surprising, the mist from the waterfall made the rocks on the sides of the river slick. He cautiously stepped onto a flat ledge that framed the northern edge of the swimming hole and sat down. He was careful not to get too close to the edge. He was more worried about his camera than he was of himself. Worlds away from his fast-paced life, he appreciated the serenity of the moment. He sat and pondered life and his current station in it.

Rays of light penetrated the vibrant trees and illuminated the water flowing over a small carved indentation in the granite lip at the top of the falls. He watched the stream crash into a deep dark pool before winding its way through the scenic valley and merging with the Androscoggin River and on towards the Atlantic Ocean. Mindful of the autumn's diminishing sunlight in Northern New England, he slowly stood up and removed the cap from his telephoto lens. To get the perfect shot, he needed to move fast.

Just then the unmistakable sound and movement of scraping rocks punctured the air, and the ground beneath him shifted. Harrison was caught off balance. He jerked forward towards the water and reached out to catch himself. He gripped a small branch directly to his right and spun around as the ground's movement increased in intensity. Panicked, he watched in horror as his camera slipped from his grasp onto the granite rock and then plunked into Frenchman's Hole. *I cannot believe Maine is having an earthquake of this magnitude and for this long. Of all places,* he thought as he slid backwards towards the steep hill leading up to the road.

The undergrowth was so thick it blocked any escape towards relative safety. Suddenly a loud booming sound reverberated in his ears and then a huge crack appeared directly in front of him, sending rock dust upwards. It felt as though a train was bearing down on him. Small rocks wedged in the undergrowth tumbled down towards him and into the water causing giant waves to ripple outwards in every direction. Unable to stand, he found himself sliding on the rough rock and back down the slope.

As he slid down towards the water, two enormous boulders split and moved upwards directly under the precipice where the water leaped into the air. Then they fell into the deep pool, blocking Sunday River's flow and temporarily moving the current towards him. He sat horror-stricken. Any escape was now unimaginable.

He grabbed onto a large branch and pulled. Cold water immediately flowed over his boots and towards his knees just as a large opening appeared between the rocks that were blocking the river's path. He stood transfixed, unaware of the increasing pull of water.

What the? he thought, watching the opening grow into a large cavern. Stunned, he was convinced he recognized the outline of a person standing upright even though the ground jerked violently around him. *What on earth?*

Harrison was in complete shock when a flash of white light catapulted from the dark opening towards him. An extraordinary lightness seemed to spread from every direction and electrify his body. In an instant, he flew upwards and directly over the river's new path. *Pfffftttt,* a loud noise reverberated through the canyon. Two badly burnt boots splashed into the swirling water as small pieces of black unidentifiable matter fluttered slowly in the air before landing softly throughout the deep valley. The rocks and boulders continued to move and grind as the earth's gravity wedged them downwards. Within a few seconds, silence filled the autumn air as the flow of the river returned to the path it'd followed for millennia.

The entire room went silent. The girl with the cat didn't move and remained near the door. Everyone stood and watched Squire Susup and the dog approach the group. His eyes were on Alek. Clearly not a McKenzie. He knew them all well.

"I'd have to say you're clearly related to the Pigwackets," said Von Piddle, stepping towards him. He'd studied Native Americans his entire life and was genuinely interested in the new arrival. The squire leaned on the tip of his ornate cane, saying nothing. He was deeply dismayed that the stranger had been reading *Whole Abounds,* one of Whole's most guarded secrets.

"Squire, it's good to see you," said Aldous, breaking the ice. "I'd like you to meet Alek Von Piddle. He's an expert on indigenous people, specifically Native Americans, *and* with locating lost artifacts."

"Mr. Von Piddle helped me tremendously when dad was—" Fletcher started to chime in before the squire nodded. He was thrilled to see his old friend who always made an appearance on Mollyockett Day and to help guide generations of McKenzie's through the passage annually on the way to Whole.

The squire reached out to greet Alek. Von Piddle immediately focused on his painted black nails while grasping onto his leathery hands. His eyes moved downward towards the bottom of the elaborately decorated gold staff. *That thing belongs in the Smithsonian,* he thought, stunned. It was an absolute historical treasure.

"Fletcher's never mentioned you."

"That was at my suggestion," said Woodrow defensively. "But up until today, he's known nothing of Whole."

The squire dropped his hand and stepped backwards while glaring at Woodrow. The McKenzie secret had been grossly violated.

"Obviously, you know things are not well," retorted Aldous. "The lives of the entire McKenzie family have been threatened."

Susup nodded knowingly and moved towards the table. "Fletcher, would you mind giving Onion some water?"

"Fletcher was almost killed last night," said Aldous. "And from what we've just been told, we don't have much time." There was desperation in his voice.

"Aldous, that's why I'm here. First, I'd like you to all to meet Lalia and her cat Humeante." Lalia nodded at the onlookers while continuing to lightly massage the cat. "She's here to help as well." He paused. "Trust me, I'm trying to do everything I can to figure out what exactly is going on. Even Mollyockett's confused and deeply concerned for the safety of your family. She directed me to come here."

"Did you say, *Mollyockett* told you to come to *this* inn?" gasped Alek.

Immediately his eyes blinked uncontrollably, bouncing his glasses wildly on his nose.

Susup furrowed his brow, intrigued by the movement.

"Yes. She's my mother," he said nonchalantly. "Why?"

Von Piddle's eyes blinked so rapidly that he took off his glasses and blindly walked in the direction of the bar. Onion stopped lapping at the white bowl Fletcher had filled with water and followed Alek.

"Squire, what do you think's going on?" Aldous asked gravely. He felt like he'd aged ten years in the last twenty-four hours. "Obviously your familiar with the incidents at your mother's grave and Snow Falls."

"We're all very sorry for what happened to her final resting place," said Woodrow.

Aldous nodded apologetically. "I'm sorry. I can't imagine how that must've impacted you."

Von Piddle nodded, confused. His now foggy mind swirled with dozens of questions. He moved sideways and accidentally bumped into Onion.

"Been pumping the old iron, haven't you Fletcher?" he whispered toward the muscular dog.

The squire moved over to *Whole Abounds* and tapped his right index finger on the open page. "Fletcher, who was there last night?" he asked.

"Well, other than the fog that gave me instructions, Tomhegan was there." He moved to his seat and sat down. "As well as two other guys named Nukpana and Tygorge. There was one other guy who looked similar to Tygorge, but they didn't say his name. Before that, the fog in my room mentioned two names: Camazotz and Uktena. It instructed me to obey or they would kill me."

Susup swallowed hard and sat down. He laid his staff on the table and began to roll it slowly.

"Then there were the two Slaughter Makers. Want me to describe them?" There was distress in his words. Susup looked at him and thought how much had changed since their visit to Whole less than three months ago. He closed his eyes as Fletcher expertly described Croft and Walton.

"I thought you would have known about what happened last night." Fletcher said. "You always know what is going on."

Susup didn't answer him.

Aldous' temperature immediately spiked. The silence spoke volumes. Other than the squire, he'd had more experience with Whole than any other person in the room. "I'll be right back," he said as he moved towards the door. "I need to call the house and tell them that Fletcher is with me. Heaven knows what'll happen if they find out he's not with Quinn and Camway."

Woodrow quickly nodded in agreement. Lucille was a ticking time bomb when it came to Fletcher and any lack of knowledge with respect to his whereabouts. He'd actually wanted to investigate the stone wall in the root cellar before coming to the inn but changed his mind. Lucille was on the hunt, and he was avoiding her at all costs.

Alek recovered his glasses with the help of Susup and clumsily sat at the table. His glazed eyes focused on the gold tip of the staff. *Simply marvelous.*

Susup quickly pulled *Whole Abounds* towards him much to the dismay of Alek who considered it a priceless artifact that needed to be treated accordingly.

The others silently quizzed him as he scanned each page. "Ah, here we are," he exclaimed.

They all immediately leaned towards the book.

"Vitamin B12," said Susup. "Fletcher, let me have your hand."

Without hesitating, Fletcher extended his right hand. The squire grabbed onto it and extended his index finger. Slowly, he rubbed it on the black-and-white drawing next to the word *B12*.

Fletcher expected the same vivid mental explosion he'd experienced in Whole when he was with Machias. Nothing.

Silently, Susup continued to move through the faded pages. He stopped and grabbed onto Fletcher's hand again. Quickly, he traced his index finger on a crudely sketched tree with the words: *maidenhair, source of ginkgo biloba.*

The impact was instantaneous.

Fletcher's mind exploded in a multitude of bright flashes of vivid, beautiful colors. Sharp electrical currents vibrated throughout his brain then bounced off his skull. Immediately he had unimaginable clarity.

It was reminiscent of the time Machias had told him to rub the ginkgo leaves while in Whole. He instantly felt the inner sanctum of his memory being tapped.

Aldous immediately knew what'd happened. He too had experienced Whole's powers numerous times before control of the passage had been transferred to Fletcher while he was medically incapacitated.

"But—" Fletcher started..

"What—" Woodrow interrupted.

"As long as Lalia is here," The Squire explained, "You can tap into Whole's powers up here. Mollyockett and Machias are sure of that. I need you to focus on last night and tell us every detail, Fletcher." He said, crouching anxiously in front of the leather bounded book.

"What's going on here?" asked Alek. He lowered his head and refocused on the half empty green bottle on the bar. "Looks a little hocus-pocus to me."

"Let me get you some water." Woodrow said, reaching for a silver pitcher siting in the middle of the table. Von Piddle protested silently.

Fletcher closed his eyes as the room became eerily silent. Aldous picked up a pen and waited. "Well, I was sleeping when a voice woke me up and then. . ."

Fletcher spoke in vivid detail for thirty uninterrupted minutes as the four other men gaped in horror. Everyone had gasped loudly when Fletcher described what he thought was Susup healing his broken body in the root cellar. Lalia knowingly smiled. When he opened his eyes, no one spoke a word. Aldous laid down his pen and rubbed his eyes. His heart was beating so fast it felt like his chest was going to explode.

My family, he thought.

"You're positive you're okay?" Woodrow asked, giving Fletcher's entire body a cursory look.

"I feel fine, positive." He glanced towards the squire. "Thank you."

Susup stood up and rubbed his forehead. Alek meanwhile was preoccupied with the three blue feathers brushing the ceiling. "Well," said Susup. "First, I agree with all of you that a barrier of sorts prevented them from leaving wherever they were sitting when they had the Slaughter Makers attack that boar. If they could, they'd have grabbed the stone star themselves. I'll ask mother what she thinks."

Von Piddle giggled then immediately looked away. Whatever he was drinking was now registering.

Susup stood up. "There's no way they're getting their hands on *Whole Abounds,* Fletcher's staff, and Vilcanota's patera."

"What's the release code mean?" asked Fletcher.

"I've never heard of a release code," the squire admitted. "I wonder who's feeding them their information."

The squire dragged the notebook Aldous had been writing on across the table and studied it. He focused on the words *Camaztoz* and *Uktena.* The two names the foggy voice had told Fletcher would kill him unless he followed his instructions.

Susup moved towards the back of the room.

"Camaztoz is the death bat. It's—"

He stopped when he noticed Alek's hand wildly waving in the air as if asking permission to speak. "What *exactly* just happened to Fletcher?" Alek slurred. "It's like the old chap was reciting directly from a book."

"The nutrients of the body," said Fletcher, looking at his father. "They feed the body and each one of them have a particular impact. Vitamin B12 and ginkgo biloba improve your memory. In Whole, however, they are super boosted."

"We've been told many times that Whole is changing just like nature itself," said Susup, clearly annoyed by Alek's interruption. He felt he needed to address Fletcher's confusion. "Unfortunately those changes are not good. Mollyockett's been working diligently to counter all the evil that's recently surfaced. Don't ask me how she did it, but *Whole Abounds* now has the unique abilities up here as it does in Whole as long as Lalia is present. You know the same—"

He was interrupted by a knocking sound at the door.

Woodrow quickly walked over and opened it.

"Thank you, Jessica, I really appreciate all your help." He carefully grabbed onto a large platter of beautifully displayed sandwiches and wrapped Paw-Paw Bars. "Please make sure we're not interrupted."

"Fletcher, the powers of the patera you used during your encounter with Tomhegan can now be accessed in your world using *Whole Abounds* if Lalia is with you."

"How'd you heal me if only I can use them?" Fletcher quizzed him.

No one had seen him jerk his right hand into his pocket. Once again, it burned painfully. Silently, he fought off the urge to scream.

"You actually healed yourself," Susup responded.

Fletcher looked confused.

"I found your broken and battered body on the floor of the root cellar after being told by Mollyockett to hurry. I immediately summoned Lalia then traced your finger on numerous vitamins and minerals to fix your broken body. It wasn't an easy task given the damage you'd suffered."

"Good heavens," Aldous gasped, horrified.

Woodrow shook his head and patted Fletcher's shoulders.

Alek's mouth fell open.

"Now, if you don't mind, I was discussing Camaztoz!" said the squire sharply. He was annoyed with the constant disruptions. "This ferocious bird originates with the ancient Mayans, who consider him to be a powerful god-monster from Xibalba, where he presides over an army of bloodthirsty bats. He's powerful enough to destroy entire civilizations but made a treaty with humans." He paused. "He brought them fire, but in exchange he demands a constant and unending flow of human sacrifices."

"Hogwash," said Alek curtly. His head was about to explode.

Aldous turned towards Woodrow and nodded annoyingly at Von Piddle. He was now questioning his presence.

"Trust me, we'll need his expertise," Woodrow whispered while shoving a glass of water in front of his old friend.

Susup and Lalia glared at Alek with extreme annoyance.

"What is Xibalba?" said Fletcher eagerly.

"Pounced *see-ball-ba*, it translates into 'place of fear' and is the name of the underworld in Mayan mythology, which was ruled by Maya death gods and their helpers. Over five hundred years ago, the entrance of Xibalba was believed to be a cave in Guatemala. Even to this day, locals associate that cave with death and Camaztoz's home."

"Would that have anything to do with the passage's southern entrance I sealed the first time I visited the Quechuan temple?" asked Fletcher.

"Perhaps. Mollyockett is still attempting to decipher deviations in the Cygnus constellation." Susup said.

"Did you say *the Cygnus* constellation?" Aldous chimed in. The puzzle was expanding. Cygnus was the name of the food empire the McKenzie family controlled for generations. Started by Thomas Gage McKenzie, a logger turned baker, he named the company after having a dream that included the northern constellation Cygnus on the exact day he baked his first loaf of Birch Bread. It was a healthy, whole wheat bread with a slight touch of Maine maple syrup.

"That's what she told me," Susup pressed on. "Obviously Camaztoz is an ominous sign."

"You think?" Alek blurted out. He quickly decided it was best to align with Susup.

Susup ignored him.

"Now, Uktena is the Horned Serpent. Surprisingly, it's not Mayan. You see, Cherokee legend prominently features this dragon-like behemoth, which they believe started out as a human being who took the serpentine shape to seek revenge on those who had wronged him. These powerful monsters are lightning fast and can devour a person with a single bite."

"And they were the ones in Fletcher's room last night?" Woodrow gasped.

"Good Heavens, the old chap is lucky to be here with us." Alek muttered. "Are you sure it was those—"

Alek stopped when Susup glared at him coldly. His brown eyes were no longer soft. "No offense, mister, no offense meant," Alek mumbled. He was dying to ask him how Mollyockett's son could be alive in this room given that he had been born centuries ago.

"If you're going to question everything, why are you here?" retorted the squire. He glanced towards Aldous. "Wait till mother finds out the secret has been violated."

"We may need his help in the future,' Aldous said. "Obviously there's not much time left." Everything was spiraling out of control and the very lives of his family were at stake. Plus, I had no idea you were on your way.

Sensing his desperation, Susup stopped and motioned towards the food. "Let's take a quick break, shall we?"

Afraid he'd be booted from the gathering, Alek moved towards Woodrow for support. While they ate, Fletcher picked up the pen and started to sketch the evil faces carved into the granite walls opposite the Slaughter Makers in the cave. Given his expanded and vivid memory, the task was fairly easy.

"So what's your history with indigenous people?" Susup asked Von Piddle who was meticulously rearranging slices of turkey between two slices of Birch Bread.

He shrugged and looked at Fletcher's sketches while answering. "Graduated with Woodrow at Balston Prep then went to Massachusetts Institute of Technology. I have my doctorate in survey engineering, particularly historical sites, and Native American studies. Unfortunately, neither are offered there anymore. Shame."

The squire studied the man's gentle demeanor. Adventure was clearly carved in the lines that graced his forehead.

"Finding the place where the two eagles nest was a sheer stroke of luck," he said jovially, remembering the task given to him by Woodrow and Fletcher three years ago. Even though they'd mislead him, he was thrilled to discover that it had actually led to the mysterious world of Whole and helped him rescue his mother and heal his father.

"What's your thoughts, Squire?" Aldous asked.

"I'm trying to figure everything out," Susup answered, looking at him blankly.

Woodrow, who was studying an old glass-framed map of Oxford County, cleared his throat. "So, if you think about it, the past three incidents *all* involve Mollyockett's life."

The squire and Aldous nodded in agreement.

"First, we have the incident at Snow Falls. Everyone's familiar with the curse she placed on—"

"Curse, what curse?" Von Piddle blurted out oblivious to the mayonnaise dripping on his shirt.

Fletcher quickly grabbed onto his right hand and rubbed it in an effort to mitigate the burning sensation. The entire group was oblivious to his trauma.

The squire rolled his eyes. "Go on, might as well tell him so he knows everything," he sighed.

"How can you grow up in Mahoosuc and not know about the curse she placed on the residents of Snow Falls?" Woodrow asked, confused.

Alek hunched his shoulders. "I may have at one time, but I'm finding time has not been good to my memory every now and them. There's a lot tucked up there."

"To make a long story short," Woodrow said through gritted teeth. "Mollyockett was caught in a blizzard in 1810. She made it to the village of Snow Falls and sought shelter. Unfortunately, every resident turned her away."

"Barbarians," muttered Alek. He was very familiar with the discrimination Native Americans experienced at the hands of the colonial settlers.

Woodrow continued, "So she moved on. She had no choice. But before departing, she placed a curse on the entire village condemning it to eternal failure. After walking for hours in white-out conditions, she arrived at the door of Dr. Hamlin's mansion on Paris hill. The county's wealthiest man welcomed her even though his infant son, just a few weeks old, was near death. Much to his surprise, Mollyockett used her knowledge of roots and herbs to heal the sick infant. Before she left, she blessed the baby saying, "may he become extremely successful and famous." He went on to become a United States Senator as well as the fifteenth vice president under Abraham Lincoln."

Alek was extremely familiar with Hannibal Hamlin's accomplishments. Not wanting to be seen as a nuisance, he listened intently. He'd already drawn the ire of Squire Susup.

Fletcher looked up from his drawings.

"Soon after she cursed Snow Falls, the large mill failed, throwing most of the residents out of work. Many moved, which contributed to the failure of the other businesses. And to this day no company has been able to make a go at it. In fact, there are less than ten structures

standing today. Down from several hundred at the time of the blizzard."
Woodrow looked towards them, annoyed the disquisition had taken
so long.

"The waterfall at Snow Falls is where the first incident took place,"
Fletcher chimed in.

"Actually, the second incident, the desecration of her grave, took
place almost at the same time," Aldous corrected him, moving towards
the map. "And both times someone got killed."

"Well obviously they wanted something aside from the symbol they
stole from the bottom of her gravestone," Susup replied coldly. "I can't
believe they actually violated her grave."

Silence filled the room out of respect.

"We all are familiar with the third incident. The very place that leads
to Whole in the root cellar," Woodrow said solemnly. "Its importance
cannot be understated in the relationship between Mollyockett and the
McKenzie family." With his finger, he drew a triangle connecting the
three locations on the glass protecting the map.

Alek leaned back. Retirement had been so simple for him less than
twenty-four hours ago. *What's happening?* He thought. *Have I actually
gone crazy?*

In the background, three emergency vehicles raced passed the
McKenzie Inn, sirens blaring as they headed in the direction of
Frenchmen's Hole.

Little did the group know that Woodrow's triangle was now a crude
square with the addition of a fourth incident—a location that was the
very heart and soul of Mollyockett's life. The *very* place where she transferred the power of the passage from her bloodline to Jackson McKenzie.

CHAPTER 6

OLLANTAYTAMBO REVISITED

EARLY THE NEXT DAY, MOLLYOCKETT WAS UP WAITING FOR PIDIANISKI. She'd been briefed by Squire Susup the night before and had spent the night pondering all he'd told her. Everything was swiftly spiraling downwards. While the squire had the unique and unexplained ability to travel between Fletcher's world and Whole, Mollyockett was restricted to the magical land. Again, one of Whole's mysteries. She was completely comfortable with the deck she'd been dealt. The trade-off also included the ability to take advantage of the nutrients it offered that extend both hers and Susup's lives for eternity.

Dark days are upon us, she thought as she inhaled a crude stone pipe. It was the Quechua pipe Fletcher had pocketed while sealing the southern passage in Whole. The following year, he presented it to her as a gift during his annual visit to her garden. It was her most prized possession.

She seriously wondered if the era of the McKenzie family controlling the passage was coming to a close. She vowed to use her last breath to keep from letting that happen. In order to save Whole, she needed to decipher the mysterious clues given to her and pass them on to Susup. The lives of the entire McKenzie family depended on her once again.

She was in her garden—the one place she needed to be during a time of crisis. Comfortably resting in her root chair, she took in a majestic waterfall in the valley below. Small fluffy clouds formed in the mist created by the aqua blue water swirling at the base of the falls. Slowly they expanded into dark gray clouds filled with water. Effortlessly, each one meandered towards enormous rows of fruit-filled trees of every imaginable type. As if on cue, each stopped directly over a designated tree and released its contents, quenching the thirsty plant.

"Sorry, I came as quickly as I could."

Mollyockett was so transfixed she'd not heard Pidianiski arrive. She stood and turned towards the voice of her friend who she helped transcribed *Whole Abounds* for her people and later, the McKenzie family, hundreds of years ago. Pidianiski was wearing a brown leather dress that matched her crude leather shoes. A thin rawhide belt was tied around her waist which secured a large hunting knife. Her dark black hair was tied into two large braids that spilt her hair down the center. They were held into place by a thin leather strip tied around her head. A brown bald eagle's feather was fastened to the back of the headpiece and stood proudly over her frame. Mollyockett was very familiar with this particular type of eagle feather. Its main ingredient was keratin, a fibrous structural protein that also made up the outer layer of human skin. She'd used these feathers many times to help burn victims recover while living in Western Maine. It was one of her many secrets that made her a legend.

Unlike others in her tribe, Pidianiski was not one to dress elaborately. She believed in simplicity and lived her life that way.

"That's an impressive knife," Mollyockett observed.

Pidianiski looked her over, taking in every detail of the pattern of red and black porcupine quills decorating Mollyockett's long leather dress. They always told a story. She was, however, taken back by her disheveled appearance and the dark bags under her tired eyes. "Obviously things are dire," Pidianiski said, arching one of her dark brows.

Mollyockett sat down and invited Pidianiski to join her. Pidianiski closed her eyes and thought of her woven root chair left behind in her circular thatched hut. She looked at Mollyockett's long pipe with disdain as a cluster of brown roots punctured the ground's crust then expertly wove themselves into an exact replica of her own chair. She quickly sat down.

"If the antioxidants down here didn't reverse the deadly results of that thing, I'd never smoke." She swallowed hard. "It calms me."

Pidianiski shook her head from side to side. She casually folded her hands on her lap, exposing her painted black nails.

Mollyockett dismissed her disapproval. "Squire was here last night," she said gravely. "Dire is an understatement." She screwed up her eyes in an effort to remember every detail she'd seen and heard from Squire and others. *Where to begin? Tomhegan. I knew in my gut he had survived that encounter with Fletcher.*

Pidianiski read her mind. "Tygorge and Nukpana?"

Mollyockett nodded. "They've conspired with Tomhegan. Never in a million years would I have expected that to happen."

"Nothing about Tomhegan surprises me."

Mollyockett reached into her pocket and passed Vilcanota's patera to Pidianiski. After a moment or two, Pidianiski knew she didn't want to hear what was about to come.

"They're demanding Fletcher's staff, the patera, and *Whole Abounds* or they're going to kill the entire McKenzie family in December."

Pidianiski rolled the disk-shaped stone in her hand. "How'd they know about this?" she demanded.

Mollyockett took a long drag on her pipe and closed her eyes. "I've no idea, I'm trying to figure it out," she muttered. "Any idea what the *release code* for *Whole Abounds* means?"

Pidianiski did not answer her immediately. She looked into her intense eyes then out towards a cloud floating casually towards a row of orange trees. *Is this the beginning of the end?* After a long pause she said, "No idea. I may have thoughts on it though. But, if they know about everything they're demanding, the McKenzie family is not the only thing that's in grave danger." She threw Mollyockett a dark look.

"Care to take a conjecture on the release code? It's vital we figure out what it is."

Pidianiski swallowed hard while thinking. "At this time, I don't. I'm sorry." Time stood still while they both pondered the situation. Pidianiski was the first to break the silence. "When I was transcribing *Whole Abounds,* I was told that everything had to be absolutely perfect. There was no room for the slightest mistake. As you know quite well, both the book and patera affords the person who holds the power of the passage unique powers *if* they know how to precisely tap into a particular nutrient that comes from Whole. However, they must—"

She was interrupted by a large colorful bird that swooped in and perched itself on a log fence overlooking the valley.

Mollyockett turned to greet Merrimack, an Australian Outback parrot that had been her closest companion for years. She immediately turned her attention back to the matter at hand. They needed to move quickly.

"You were saying."

"They must tap into the correct nutrient or the results could be devastating." She rolled the patera over in her hand and closed her eyes. "Just like that time when Fletcher encountered Tomhegan and needed incredible strength. He quickly needed to tap into the proper amino acids that make up proteins to expand his muscles. Amino acids are wonderful things, there are twenty of them and—"

"I'm very familiar with amino acids that make up proteins," Mollyockett said with slight impatience. "Your thoughts are wandering."

Pidianiski continued, "They're the very building blocks for proteins that constitutes one of the seven nutrients of life itself. One of the twenty amino acids is phenylalanine. It's wonderful when connected to other amino acids, but alone it can cause immediate adverse reactions with some people."

"Why are you giving me this dissertation on proteins?" Mollyockett asked.

"Because we can use what we know against them."

Against them, Merrimack imitated her words.

"Pffft," Mollyockett said, smiling at her pet. Merrimack happily jerked his head up and down rapidly."

Knowledge is power, Mollyockett thought. The very words she'd left in a note to Jackson McKenzie centuries ago.

Pidianiski continued, "There are molecules in phenylalanine that can kill you if maximized. Stupidly, humans have turned it into a non-carbohydrate sweetener for many soft drinks, which is carcinogenic to the brain."

Mollyockett was now tuned into what she was saying.

"Cancer," she muttered.

"Exactly. Had Fletcher tapped *just* that one particular amino acid while attempting to expand his strength, he'd have died of brain cancer on the spot."

Mollyockett smiled. Pidianiski was one step ahead of her. *While the nutrients are the essential components in foods that organisms use to survive and grow, they can be used as weapons too. Perhaps, we can turn the patera into a weapon against them. A perfect Trojan Horse of sorts. Chances are extremely slim they know how to properly use it.*

"What are you thinking?"

"I think we need to fully understand everything Squire relayed to you last night."

"Again, thoughts on the *release code* he mentioned. I've never even heard of it."

"I'm as confused as you," Pidianiski answered and thought back to the time when the two of them translated *Whole Abounds.* "I recall something about the book being a *key* to something, but Kozart didn't call it that."

A thoughtful look came over her face as she gazed down at the patera she had been rubbing. "They could've been mistaken. You're sure that is what they meant?"

Mollyockett nodded her head. "Positive. Tygorge and Nukpana are never confused. I'd stake my life on it."

She took the patera from Pidianiski's hands, wanting her full attention. "They've reunited the five principal nations of the Wabanaki Confederacy: Mi'kmaq, Miliseet, Passamaquoddy, Abenaki, and Penobscot. Just like your father had done."

Pidianiski's mouth opened in disbelief. "That's impossible. How?"

"You question Whole? There are parts that remain a complete mystery even to this day. Trust me, the reunification has happened."

Pidianiski's eyes narrowed. It was all coming together in her mind. "With the most evil chief each nation had ever produced now turning up," she said as she turned pale.

"They've also desecrated my grave and removed the symbol from the bottom of my stone."

"Wait! What!?" Pidianiski exclaimed with a horrified look. She hadn't expected the reunification of the five Wabanaki nations. An ominous sign predicted by Machias many years ago. One that she had dismissed as ludicrous. Now this. *Why on earth would they need to desecrate her grave?*

"Ashes to ashes, dust to dust," said Mollyockett, casually brushing off the response.

Pidianiski was suddenly reminded why Mollyockett had been chosen as caretaker of Whole. She fully understood it for the most part. It's powers, secrets, and beauty. She was the perfect person.

"After they violated my final resting place, they left two symbols on the back of my stone. One was the Thunderbird we're both familiar with. The other is the Hopi Maze that represents Mother Earth."

Pidianiski nodded and furrowed her brow. "What's the significance of that?"

"It's obvious. The Thunderbird symbolizes a sign of war and domination. The maze represents the beginning of a journey into nature or Mother Earth." She focused on Merrimack who silently watched her every move. "Clearly, the two are a metaphor for the new confederation's move to eliminate the McKenzie family and their allies by declaring war for Whole itself."

Pidianiski studied Mollyockett's dark eyes. She'd never seen her old friend look so exhausted.

"If we put our minds together, our chances are good."

Mollyockett laughed. "There's more, which is why I asked you to hurry."

There's more? Pidianiski said.

"Fletcher's bedroom was visited by some type of fog that directed him to the root cellar. Under the threat of death, he was forced to use the star he'd taken when he sealed the southern passage to enter a mysterious cave of sorts. Nukpana, Tygorge, Tomhegan. and another unidentified man, along with their *friendly* Slaughter Makers, were waiting for him."

They looked at each other, attempting to fit the pieces of the growing puzzle together. "So this is where you come in."

Pidianiski sat on the edge of her seat and listened intently.

"The fog in his room was very clear that if he didn't do as told, Camazotz and Uktena would kill him."

Pidianiski immediately knew why she'd been called to this side of Whole. Aside from Fletcher, she was the only other person who'd been to the southern passage. In the Quechuan valley in Peru, there was a small town called Ollantaytambo. Its people had been the guardians of the southern passage before being wiped off the earth by European conquerors. Deadly diseases and war swiftly took their toll. Unlike Mollyockett, who foresaw the demise of her people, the Maya people of Ollantaytambo disappeared so quickly they didn't have time to react to the threat and protect the southern passage. The ruins of the town were soon lost to the immense jungle until "discovered" by Muriel and Von Piddle. Their ruse had paid off. Instead of massive deforestation, which likely would have led to the passage's discovery and possible destruction, the civilized world demanded that the entire area be given protective status as a major historical site. Immediately, it was flooded with historical buffs and international tourists. It's believed that Camaztoz, the god-like monster who presided over an army of bloodthirsty bats, originated in the small Peruvian town. Uktena, however, was Cherokee. Mollyockett would focus on that aspect of the mystery.

"Given the fact that they used *and* wanted the sixth star from the southern passage when they visited Fletcher speaks volumes," quavered Mollyockett. "Camaztoz's involvement is definitely an ominous sign."

Pidianiski knew what was next. "You know as well as I do that I cannot visit the location where the southern passage was located. Only the holder of the power of the passage can do that. You're not thinking about bringing in Fletcher?" asked Pidianiski nervously, moving over to stroke Merrimack's vibrant feathers. He sensed the seriousness of the expressions between the two women and remained silent.

Mollyockett moved with her and gave a forced chuckle.

"I'm planning on it."

"He'll be killed," Pidianiski whispered. Merrimack immediately flew off towards the fruit grove.

"Do you have any other options given what we know?"

"Battling Tomhegan is one thing, but *all* those chiefs together is another completely." Exasperated, she folded her arms. "Even the two of us working together don't stand a chance. And we have centuries of knowledge on our side." Mollyockett closed her eyes, thinking of the very first time she'd taken Fletcher to her garden and removed the cast on his leg. *Innocent was an understatement.*

"So why am I here?" said Pidianiski flatly. She was contemplating walking away but knew she physically couldn't. There was too much at stake and it would take them all to overcome what was expected in the very near future.

"Late last night, I had a word with Machias. As you're aware, he knows more about Whole than almost anyone." As she said this Pidianiski thought of Machias dressed in animal furs and his horned mask holding *Whole Abounds* high over Fletcher's head as Mollyockett transferred the power of the passage to Fletcher. "He's absolutely convinced," exclaimed Mollyockett, "that the restriction preventing you from returning to Ollantaytambo is no longer there given the star's power is now aligned with the symbol in Fletcher's root cellar."

"Based on what?" Pidianiski asked. She too had held the power of the passage at one time. Centuries later, its mysteries still confounded her.

"He's seen signs that lead him to believe—"

"What signs?" Pidianiski interjected. She was almost as knowledge-able as Machias, and the current situation had simply appeared without warning. She'd seen absolutely no signs of the impending danger.

"We didn't have time to go into details," said Mollyockett evasively. "Once I relayed what Squire had told me, he said he had urgent matters to attend to and rushed off."

"Did he say what I was to do when I got to Ollantaytambo, or am I to *just* feel my way in the dark?" Pidianiski asked sarcastically. She absolutely detested *flying by the seat of her pants* as Mollyockett called it. A term she'd learned from Aldous.

"He's convinced the Quechuan people are somehow involved, given the use of their stone star and the presence of Camaztoz on the same night in the McKenzie house. If that's the case, I'm quite positive their involvement is innocent."

Pidianiski nodded in disbelief. "They're gone. Extinct as dinosaurs."

"Machias has his thoughts."

"Well, hopefully they have not been resurrected as Slaughter Makers." Annoyed that her question had not been answered, Pidianiski moved to face Mollyockett. "You both know I'll do whatever it takes. I'd even give my life for Fletcher and Whole, but I need to know what my mission is. The place is massive." She thought back to the year 1707 when she was transcribing *Whole Abounds* from crumbling birch scrolls. She'd been studying Kozart's notes, readying them for translation, when references to a small town in Peru named Ollantaytambo appeared. According to Kozart, its inhabitants, who were on the verge of extinction, also had the unique ability to access Whole. She studied the notes and made the grueling journey to the Quechuan Valley. The temple was stunningly magnificent and eerily silent. Hidden by the thick South American jungle, its peaceful people had vanished from the face of the earth. The temple and its surrounds were truly one of the great wonders of the world.

Mollyockett nodded.

Pidianiski prodded further. "Does he think the Quechuan people are somehow against us now?" She laughed slightly. "Given that they're extinct, I'm a little skeptical." She turned and searched for Merrimack in the valley below while making a list in her mind of everything that needed to be done in preparation of her unexpected journey. *There's a lot to be learned before I leave.*

"He has no idea if the Ollantaytambo people or anyone associated with them are involved. He just wants you to quickly visit the area and see if anything has changed."

"When?"

"Right now," Mollyockett whispered.

Pidianiski had no choice but to move swiftly. Her long black braids rippled behind her as she entered Entreat Point, a long stone point hanging directly over Sixth Day in Whole. It was the very location where power of the passage was transferred from one person to another. While she had been the caretaker of the passage, Entreat Point was the *only* place that allowed you to travel *back* to places you'd visited in the past by simply closing your eyes and wishing it. Also called Mortaise Realm, it disassembled the billions of cells in your body and immediately transported them to any location you desired, just like Flow travel (short for *hyper-metabo-flow plume*, which allows for rapid transport at the cellular level). She had used Flow travel on her first trip to Ollantaytambo because she had been the holder of the power of the passage at that time and had never been there. Now, she was relying on Mortaise Realm due to the fact that Fletcher was now the passage's caretaker. Only he could travel to the southern passage through Flow. She was relying on the instructions relayed from Machias to Mollyockett. *Machias better be right* she thought.

The rule of Mortaise Realm was that any person while visiting Entreat Point could revisit a particular location they'd been before—much like Fletcher's introduction to *Whole Abounds* at Christmas Cove, Maine, before he traveled to the Quechuan Valley. Whole and the McKenzie families very survival depended on this exploratory visit. Since she no longer controlled the power of the passage, what time period she would arrive in was still a mystery. She'd always known that Whole was always on the move, changing constantly. Signs were everywhere and closely monitored by Machias. She was hopeful he was leading her in the right direction as she contemplated her journey.

Before closing her eyes, she thought of Vilcanota's patera and *Whole Abounds*. *Wishful thinking*. As protector of the passage, only Fletcher could access their powers. She took in the vibrant field below and then thought of the lost temple she'd visited centuries ago. In an instant, her body disassembled itself, speeding effortlessly through Whole's atmosphere. Surprisingly, she was able to take in flashes of the realm's enormity as if watching a slide show stuck on fast-forward. She caught a glimpse of the Valley of the Ferns, the place she called home, before noting the swirling and dangerous currents of Umbegog Gulch— Whole's unique and very accurate alarm predicting eminent danger. It had never been wrong. She swooshed over a multitude of vineyards, gardens, orchards, rivers, and forests. Every imaginable living creature passed by her. The very lifeblood of Earth itself. Shockingly, she found herself caught up in Flow's blue rays during her journey. A first in the history of Mortaise Realm.

Suddenly, everything went ominously black and eerily silent. Pidianiski's was fully conscious as the cells of her disassembled body aimlessly searched for each other, looking for the exact spot to attach itself. As the agony increased, Pidianiski was on the verge of blacking out. For a second, she was convinced Machias had misread the signs.

She summoned what little energy she could muster as her soul floated above the massive cluster of cells that continued to bounce in every direction. A violent battle ensued between her own energy and the pain that was causing her mind to shut down and slowly ebb into nothingness.

Then even the pain was leaving her...

It's over. If this is what dying is like, it's wonderfully peaceful, she thought before completely blacking out.

Her tiny body lay crumpled at the base of an elaborately carved wall. Tiny fireflies and lizards were chiseled on the hard floor below her. Her limp right arm was wedged into a tiny crevasse. A tiny drop of water falling from high above, landed on her neck, causing her to flinch.

Am I dead? she wondered.

Slowly, she opened her eyes. Her heart beat rapidly. She pulled herself into a sitting position against a cold wall and listened to the dank silence.

Machias is absolutely amazing, she thought as her eyes adjusted to her unfamiliar surroundings.

To her right was the exact symbol that had been on the bottom of Mollyockett's grave and in Fletcher's root cellar. There was also an oversized replica in the middle of Sixth Day which served as the chosen location where Fletcher had been given his powers by Mollyockett and Machias—a closely guarded secret passed down from generation to generation.

Pidianiski was absolutely positive she was in present time due to the fact that the upper star was missing from this particular symbol. While at Christmas Cove she had instructed Fletcher to remove it.

Pidianiski stood and moved towards the symbol.

The sounds of her steps echoed on the hard floor. She walked slowly trying to take in as much as possible. Machias and Mollyockett would demand details.

Enormous blocks of stone jutted out at the base of all four walls before rising upward at an angle.

The lost pyramid is still intact, undiscovered. She thought, extremely pleased.

Hundreds of meticulously chiseled snakes, lizards, birds, animals, fish, and plants, the works of master craftsmen, graced every surface.. She thought of the peaceful people who'd once lived there and spent centuries creating the hidden treasure.

While credit was a given to Muriel and Von Piddle for *discovering* the lost village of Ollantaytambo above her head, this part remained hidden from civilization due to Fletcher's heroic actions of permanently sealing its entrance.

The very survival of Whole depended on it.

Even the smallest sounds were greatly amplified in the dimly lit vastness. A slender ray of light illuminated a long stone shelf protruding from the center of the wall. Majestically carved vines scrolled around and under two supporting blocks.

The phrase *guaduim et spes* was etched under the shelf.

"Joy and hope," she whispered.

As she rounded a corner, she came to a sudden halt. Set in the center of a small room with towering walls lay a long rectangular rock. Directly behind the stone, a grotesque depiction of a man about to be beheaded. A pair of executioners were adorned in elaborate ceremonial dress. They stood over the man with long swords raised, ready for the kill. She immediately recognized the Maya headdress covering the upper half of their long hair. Large Golden-headed Quetzal tail feathers were arranged into beautiful patterns. She studied the stone carving more closely. Mayan men grew their hair long but burnt the hair off their foreheads to accentuate their elongated profiles. A powerful sign during war.

Pidianiski focused on what appeared to be a massive pool of coagulating blood flowing over the side of the block and onto the floor. *Something recent had happened here. More than one person had just met a violent demise.*

Instinctively, she grabbed her long hunting knife and pulled it out of her rawhide belt. The shadow of the eagle feather in her headband danced in the pool of blood as she looked behind her. Wanting to jump back into the unexpected blue rays of Flow for a quick escape, she remained in the doorway of the small room. She knew that Whole was changing but had no idea if Flow travel would work for her again.

Machias was dependent on a full reporting.

This has to be somehow related to the Wabanaki Confederation she thought.

She took a step closer towards the blood, looking for clues that could shine light on the horrific aftermath.

"The code or you die, *Chief Camaztoz.*"

A cold voice spoke with a rasping tone.

Instinctively, she pivoted.

"Do what you're told, Pidianiski, if you value breathing."

The whisper came from behind her and was barely audible.

A blue fog appeared directly beneath her feet and rolled towards the darkness in front of her as she turned and stepped further inside the room. *I wonder if this is what Fletcher saw in his room the other night?*

There was complete silence in the black void behind the executioner's stone, but she felt something watching her every movement.

The stench of rotting flesh hit her face. She held her breath and her heart skipped a beat. She bravely took a step forward to the very edge of the coagulating blood hardening on the floor. As she moved into the room, she could start to make out three shadows in an arched opening leading to a back chamber.

Barely breathing, she stared them down. The stench flooded her eyes, causing them to slightly sting.

"Your confederation has underestimated us," she called out. "I'll die before helping you." As she spoke, the three shadowy figures moved closer to her. Outlines immediately formed. *What? What on earth?*

"Very well, have it your way," the voiced hissed angrily. It was now emanating from the small ledge above the Latin inscription.

She stumbled backwards just as three moose-like beasts moved towards her in unison. Venom etched in their black eyes. As the voice spoke, their bat-shaped ears twitched as if cowering to a military command.

She studied their movements and slowly moved the knife in her hand. The beasts followed the turning blade with their eyes as she raised it over her head.

With explosive power, they sprang towards her. The earth rumbled under their feet as they jumped, causing a massive stone to crash down from the elaborately etched wall.

Pidianiski immediately fell backwards, dropping the knife onto the stone floor.

"Spare nothing!" she heard the voice screaming.

The Slaughter Makers reared their hairy heads, growling angrily and emitting a foul smell.

She quickly crawled towards the knife then kicked off the flat side of the rock. She rolled to the right and stood up. Suddenly, something slammed into the top of Pidianiski's head, causing her to stumble forward. She was on the verge of blacking out but fought it off. Small black circles floated in her eyes as if winking at her. A small trickle of blood dripped down her forehead as she stumbled towards the entrance of the killing chamber. While passing through the opening, a claw tore into the back of her leather dress, ripping it open and pulling apart one of her long braids. Pidianiski's head jerked backwards violently.

The beasts roared in anger and the noise reverberated off the walls. Pidianiski regained her footing and ran towards the exit. A thick and salty smell of blood filled her nose, just as a warm sensation reached her back. She kept her fix on a small opening in the far wall, unaware of the blood dripping from the gaping wound in the center of her back. The claw had ripped through tissue and muscle and part of her spine was exposed.

She stumbled forward as the distance between her and the Slaughter Makers decreased. The center one lowered his head and charged. Hurtling at full speed, he immediately found his target. The top point of his furry antler poked into Pidianiski's back, puncturing her lung. She gasped and tried to fight off the searing pain just as a smaller antler point pulled apart her right thigh. A second Slaughter Maker charged. Its horns tore one of her ribs from its cage. The force hurtled her upwards and towards the opening she'd been aiming for.

As she lost consciousness she thought, *Fletcher, I tried. Honest.*

Much to her surprise, a sense of calm came over her as vicious snarls of the Slaughter Makers continued to fill her ears. Oblivious to the flashing blue light, they were slowly pushing her towards the entrance to Flow in a savage effort for fresh meat.

Suddenly, a brilliant flash filled the room. A cracking sound reverberated off the temple's walls. Blue and white beams of light fractured into thousands of shiny circles and enveloped Pidianiski's limp body. The Slaughter Makers immediately reared up and stepped backwards as they cowered from the annoying flashes of light.

Pidianiski continued to hold onto her knife unaware that the violent explosion was now tearing at her cells. She no longer felt any pain as she lay crumpled in the small opening as the vivid flashes of light disassembled her cells. And then silence.

The Slaughter Makers had disappeared back into the black void behind the killing stone. A long trail of red came to an end where a bent hunting knife lay covered in a massive pool of blood. Its owner was gone.

CHAPTER 7

JONATHAN SNOW'S DEMISE

"WHO ON EARTH DO YOU THINK YOU ARE?" REFINNA BOOMED ANGRILY.

The plump faces of Ogden and Oberon snickered behind her.

"But, Mrs.—"

"It's *Ms.* McKenzie," said Refinna, cutting the timid school nurse off. She quickly zeroed in on the name Greta pinned to the woman's chest and gave her a cold look. "Not from around here are you?"

"Err, no…Actually I grew up in—"

"*Reeeallly,* well, it's quite obvious you've no idea who I am!" Refinna continued, glaring at the Greta who was now cowering behind her desk. "I demand you change their charts right this instant!"

"Change their charts? But a body mass index *can't* be changed with a stroke of a pen," she said, opening the white folder for Oberon. "A person's BMI is universally accepted as—"

Refinna took a step closer and raised a thick index finger in front of the nurse's face. "Obviously, you're an expert with *universal* things—"

She stopped talking and condescendingly raised her left bushy brow. "But in this part of the world, public servants respect authority."

Ogden feigned a cry followed by a loud whimper. Immediately, Oberon joined in.

The distressed sounds coming from the oversized, red-headed twins sent Refinna into a frenzy. Incensed, she scooped up the two folders, pushing them into her giant leather purse. "Let me tell you something, Missy, it's one thing for an *American* to try to prevent my precious darlings from learning to scuba dive while on a cruise, but to have a foreigner do it is completely mind boggling. I'm sure I'll find a *competent* doctor or nurse whose BMI charts will gladly satisfy the instructors on the boat. Had the Coronavirus pandemic not happened, we would have taken this trip long ago. We've waited two long years for this to happen. How dare you?"

Greta gasped. "You can't just take medical records with you, Ms. McKenzie, it's against school policy." Her protests fell on deaf ears.

"Well, since *we* pay your salary, I say *we* are changing the rules," Refinna replied curtly and turned towards the door. "I'll be sure to let the school board know exactly how the medical department is treating parents nowadays."

Oberon and Ogden smiled as they scowled at the nurse.

"Come on boys, let's go get some fudge at the factory. Your aunts are tasting a new recipe," said Refinna, glaring at the nurse. "Disrespect invites hunger." As she turned to exit, she ran right into Fletcher.

"Well, look who's here? What happened? Fall off another cliff?" she asked as Camway pressed a wet towel against his left eye. "Another one who'll do anything for attention. Birds of a feather—"

"If you don't mind," the nurse said trying to squeeze past Refinna, who was blocking her way. "I must attend to his eye," she said weakly.

"Oh, please," snarled Refinna. "Clear as day they're either attempting to get out of something or looking for attention. Again."

The twins exchanged a satisfied look.

Fletcher quickly stepped aside to let the trio pass. He'd learned years ago that arguing with his aunt was a lost cause. She always had the last word. *What's she doing here?* he thought, stealing a glance towards Camway's good eye.

"Getting the twins revved up for their diving lessons in the Caribbean," she stammered as if reading his mind. "You're not the only McKenzie with athletic abilities. At least they've got brains to match *their* brawn."

Fletcher remained silent and glanced at the nurse whose mouth was now open.

"I've been trying to get in touch with Uncle Woodrow for the past week. Have you seen him?"

Fletcher's spirits plummeted. Any chance of a quick departure on their part was dwindling. Given the events of the past week, he chose his words carefully.

"Well, I . . . um." Refinna furrowed her forehead and glared hatefully at him. "Well, have you seen him or have you not seen him?" she squeaked, mimicking his voice. "This is not rocket science, Fletcher."

The twins laughed loudly.

"I saw him during the fall festival on the town common," he replied dishonestly. She zeroed in on his pupils. "Why?"

Refinna took a step backwards and laughed loudly. "It's none of your business why I'm looking for him. Clear as day you're up to your old games again. You ought to change your manners and act like Ogden and Oberon. You could learn—"

Fletcher let out a slight giggle. Camway, sensing what was about to come, slid towards the nurse who was now dialing furiously for security.

"Aunt Ref—"

"LET. ME. TELL. YOU. ONE. THING!" she thundered, knocking the two medical folders out of her purse. She took a step closer and stepped on them. Spit sprayed on Fletcher's face. "How dare you disrespect me, young man. Especially, after I took *all that time* off my life to help raise you. And during a time when I should've focused on Foods for Fun. You disrespectful little snit."

The twins, thoroughly pleased with the punishing scene, moved towards the door's entrance for a better view of Fletcher's face.

Fletcher cringed and backed into the space vacated by the twins. He wanted to flee the scene but was blocked by Oberon's and Ogden's massive bodies.

"I was only laughing at—" He was digging the hole deeper.

"AND THAT LITTLE TRICK YOU PLAYED ON SERENA, WINOLA, AND MYSELF AFTER WE INTERRUPTED OUR CAREERS TO RAISE YOU!"

Fletcher swallowed hard. His aunt's face was now a dark blue, and her eyes were bloodshot. He'd known this moment would eventually come, but he never thought it would happen on school grounds.

When Muriel and Nimsy had gone missing in the Quetzal and his father was medically incapacitated, the terms of succession for Cygnus dictated that Winola, Refinna and Serena "raise" Fletcher while running the company until he reached eighteen. Gladly, they let Muriel's parents, Edmond and Lucille, take care of him in the McKenzie home. They, however, kept a tight leash on him and subjected him to long and miserable hours at the Cygnus factory. Additionally, with Aldous missing from the scene, the hefty sisters turned the attention of the well-respected company towards massively profitable, unhealthy, and fat-laden foods. In their efforts to quickly shed Cygnus of its signature healthy foods, they created Foods for Fun, a fast-growing spin-off company the three sisters owned and managed. It was financed by the sale of Birch Bread and many other beloved healthy foods that were part of the Cygnus portfolio. Unbeknownst to them, Aldous, when he was at the helm of Cygnus, was one step ahead of them. Well aware of the potential antics of his three sisters should something happen, his prior planning led them to believe that Aquidneck Kitchen, the Rhode Island food company owned by Quinn's father, was purchasing Birch Bread and other healthy Cygnus products. In reality, a trust had previously been set up for Fletcher by Aldous and Muriel that discreetly owned Fifth Ward Whole & Healthy. Quickly, Fifth Ward scooped up Birch Bread, New England Oak Cakes, Maine Maple Honey Nut Bars, Casco Bay Whole Grain Clam Cakes, and Goose Eye Granola Mix. His three aunts had only learned months ago of the corporate switch, a move that as a matter of pride enraged them even though they had zero interest in the healthy products that'd been sold. It was the sole fact that the sale exclusively benefited Fletcher that sent them into a tizzy.

"You think you can take advantage of us while we're preoccupied creating delectables people *actually* want!?" she thundered, towering over him. "Well, this isn't over young man. Trust me when I tell you that there will be a time when Foods for Fun will rule the roost, and you'll come begging when that piddle company of yours shutters its doors. Forever!"

Fletcher swallowed hard. Images of her peddling Blueberriola Sugary Sham Shams flooded his mind.

"Ha! Scrubbing toilets, that's what awaits you." She turned and glared at Greta, as if suggesting the same fate for her.

"What's going on here?" said a winded voice from outside the door. Refinna turned, attempting to find the source of the voice. *How dare someone interrupt me.*

An older security officer was moving towards her; he immediately recognized the fear on the faces of Fletcher and Greta. Disdainfully, he sneered at the twins. *The bullies of Balston Prep.*

Refinna huffed and jerked the straps of her purse over her shoulder.

"Boys, let's go," she exclaimed, breathing like a winded elephant. The massive twins sniggered then stepped aside, allowing her to pass. As Refinna stepped into the hallway, she clipped the arm of the officer, knocking him backwards. Oblivious to the crowd that had gathered in the hall, she strode toward the exit, unaware that the two medical folders were still on the floor in Greta's office.

Fletcher wiped the sweat from his forehead with his shirtsleeve.

"You're related to her?" Greta asked, completely confused. Everyone had forgotten about Camway's eye.

Fletcher nodded.

"Unbelievable." The nurse shook her head, watching the officer follow the portly trio around a corner and towards the school's entrance.

With all the drama, Camway had completely forgotten about his injured eye.

"So, what happened?" she asked.

Just then a voice came over the loud speaker, requesting Fletcher report to the front office. Camway and Fletcher exchanged nervous looks. *Now I'm in trouble,* Fletcher thought. They'd been horsing around in the gym with Lautaro Silva, Fletcher's new neighbor from Argentina. Lautaro accidentally elbowed Camway in the eye after he'd jimmied the doors to the locked basketball court after lunch and before the start of classes.

Camway chuckled at the announcement.

"What?" Fletcher asked.

"I just hope your aunt isn't at the office." Camway's good eye widened.

Greta immediately stopped opening a cold pack and swallowed. *This is not going to be good.*

Fletcher's day was going from bad to worse with each passing minute.

He walked down the long hall and tried not to think about a possible second encounter with Refinna. He could handle the principal but couldn't deal with Refinna again. As he walked, he spied Lautaro quickly sneaking out a back door in the cafeteria. *Well, isn't that just ducky.*

"Fletch, what's going on?" Cicely said, poking her head out from her European history class. "I heard Cam got hit in the eye with a baseball bat. He okay?"

"No and yeah."

Cicely threw him a totally confused look. "Which means?"

"No, he *didn't* get hit by a baseball bat. Lautaro elbowed him while we were playing basketball," he paused, "in the gym when it was closed."

"Yikes."

"I know, and yeah, he's okay. Just a black eye."

"Geez, good luck Fletch." She now understood the announcement instructing him to report to the office. "If there's anything I can—"

His heart quickened as he touched her arm.

"Yeah, track down that chicken from Argentina. I just saw him sneaking out of school."

Cicely laughed. "Way to make the situation worse."

"Not really. As far as I know, no one knows he's involved. Listen, I gotta run."

"Well, let me know what happens. And Fletch, good luck."

He grinned at her and quickly resumed walking in the direction of the front office.

As he approached his destination, he noticed a small gathering just inside the front entrance to the school's main building. It was his father, Uncle Woodrow, and Alek Von Piddle. He picked up the pace.

"What took you so long?" Woodrow said, hunching his shoulders. Once again, he was wearing one of his signature blue sweater vests. "The building is not *that* big."

"What's going on?" Fletch asked, anxious to change the topic. "Why are you all here?"

"Apparently, that little earthquake in the area of Frenchman's Hole the other day resulted in a tourist from Massachusetts going missing," Aldous replied. "All they found were his scorched boots and camera in the water." His father looked like he'd aged ten years since yesterday's gathering.

Scorched boots? Missing? Fletcher's head was swimming.

"We've just had a gander at that handsome stone wall in your root cellar and now we're taking a little jaunt to Snow Falls," Von Piddle announced, wiping his glasses. He looked extremely tired, and surprisingly, he was wearing the same clothing from the last meeting at the inn. Thick white tape now held his glasses together at the bridge.

"We just noticed your aunt Refinna pulling out of the parking lot with the twins. Any idea why she was here?" Woodrow asked, stepping from the small space that hid him from the outside. "Thankfully, she didn't see us."

"You find anything in the basement?" Fletcher asked, thinking it best to ignore the question.

"Just two elongated cracks in the upper rocks," Aldous said. "Other than that, nothing's changed."

"Place is busy." Woodrow chimed in, watching Jean Vincent pull in front of a fire hydrant just outside where they were standing. "I say we continue this conversation in the car."

Fletcher's heart raced.

"What happened to Cam?" Mrs. Vincent asked Fletcher the second she entered the door.

"Er, he got hit in the eye while playing basketball."

Alek smiled wide. "Boys will be boys," he said jovially. "Reminds me of the time when my father took me on my very first expedition. I was right about your age Fletcher when—"

"Put a sock in it, Alek," Woodrow said. "We've got to head to Cygnus."

"Cygnus, I thought we were going to Snow—"

"We are," Aldous interrupted. "Good day to you Jean. Let me know how Camway is, ok?" He was anxious to leave the questions behind.

"Absolutely," she replied. "He's had worse."

"What's mom and Grans going to say when I don't come home on time?"

"We're Lucky, Fletch," answered Aldous. "They're all in Portland at The Good Cause Thrift Store for some check presentation. You know how dedicated your mom is with McAuley Residence."

"I actually bought an old colonial hammer and stake there once. Genuine treasure. For ten dollars. Poor ladies had no idea what they were selling," Von Piddle said. "I gave them a hundred and told them to keep the change. My conscience was stabbing my brain."

Woodrow shook his head and laughed.

"Any idea who the person from Massachusetts was?" Fletcher asked as Aldous drove south on route twenty-six.

Woodrow nodded. "They're not releasing the name until his next of kin is notified. His rental was found abandoned in the parking lot."

"I was at Ye Old Boot this morning and heard the ol' chap was a photographer from Boston," Alek announced while tightening the tape on his glasses.

"Wait, what? You were at the Boot this morning?" Woodrow asked, rolling his eyes.

"Well, after learning what I learned at your inn, be glad I didn't move into the Boot for good," Alek sincerely responded. "And that Squire, he's honestly Mollyockett's son?" He'd still not wrapped his mind around the surreal situation.

"They know what happened to him?" asked Fletcher.

Silence filled the SUV.

"So apparently the Walton and Croft circle is getting bigger."

"Let's not jump to conclusions," Aldous reasoned with him. "He may just be on a long hike."

"Yeah, a long hike" Fletcher laughed. "After burning your boots and tossing what's left of them along with your camera into Frenchman's Hole. Sounds like an expert hiker to me."

"Poor chap," Alek whispered while taking in the large telephone statue in the center of Bryant Pond. *Sculptor should be shot.*

"How do you think Lalia is able to enable me to use Whole's powers up here?" Fletcher asked as they passed a logging truck on an uphill climb.

"Susup did say Whole, like nature, was always changing," Aldous answered.

Woodrow nodded.

"Let's just be glad they figured that out. I mean, it can only help us. And boy, we could use all the help in the world right now."

Woodrow nodded again.

"Almost a little too hocus-pocus for me!" Von Piddle exclaimed. "Still can't wrap my mind around it. I bet it's that black cat. Totally gives me the creeps. Reminds me of the time I accidentally walked into that smelly voodoo parlor in New Orleans."

They all ignored him.

Aldous looked at Woodrow and cleared his throat. "Fletcher, the reason why we're going to Snow Falls is to take a look around. Every bit of information we can muster up will help us determine what the next steps are. We've no idea when Squire Susup will meet up with us again, but we just can't sit around doing nothing."

"Here, here." Alek called.

Fletcher ignored Alek's blinking eyes and bouncing glasses. "So, have the police learned anything from Chesley Snow?" Fletcher asked. "He's got to be involved somehow."

"From what I've read," Woodrow answered quickly, "nothing really. But, with his record, I'm sure he's nervous. It'll only be a matter of time before the authorities connect the fate of all three men."

"How can they *not* already," Von Piddle blurted out matter-of-factly. "Like, there's dozens of people who suspiciously disappear in Oxford County, leaving only burned footwear as a clue. Bunch of dimwits, you want my opinion."

"Even if they do connect the dots, think of what they'll find?" Woodrow responded to his old friend, playing devil's advocate. "It's not like a giant hole in the ground is going to open up, welcoming them to Whole."

Good gracious, how on earth did I get here? Aldous thought.

Fletcher swallowed hard. As holder of the power of the passage, he guarded it closely. Aldous turned and nodded at him as if reading his mind.

"I forgot to mention," Woodrow announced gravely, "According to Stanley Mull, the *Newry Tribune* is running a front page article tomorrow morning suggesting that something is afoot now that three people have gone missing. He was poking around with the guests at the inn this morning, asking if they'd been to Frenchman's Hole lately."

"Uncle Woodrow, how could you forget something like that?" Aldous's asked. "Clearly, that would be the biggest story of the year in Western Maine."

"There's just so much going on. I'm having trouble keeping everything in my mind," Woodrow replied defensively. "I'm sorry Aldous."

"Well, it was only a matter of time. Quite honestly, I'm surprised the paper didn't issue a special edition given what's happened."

Silence once again filled the SUV as they passed a sign: *West Paris, the gem of Western Maine.* As they approached the trailhead, surprisingly, the parking lot was empty.

"Listen," Woodrow announce. "If anyone asks what we're doing here, just tell them Mr. Von Piddle is planning an archeological dig at the old factory and asked us to help."

"Why don't we just say it's for a school project for Fletcher," Alek laughed, winking at him. He'd been personally conned with that excuse when Woodrow asked for his advice while searching for the entrance to the passage. "You remember, where two eagles nest."

Woodrow chuckled loudly. Never in a million years had he expected to welcome Von Piddle into the world of Whole.

Silently, they all walked towards a log footbridge spanning the raging water, searching for any clues. Long strands of yellow police tape still attached to several trees blew aimlessly in the breeze.

Von Piddle turned towards a closed restaurant on the opposite side of the road before focusing his gaze on four small cabins standing north and beside the river. "So this was once a thriving town? Absolutely amazing."

"And the very heart of it was a large mill right over there," Woodrow stated, nodding towards the other side of the small river. He thought of Mollyockett passing by this very spot in search of shelter during the crippling blizzard.

Alek immediately spotted dozens of granite blocks with chiseled indentations made by the rope pulled by teams of oxen. A moss-covered stone wall ran along the fringe of a wooded area marking a forgotten property boundary. "Unbelievable! I've driven right by this place thousands of times, but I've never been here before. And so close to Cooper Farms," he remarked.

As they walked downward, the sound of falling water intensified, giving the distinct impression of a long drop. The four men came to a sudden stop in the very center of the bridge and looked over. Blue and yellowish water glided over hundreds of hidden boulders just below the surface before leaping over a forty-foot waterfall. It crashed into a deep pool, creating millions of tiny bubbles that danced on the surface before meandering towards South Paris. Mist from the falls crept upwards, fading just below their feet. Additional yellow tape stood out in the autumn leaves, marking off an area directly to the right of the pool of water. Downstream, clumps of mangled trees lay in the middle of the river blocked by jagged rocks protruding upwards like scars inflicted by war.

"I wonder what happened there?" Fletcher asked, nodding towards the yellow tape. A black burnt streak ran down the center of a large flat rock as if recently struck by lightning.

No one responded.

"Let's see if there's a path that'll take us down," Aldous suggested. He was desperate for any clue that would help ease his mind.

Von Piddle's eyes widened. "Splendid idea, good sir!" He yelled. "No Everest, but I'll take it just the same."

Woodrow rolled his eyes. "Just be careful, Alek. Like Everest, there's no getting airlifted from down there."

"Ah, Woody, that's why you've ran an inn all these years, while I've literally risked my life time and time again in search of beautifully lost history. A little worry wort you are." He winked at Fletcher. "Are you with me or are you against me?' He pointed towards a precipitous path that began at the old mill's crumbling foundation. It was clear to everyone that the haphazard trail downwards had been created by a recent collapse of the canyon's walls.

Woodrow scowled at the obvious danger.

"Okay, let's take it slow," Aldous conceded. He knew they needed to investigate everything before they left.

"I'll see what I can find inside the footprints of the mill, if you don't mind. There's a lot over there," Woodrow offered. "Just be careful Fletch." An image of him falling off Devil's Leap during the Hamlin State Park cleanup was forever etched in his mind. Additionally, he knew he had Lucille to contend with if anything went wrong.

"These rocks have been upended quite recently," said Alek after skillfully grasping onto small bushes and making his way to the bottom. "You can tell by how clean and sparkly they are." He rubbed his wrinkly hand on the very top of a block shaped stone. "Hmm."

"See anything dad?

"I've never been at its base, but the falls looks exactly like I remembered it as a kid."

"Ah, take a closer look," Von Piddle chimed in, pointing towards the area around the dropping water. "Slight disagreement with you old chap. Clearly most of them have recently been displaced and quite violently. Normal erosion wouldn't create those pointed spikes."

Fletcher and Aldous turned their attention to where the elderly man had just directed their attention.

"Additionally, even though they're wet, there's no debris or algae on them like there should be. The other rocks surrounding them clearly have been here for millennium. Here, look." Alek expertly bounded towards them. His nimbleness caught Aldous completely off guard.

"Unbelievable!"

"Take these gray rocks. If you notice, they're not as light as those over there, and they're very slimy. It's a sign they were *right here* even when Mollyockett walked past them during that snowstorm."

"So what do you think happened and *when*?" Aldous quizzed him, lowering his head in an attempt to see into the small crevasse behind the falls. His jaw dropped as Von Piddle crawled over an enormous black rock then walked chest high directly under the falling water and right on the edge of the hidden ledge in the deep pool.

"Dad!" Fletcher shouted. Von Piddle disappeared behind the flow of water gushing downwards. "What's he doing?"

Aldous scrambled clumsily towards Alek then sat directly on the edge of the falls unaware of the old bearded man watching his every movement from the thick woods high above them on the opposite side of the river. Soaked, he squinted into the dark void looking for the eccentric man. *This cannot be happening,* he thought. Intuitively though, he was pleased Von Piddle had joined them.

Fletcher looked at the falls. "He's not serious?"

Aldous swallowed hard. "Uncle Woodrow has known Mr. Von Piddle his entire life. Said he's got this knack when it comes to locating things. I hope he's okay."

"You got that right. I found that out when he helped me locate the entrance to the passage. What a weird guy."

"Fletch, everyone's a little different. I wouldn't say he's weird; he's just Alek Von Piddle. And remember, he's the one who helped save our family," Aldous said brightly.

Fletcher smiled and nodded while remaining focused on the falling water. The scene was spectacular with the autumn leaves exhibiting their vibrant colors.

"You find anything?" Aldous asked Woodrow who was crossing the bridge towards the road."

Woodrow shook his head as he scanned the scene below him. "Where's Alek?" he yelled.

"Under there!" Aldous shouted, nodding his head. He pointed towards the bottom of the falls.

Woodrow shook his head in disbelief, chuckling. "I'll scout out this side of the river."

Fletcher turned towards the fresh black mark recently made on the flat rock. He studied the pattern, wondering if it had any significance. The yellow tape fluttering in the wind reminded hm of the seriousness of their visit to Snow Falls.

A piercing scream rose above the noise of the falls. Von Piddle was in trouble.

Aldous immediately jumped into the river and crawled towards the spot of the noise as Fletcher wheeled around and scrambled forward. They both came to a sudden halt as Alek quickly emerged from the blackness. Eyes blinking wildly, his glasses hung precipitously off his left ear. His wet clothing clung tightly to his aged frame.

Aldous stepped out onto an underwater ledge towards him. The frigid water now fully registered on his body.

Alek shook his head violently to stop him. "Stay back!" he called out. Although he was white as a ghost, he cast an amused eye towards the two of them, completely confusing them. Aldous stood tense, but Von Piddle's smile only widened.

The others didn't grin back.

"Unbelievable," he shouted in disbelief. "And I thought the *discovery* of that Quechuan village was the find of my life."

"Are you all right?" Aldous yelled, still completely baffled by the scream.

"Well, I'd say there's more to that curse than what I've been told." He shook his head in surprise. "The entire place is a death chamber that would rival those in ancient Roman times. You should see all the bones under there."

Fletcher's jaw dropped. "Bones!? As in *human* bones?" he asked.

Alek nodded, extending his hand towards Aldous for help out of the swift moving current. "And there's something still alive under there, and it not Bambi."

Aldous stared at him, swallowing hard. The place was definitely not a safe place for a young boy. "Fletch, head up right now."

"The bones of at least a hundred people are under there. And they didn't just die of old age," Alek said gravely, studying Aldous' eyes. "It's clear from their clothing and guns that some have been there for several hundred years."

Aldous gasped. "Guns?"

"Well, a few muskets from what I noticed. Revolutionary War ones with the bayonets still attached. It's unfathomable." He stepped off the rock and shook the water off his white hair while banging his head to get the water out of his left ear.

Aldous grasped onto the old man's hand and pulled him towards the path. "Let's go."

"We need to call the police," declared Alek, stumbling towards a small bush after being jerked forward.

Aldous wheeled around and stared at him. "Listen, the last thing we need right now is to get others involved. Just think of what you're saying. Okay?"

Alek nodded. He hadn't thought of that.

"Any idea what's alive down there?"

"No idea. But whatever it is, it is huge and needs to gargle. You should've smelled its breath. I almost fainted."

"Do you think it was—"

"A Slaughter Maker?" Alek grasped onto a small tree and glanced behind him. "No idea. It was somewhere behind the bones in a dark spot. But trust me, it was not pleased with my little visit. I hoofed it out immediately."

"How could you see? It looked completely dark behind the water."

"That's the weird thing, Aldous. The walls in the front of the cave were glowing green, which helped shine light on the crypt. Strangest thing."

Quickly, they made it to the top of the path where Fletcher was waiting for them.

"Do you think some of the bones belong to Croft?"

"I thought that for a second, Fletcher, but they've been there for quite some time." Alek attempted to catch his breath. "The clothing clearly confirms this." Water sloshed out of his shoes with every step.

Fletcher furrowed his forehead.

"They look like what people would've worn in the seventeenth and eighteenth centuries. Clearly, many of them are Revolutionary War soldiers."

"Hey, over here," Woodrow yelled, wildly waving his hands above his head from the top of the hill next to the highway. He was completely oblivious to the dramatic discovery by his old friend.

"I don't know if I can handle any more surprises," Aldous announced. Completely soaked, he crossed the bridge cautiously while looking over the side. "You two be careful and stay in the middle. Let's see what he's found and get out of here."

Von Piddle stepped forward eagerly. A trail of water followed him. As they approached Woodrow, their drenched bodies and look on their faces made him step back. "What's wrong?' he asked. Aldous, Fletcher, and Alek all launched into rapid explanations of the old tomb hidden under the falls.

"I'd bet my life it was a Slaughter Maker," said Woodrow. "We need to go, but first look at this." He pointed towards a large rock with a square, weathered green plaque attached to it. "I must've driven by this a million times and never even gave it a thought."

Immediately the group assembled in front of the rock.

"This is where the name of the falls comes from," said Woodrow reading the plaque aloud.

> *Snow Falls*
> *Named For Captain Jonathan Snow*
> *Massacred by the Saint Francis Indians Here In 1755*
> *West Paris Bicentennial Celebration 1776 – 1976*

"The name *Captain Snow* was embroidered on one of the military uniforms," Alek gasped, cupping his mouth. "Bones were a mess. It was the one closest to the entrance and a crude arrow was sticking through his left eyehole."

"Holy smokes!" Aldous heaved, rubbing his hand over the plaque. "I always thought the name came from the falls being frozen at times in the winter. Poor guy."

Von Piddle shot him a glance. "You have to remember that there are two sides to every story. Most likely Captain Snow didn't just come here to enjoy nature's beauty." He paused and looked at the footbridge he just crossed. "The Native Americans who lived here for thousands of years were savagely driven off their land by the newcomers—quite often by deadly force at the hands of people like Mr. Snow. Reminds me of the time when I was in northern Australia searching for the remains of an aboriginal—"

"Let's get out of here," said Woodrow, cutting him off. "I don't know if what you found is connected to this, but I suggest we leave. And remember, not a word to anyone. Try to act as normal as possible. They last thing we need right now is mass hysteria. You can dry off at the inn."

"You're kidding," Aldous chimed in, shaking his head. "Are you out of your mind. Of course it's connected." The lives of his entire family were at stake and his patience was running thin. The Moon of Popping Trees was fast approaching, and he was desperate for answers.

CHAPTER 8

MAHOOSUC HYSTERIA

"Your late. Again," said Professor Lintine dryly. "And what's the excuse this time, Mr. McKenzie, hmm?" He lowered his head and looked over the top of his thick, black-framed glasses.

Lautaro Silva snickered.

"Something funny Lautaro?" Mr. Lintine quickly moved up the aisle, sizing up the Argentinian. "I'm sure your father will be absolutely *thrilled* when I call him *again.*"

Fletcher, taking advantage of the distraction, quickly took his seat between Camway and Cicely. He was tired. At breakfast, the brown spot on his hand burned so badly he couldn't eat. Alarmed and confused, his grandmother had Muriel drive him to the local urgent care, who had difficulty diagnosing the source of the pain. He was discharged with a white ointment and a small card reminding them of a future appointment.

Lautaro grunted and lowered his head.

"I believe I asked you a question, Fletcher? This is the third time this week you've been late." The professor moved towards the front of the room and picked up a long piece of white chalk from the base of the blackboard. He closed his eyes and inserted the chalk stick into his mouth and inhaled deeply. Opening his eyes, he exhaled as if puffing a cigarette.

"All of you have signed Balston Prep's Student Expectations Agreement on day one of your enrollment. Clearly, a few of you have underestimated my deep respect for that document. Fletcher and Lautaro, I'll see you both after school dismissal this afternoon. The interruptions in my class will come to an end."

Fletcher had promised his father and Woodrow he'd meet with them at the inn after school to formulate a plan under the guise that they were helping ready the property for the upcoming winter. Von Piddle was in Augusta pouring over historical documents at the State of Maine Historical Society. The curator respected Alek and would give him unfettered access to its priceless documents.

Lautaro began to object. "But Mr. Lin—"

"I believe it's called detention, Mr. Silva, if that's the word you're looking for. Hmm…"

"Professor, but I was . . . You can't really be—"

"Don't tell me how to run my class. You may both think that the classroom is yours to disrupt in any fashion you desire. But let me very clear. We are here to learn and learn only. *Not* to perform a charade at the expense of others."

The classroom remained deathly silent while he took a long drag on the chalk stick. Mr. Lintine's nutrition class was mandatory at Balston Prep, and everyone dreaded it. Lintine was an extreme advocate of natural foods. He even traveled to Missouri to oppose Monsanto Foods whenever there was a protest against genetically modified foods. A silver kale blender was prominently displayed in the corner of his classroom as a constant reminder of his favorite healthy food. A chain smoker in his early life, he substituted mock chalk smoking to satisfy his cravings of the deadly habit.

Fletcher turned towards Cicely and slightly shook his head in protest.

"What's up with you?" she whispered during the mock cigarette exhale. "You know what a pain Mr. Lintine is."

"Care to join them, Ms. Parker? Hmm?" asked Professor Lintine, mockingly. His beady blue eyes darted directly at her. "Save your gossip for the hallways or our little group will grow by more than a third."

Cicely's face reddened. "I'm sorry."

"I hate to announce this, but the plant and root field trip to the boulder fields has been postponed indefinitely given the current state of affairs in the Mahoosuc Valley. The last thing this school needs is one of its students to be added to that growing list of missing persons. Dreadful."

Fletcher, afraid that he'd be singled out as part of a conspiracy, crouched in his seat and stared directly at the map of the world hanging from the wall. *Dad will have to call Mr. Lintine with a good excuse to get me out of detention,* he thought.

"So, can anyone tell me what a calorie is? Hmm?" He moved from his desk and stood in front of a large diagram of the human body, chalk in hand.

"It's a tiny piece of food," Raymond Peavey immediately yelled from the back of the room.

Mr. Lintine's lips curled into an angry frown. "I see some of you have failed to take this class seriously. Tut, tut, tut."

He ignored Fletcher's waving hand.

"Anyone else? This is *not* rocket science." He sucked on his chalk and closed his eyes. "You know what I find absolutely astounding? *Your* generation is the first generation in the history of the United States to lose life expectancy. And that decline in your ability to walk on this amazing planet is due solely to the poor dietary habits you all are choosing. So as you gorge on that enormous bag of potato chips in your backpack, Mr. Peavey, I highly recommend you read the books assigned to you." He gracefully moved towards the blender and proudly patted its black plastic top.

"Instead of using *Basic Nutrition* as a tabletop to hold those Tweedle Cakes and Blueberriola Sugary Sham Shams while you plop yourselves in front of your televisions and cell phones for hours on end, I suggest you follow the curriculum. Your body will most likely thank you for it for years on end."

Silence followed his speech. Cicely and Fletcher exchanged raised eye brows.

Camway, quietly flipping through the pages of chapter two in *Basic Nutrition,* stretched his hand over his head and waved it wildly.

"Yes, Mr. Vincent," Lintine said dryly. "Nice eye by the way. Unfortunately for you, there's no known nutrient which will offer a speedy recovery to your most unfortunate incident. I just hope you put an ice pack on it immediately after it happened."

Laughter exploded throughout the room while Camway nodded.

Mr. Lintine moved forward , studying Camway's eye. "So, I ask you, what is a calorie?"

"It's a unit of energy."

"Go on. There's more."

"Err…" Camway discreetly darted his eyes to the page opened in front of him. "One calorie is the amount of energy required to raise one gram of water by one degree Celsius."

"Well, Mr. Vincent, there's good news and bad news." His right arm flailed wildly as he wrote the word *calorie* in cursive writing on the blackboard. "The bad news is you get no accolades for cheating. Clearly, you're spending too much time at Ketchum Ski and Board happily trying out your father's latest gadgets. Hmm? The good news is that you are absolutely correct with your definition of what a calorie is. It is a unit of heat." He paused and wrote out the definition on the board. "Additionally, you've expended at least five calories scanning the pages of your book and waving your hand. So, Bravo, Mr. Vincent."

A few people giggled; Fletcher caught Camway's eyes and rolled his upwards.

"Anyone know how many calories are in a pound of body fat?"

Fletcher and Cicely, as well as a few others, immediately raised their hands.

"Yes, Ms. Parker, enlighten me."

"A pound of body fat is 3500 calories."

"Very good. And if you eat 500 calories less then you burn every day, how much weight will you lose in one week?"

Cicely paused, regretting being a volunteer. She know what was about to come.

"There are seven days in a week, so if you eat 500 calories less than you burn every day, you will lose one pound of body weight each week."

"And where did these jumbled numbers come from? Just pulled them out of thin air from your head, hmm?"

"Er, umm … no. Five hundred calories multiplied by seven days in a week equals 3500 calories, which are in a pound of fat."

"But Ms. Parker, I'm absolutely confused when it comes to foods categorized as fats. Care to help me out, hmm?"

Cicely swallowed hard. She'd spent the evening with Fletcher going to the movies when she should've been preparing for today's lesson.

"I've heard somewhere that there are good fats and bad fats. What's that all about. Hmm? Please enlighten me."

"There are saturated fats and unsaturated fats."

"They sound very familiar, so why should I be concerned with which one I slather on my delectable Belgian waffles?"

Lautaro giggle loudly. Immediately he lowered his reddened face and refocused on *Basic Nutrition.*

"What's so funny, Mr. Silva? Enlighten us all will you? Or are you bored with this little conversation we're having?"

"Um, no," said Lautaro quietly. "I'm sorry."

Mr. Lintine rummaged through some items in a brown bag sitting on his desk. After a few tense moments, he pulled out a small brown jar.

"So Mr. Silva, if I were to spread this almond butter on my delectable, whole-grain Belgian waffles, which one of the fats that Ms. Parker just blurted out would this be?"

"Agh, I would say—"

"Yes?"

"Um, it's a un . . . um—"

"Well, I see we've found something for you to read later this afternoon, haven't we? Hmm?"

The entire class remained motionless, afraid they'd be the next nutritional victim. All eyes focused on the circular clock directly over the door and wished the dials a speedy trip to the end of the hour.

"So which category does my little jar of almond butter fall into, Ms. Parker? Hmm?"

"It falls into the unsaturated category, which is the healthy one."

"Saturated means that it's combined with something. What is it?"

Cicely closed her eyes and inhaled deeply, praying for a quick end to the lesson. She vowed to never raise her hand again in Lintine's class. She lived the lessons when it came to her personal nutritional choices, but she wasn't a nutritionist as was now being demanded of her.

"Hydrogen?"

"Bravo. You get a coupon for a free bag of kale chips from the cafeteria. My favorite."

Fletcher discreetly pinched his arm to prevent himself from breaking out in uncontrolled laughter.

"Can you name five healthy fats, Ms. Parker, now that you're on a roll?" He sucked on the chalk stick and happily closed his eyes. "And not including my little jar of almond butter."

"Avocados, olive oil, nuts, fish and, um … canola oil?"

"Hmm, I notice four fats there. But isn't fish a protein?"

"Yes, but it also contains fat, which falls into the healthy category."

"Excellent. As long as the fish isn't fried like that hellish sandwich over at Kemo's Variety that all of you love to suck down with those artery-clogging fries." Lintine pivoted and refocused on Cicely once again. "If there are 3500 calories in a pound of fat, how many calories are in a pound of muscle?"

"Pffft …," Cicely exhaled angrily, while Lintine ignored the sound.

"While there are 3500 calories in a pound of body fat, there are around 2500 calories in a pound of muscle."

Lintine placed the back of his palm on his forehead and feigned being baffled. "I've lost you. Isn't a pound a pound? what's the difference when it comes to making up the caloric content of muscle and fat?"

Fletcher held his breath and wished her the answer. Heart hammering, she tapped her pen on the desk. "Well, I . . . uh—"

She was joyously interrupted by the loud ringing of a bell.

"That'll do. Tomorrow we'll discuss proteins and muscle. I'm still very confused why they have fewer calories per pound." He paused and took one last long drag on his chalk. "It's in your best interest that every one of you be prepared. Unlike today. Hmm?"

Pivoting to his right, and starring down Lautaro, he warned, "You *never* know when your name will be called."

Lautaro turned a deep shade of red.

"Dismissed."

"God, that was brutal," said Fletcher once he was in the hallway. He immediately turned on his cell phone to call his father. He had no intention of serving detention later in the day, nor was he going to share with Mr. Lintine that he was secretly meeting with his father, Mr. Von Piddle, and his Uncle Woodrow most mornings at Kemo's.

"I'd rather be mangled by rusty barbed wire than go through that again," Cicely huffed. "I'll never raise my hand again."

Fletcher laughed loudly. "Well, he just ignores it when I raise my hand, which is fine with me."

"I wonder why? He knows you study the lessons."

"Promise you'll keep a secret?"

"About what?" Cicely asked.

"You need to promise. The last thing I want right now is for this rumor to circulate throughout Balston. Lintine will massacre me.

"Okay, I promise. Cross my heart, Fletch."

"Very good," said Fletcher. "Mr. Lintine had a crush on my mother a long time ago. According to my grandmother, he left a dozen roses on the front porch with a note for her while she was home on summer vacation from college."

Cicely broke into uncontrolled laughter, envisioning Muriel McKenzie and Mr. Lintine together. "Shut up."

"No and get this," Fletcher giggled. "She returned the roses personally and told him she had a crush on my father."

"No way! Was she polite to him?"

"I dunno. I just know he doesn't like me that much."

"Well, that's obvious. I wonder what you'll get for a final grade?"

"Who really cares at this point. My only concern is getting out of detention tonight."

"Boy, he'll be peeved when he gets a call from your dad."

The seriousness of his current life's circumstances suddenly jarred his mind.

"You okay, Fletch?" Cicely asked, concerned by his demeanor.

"Yeah, just a lot going on right now."

He paused, gazed cautiously around the crowded hallway, and continued walking.

They exchanged nervous looks.

"What do you think's going on, Fletch?"

Fletcher paused again, pursing his lips, searching for the right words. "Meaning?"

"You know exactly what I'm talking about. The three men who've just fallen off the face of the earth." She stopped and grabbed his hand. "My father said this morning that burnt footwear was all that was left. It's creeping me out."

Fletcher nodded knowingly. "I know. None of it makes any sense. I've met one of them once."

Cicely stopped dead and gasped.

"What? Which one?"

Fletcher immediately regretted what he just said. "Mr. Walton. At a fundraiser at my uncle's inn." He studied her eyes to see if she'd picked up on his deception.

"That's awful. What was he like? The paper said he was originally from Bar Harbor and moved to Andover when he married his wife." She was flabbergasted.

Fletcher nodded. "I don't remember much about him, just that he had a thick Down East accent. Hardly knew what he was saying."

"Well, everyone's afraid to go near the woods. Like they're going to be struck by lightning at any moment."

"Hey guys, wait up," said Camway, running towards them.

"What took you so long?" Fletcher asked, relieved at the interruption.

"Mr. Lintine demanded an explanation for my black eye. He wanted to make sure I hadn't been involved in a fight or something at school."

Fletcher moved towards him. The last thing he needed was to have his name associated with anything bad when it came to Lintine. "What did you tell him?"

"The truth," said Camway casually.

Fletcher gasped. "What!?"

Camway laughed. "Relax. I told him it happened during a basketball game."

"Not really a lie," said Cicely eagerly. "Just not the whole story."

She glanced at Fletcher and then at Camway. "We were just talking about the three missing men and what happened to them."

"It's killing my dad's business. None of the fall tourists are renting mountain bikes," Camway announced. "I bet it's part of a cult or something."

"Where'd you get that from?" asked Fletcher, blinking at the two of them in an attempt to put on a good show.

"Well my mother said that all three places where they disappeared are associated with Mollyockett somehow. She thinks it may be some weird cult that's obsessed with her."

Fletcher was blindsided. Others were now connecting the dots.

"What!?" Cicely asked, completely confused. "How are they connected to *her*? She's dead."

Fletcher remained silent, eager to hear Camway's answer.

"Well, she mentioned a curse or something that she put on Snow Falls one winter. Next, there was the incident at her grave and then there's Frenchman's Hole."

Fletcher's body went numb. "What's Mollyockett got to do with Frenchman's Hole?" He asked naively.

"Well, she said that the *Newry Tribune* discovered that she would often camp out at the hole for weeks at a time."

Cicely laughed loudly. "Where'd they get that from? Her diary?"

"Dunno. That's just what she said. Kinda makes sense if you think about it."

There was a long silence. Then Cicely said, "Well it's freaking everyone out. Might as well quarantine everyone to their homes. Just like two years ago during the pandemic. My father's more nervous that it'll hurt season ticket sales at the ski resort."

"That's a far stretch," Fletcher said, rolling his eyes.

Camway reached into his red backpack and pulled out a protein bar. "Well, Stanley Mull told my father that the state is bringing in the big guns. They're visiting the scene at Snow Falls tomorrow. I guess he's been assigned to the story."

Fletcher looked as though the Boston Red Sox had been relocated to New York City. His entire body went numb.

Cicely gaped at him. "Fletch," she called out. "You okay?"

"I . . . um . . . I'm just surprised that the state of Maine would ask for help. I mean, lots of people go missing every year." He made every attempt to right his mind.

Cicely was not convinced. "Rubbish. You're not telling us something. I know you too well."

"Well, my dad's been told that the falls have changed with a recent rock slide, so he's going with Stanley to see if a kayak can now go over it. He could definitely use the additional business. I'm going with them after school tomorrow."

"No!"

Cicely recoiled. "Fletcher, what's going on? You're scaring me."

"Yeah, you've been there many times," Camway announced sagely, totally confused by the sudden outburst.

Fletcher shrugged. "It's just that everyone needs to be careful until they get to the bottom of things."

"You're still not telling us everything, Fletch," said Cicely impatiently. "I know you too well."

He grinned guiltily at them. "I'm just saying that Grans said that the news has advised everyone in Oxford County to be careful until the mystery is solved. If Cam wants to go to Snow Falls, what do I care?"

"You guys wanna come?" Camway asked. "Dad won't care."

"No, I'm good. Plus, I have something to do at home."

"I'll go." Cicely said, nodding her head. "I want to see how the falls have changed, and I can get some good autumn shots at the same time. I need to start posting more."

Fletcher's heart sank.

Cicely studied his demeanor.

"Awesome, we're leaving directly after practice. I'll tell my dad you're coming." He glanced at his watch. "I'm going to be late. Fletch, I'll see you at the cross-country team meeting before your detention."

"I won't be there tonight."

"What? You know how coach Parmenter is. You've even missed practice twice last week."

Cicely remained silent.

"I know. My dad has some legal things that need to be signed for

Cygnus. He said it's important that I'm there." He hesitated. "You do realize that I'm part owner of the company?"

"And you can't sign them when you get home tonight?"

"Cam, if I could, I would. Trust me."

"Hey, why don't you both come over after school tomorrow. You guys can help me taste a new product the bakery is making?"

"Umm, no. We're going to Snow Falls, duh," Camway said, laughing. "And didn't you just say you had something to do at home?"

"Yeah, it's the tasting along with other stuff. He wants my opinion, and it'll be fun." He was wavering in his words.

"I just got beaten up over healthy fats, Fletcher. The last thing I need right now is to give my opinion on a new food that Cygnus is baking," said Cicely, unconvinced. "Plus, just have them put the item in the fridge and join us at Snow Falls. Chill out, will you?"

"Yeah, I'm sure your father will understand."

Fletcher hesitated. "Okay, I'll go with you tomorrow. You sure you got room?" *I'll keep them away from the falls and near the old mill's foundation,* he thought.

"Well, that was much harder than it should've been," Cicely blurted out. "I still say you're hiding something."

Fletcher ignored her.

"Listen, I gotta run," Camway said. "I'll make up a better excuse for you at the team meeting, Fletch."

Fletcher unzipped his backpack and stowed his textbook *Basic Nutrition.*

Cicely was looking at him in a way completely foreign to him.

"Listen, Fletch, I'm not one to pry. You know that. But what's going on?"

"I've no idea what—"

"You've been late for class more times than I can count," said Cicely. "Now you're skipping cross-country practice." She paused and folded her arms. "It's like you're in a constant fog *when* your around."

He was at a loss for words. "Listen," he replied after a few uncomfortable seconds. "There's just a lot going on at Cygnus, and Dad's depending on me right now."

"Okay, just know that I'm here if you need to talk."

ATTENTION PLEASE: CROSS-COUNTRY AND FIELD HOCKEY PRACTICE HAVE BOTH BEEN CANCELED FOR THE NEXT SEVEN DAYS. ADDITIONALLY, THE CROSS-COUNTRY MEET SCHEDULED FOR THIS SATURDAY HAS BEEN POSTPONED AND WILL BE RESCHEDULED AT A LATER DATE! The public announcement system blared throughout the school.

Fletcher wrinkled his eyes at her. "I wonder what that's all about? Canceled for a week?"

"Why would they cancel field hockey for that long? We're ranked number one." She scowled, looking around for other team members.

"What's going on?" Camway and Caia Van Ives asked in unison as they ran down the crowed hallway.

"Cicely, I can't believe they'd cancel practice for that long," Caia huffed angrily. "Championships are in two weeks."

"As are ours," Camway exclaimed. "We've not been this good in years."

Within minutes, the entire school was abuzz with not only the cancellation of cross-country and field hockey practices but now football as well. Frenzied rumors swirled, changing drastically as they moved from person to person.

ATTENTION PLEASE: FLETCHER MCKENZIE, PLEASE REPORT TO THE FRONT OFFICE IMMEDIATELY. The public announcement blazed for a second time in minutes.

"Now what?"

"Want me to go with you?" asked Camway.

"No, I'm good. It's probably just my dad picking me up."

"Okay. I'll see you tomorrow – wait. Don't you have detention?"

Fletcher smiled.

"Boy, I wish my last name was McKenzie," Camway said, punching Fletcher's left shoulder. "Wait till Lautaro finds out you bailed."

Cicely rolled her eyes and tossed her hair back. "Just don't be late for his class again and read the next chapter, will you? You're on borrowed time. Once he finds out you're skipping detention, he will make your life miserable."

Camway cleared his throat. "So, are we on for Snow Falls tomorrow? I'll see if we can leave earlier now that none of us have practice."

"I'm in," said Fletch

"Me too," Cicely and Caia said together.

"Listen, I gotta run," Fletcher said, picking up his backpack.

As he hurried to the office for the second time, Camway's words about Mollyockett played in his mind.

It was getting far more serious.

Uncle Woodrow was standing at the end of the hallway near the front entrance.

Fletcher immediately picked up the pace.

"What's going on?"

"Let's go," he said, looking Fletcher over to make sure he appeared emotionally stable. "I'll tell you in the car."

Woodrow quickly pulled out of the visitor parking lot and headed towards the inn.

"There's been another incident."

"Where?" responded Fletcher. "How bad?"

"Fryeburg. On the banks of the Saco River."

Fletcher swallowed hard. "Mollyockett's original home."

"Yep."

"Any idea what happened?"

His uncle did not answer immediately. He looked straight ahead, pondering what to say. "No idea, yet," he finally said. "But, from what I've been told, there's three victims this time." Just then he pulled over to let a speeding emergency vehicle pass.

"How do they know it's related to—"

"Witnesses reported seeing a flash of bright light streak across the river and directly at three canoeists who were stowing their boats on the banks of the river. It's all over the news."

Fletcher threw him a dark look. "Did they die?" he asked.

"No idea. They've yet to be found. All that remained was six burnt shoes in the muck."

"Three. Holy smokes." Fletcher ran his left hand through his hair. "Does Dad know?"

"He does. He's picking up Alek to meet at the inn."

"Maybe they're in the water," said Fletcher earnestly. "They could've just drowned."

Woodrow shot him a knowing look.

"So the Slaughter Makers have doubled. It's only a matter of time before it happens to us."

"Fletch, let's not jump to conclusions. But we also have to err on the side of caution."

"How can we not?"

"Let's just see what Alek has found in Augusta," Woodrow said quickly. "Hopefully Squire Susup reappears soon."

Fletcher gulped, unable to respond.

"Your father has made the decision to fill your mother and grandparents in on everything."

"Wait! What!? Why?"

"Because of what happened to you the night you met the Slaughter Makers, he feels it's best to move the entire family in to the guesthouse behind the inn."

Fletcher nodded, relieved. "Do you think it'll help?"

With a downcast face, Woodrow said, "I've no idea. He wanted to wait for Squire Susup to return, but we've no idea when that will happen. All of this is completely mind-boggling. People are dying and many others are at risk of being killed." He shifted into fifth gear and stepped on the gas. "Your father is completely beyond himself."

"Grans and Gramps are going to kill me for lying to them for all this time," said Fletcher. "That's if they actually believe everything. I mean—"

"Once they hear the entire story," Woodrow chuckled, "they'll be immensely proud of you, young man. Especially what you did to rescue your mother."

Fletcher suddenly realized the enormity of what was going on. The circle of conspirators was growing.

"I remember when I was a young man, right about your age," Woodrow said, "when I first found out about Whole and it's unique world. I was confused and quite honestly, frightened. I couldn't comprehend the immense responsibility passed on to our family by Mollyockett hundreds of years ago. It took me a long time to mentally grasp everything."

Fletcher turned, taking in his words. "Can I ask you a question?"

"Anything. You know that."

"Why don't we just give them what they want? So what if they have them?"

Woodrow shivered. "Trust me, that's crossed my mind, and your father has even mentioned it. But it's not worth the risk."

"How come?"

"We're dealing with savage killers, Fletch. Additionally, you've always known that knowledge is the key to control of the passage. Our family is the only one that's possessed that knowledge since Mollyockett has passed it on."

"Meaning?"

"Meaning that the only way to destroy that knowledge is to eliminate those who possess it."

Fletcher looked up as they drove through the covered bridge towards the inn. He thought of the first time he'd met Alek Von Piddle and how he wildly waved his hands in the air, describing how he was painting the touristy bridge to help stimulate his mind.

"You all right, Fletch? You're very quiet."

"Did it happen this morning around seven?"

Woodrow looked sternly at Fletcher. "I know it happened this morning, but not sure of the timing. Why?"

Fletcher bit his lip and rubbed the brown spot on his hand.

"Because every time there is an incident with the Slaughter Makers, the mark on my hand burns. This morning it was worse than ever."

"How bad?"

"It was so bad while I was eating breakfast, Grans told Mom to drive me to the urgent care."

Woodrow stared at him.

"What did you tell them?"

"That my hand hurt. That's all. Grans could tell it was serious by the look on my face. So could Mom"

Woodrow formulated the order of events that would take place after Muriel, Lucille and Edmond were informed of everything. It would be a delicate balance of hysteria and disbelief on their part. He knew them too well.

"When are we moving into the house behind the inn?"

"Tonight. Your father doesn't want anyone living in the house given that it's built directly over the passage."

"Let me know how I can help," replied Fletcher, grinding his teeth. "I didn't expect everything to be happening so quickly."

"Do we have a choice?" Woodrow gave him a grave look. "Ah, good, they're here," he said, spotting Von Piddle sitting in a white Adirondack chair and sipping on a cup of tea.

Woodrow pulled the Land Rover into the circular drive and pulled back the emergency brake. "It's good to have you here, Fletch. We'll all get through this. Okay?"

Fletcher nodded. What he feared most was the loss of his parents again. He was an only child, and they were all he had. The time his father was medically incapacitated, and his mother went missing was the worst time of his life.

"Ahh, 'bout time you showed up," Von Piddle exclaimed as he approached, holding his cup of tea. He was wearing a new pair of glasses. "Always loved that snappy rig of yours. Used to have one when I was living in the Sahara Desert while exploring the Ghoraf Ouled Soltan in Matmata, Tunisia."

Fletcher enjoyed the moment of levity.

"Where's Aldous?" Woodrow asked, ignoring him.

"Inside. Taking a call."

Woodrow smiled feebly. He spotted a canvas satchel leaning against the Adirondack chair. *Hopefully he found something,* he thought.

Von Piddle stepped aside, allowing Fletcher to open his door.

"Absolute travesty what's going on. Never, ever expected that my wildest adventure would be right here in my backyard." He held his feeble hand out to assist Fletcher as he stepped down.

"Did you find anything Mr. Von Piddle?" Fletcher asked, with all seriousness.

"I did, young man. Absolute stroke of luck."

"Do you think—" Fletcher stopped when he saw the shock on his Father's face.

"Don't tell me there's more." Woodrow said flatly.

Aldous shook his head. "I just heard on the news that there were more than three victims in Fryeburg."

An eerie silence filled the air, only broken by a flock of Canadian geese heading south.

Von Piddle spoke first. "For heaven sakes, good man, what happened?"

Aldous glared at him and then explained, "A group of rafters on the Saco has also gone missing. They were part of a fall foliage flotilla."

"How many?"

Aldous hesitated, waiting for them to join him on the porch. "Six. Apparently they were just downstream of the canoeists."

"Good God!" Woodrow yelled. "Do they know what happened?"

"No, but remnants of their tattered raft was found downstream in a clump of trees." His words drifted off. "It was burnt and charred."

"Anything else found?" Fletcher asked.

"No, just the raft. What's left could have floated downstream. The lightning strike was so severe, it took trees down on both sides of the river."

"Right, lightning strike," Woodrow said sarcastically. "What do we do now?"

"Let's see what Alek has found. Then I need to head to the house for the most difficult conversation I've ever had," Aldous replied, moving towards the inn's entrance.

"Alek has found a few important discoveries regarding Jonathan Snow and Snow Falls while in August. Perhaps Squire Susup will help us connect the dots when we see him again," Aldous said, nodding towards Von Piddle after they assembled in Woodrow's private dining room. Secrecy was now paramount.

Alek stood up. With a grim look on his face, he started, "Well, where to begin?" He stopped and wiped his glasses. "I was quite fortunate to be given private access to state documents not yet electronically added to its new computer data base."

Aldous' finger tips tapped the table impatiently. He'd heard what Von Piddle had discovered while on the drive over and his mind was elsewhere. "Oh, I'm sorry," he said, now aware of the annoying interruption.

"When Woodrow discovered the monument to Jonathan Snow at Snow Falls, I was quite surprised to see that he'd been *murdered* by the Saint Francis Indians." He rifled through the large stack of papers before continuing. "Actually, I was stunned. They are also associated with the Abenaki tribe and are one of the five members of the Wabanaki Confederacy. There are different subdivisions of it throughout the entire eastern United States, but I'll not bore you with naming them all."

"Thank you," Woodrow blurted out.

Alek glared at him slightly annoyed. "I'll focus on only two. First is the Pequawket, also known as the Pigwackets, which—"

"Mollyockett's people," Fletcher chimed in.

Von Piddle nodded at him and smiled before continuing. "They lived along the Saco River," he paused, swallowing hard. "In the White Mountains of Maine and New Hampshire with their principal village being on the upper Saco River near present-day Fryeburg, Maine."

"Exactly where the Slaughter Makers reared their murderous heads this morning," said Woodrow, pulling a sheet of paper closer to him.

"Well if what Fletcher said happened to him down in the root cellar is true," Alek immediately corrected him. "It's Tygorge doing all the killing with his *pretty little wand* and not the Slaughter Makers. They're only the end result, so to speak."

Fletcher cleared his throat. *If what happened to me is true?* he thought. "Do you think it was him in Fryeburg this morning?" he asked.

"No idea, but it certainly looks like it. Let's get back to what I found. It only makes sense that it would be the Pequawket who raided Snow Falls since the falls were sacred to them. *Not* the Saint Francis Indians."

"Why wouldn't the Saint Francis Indians make sense?" Woodrow asked respectfully, careful not to offend Alek a second time.

"Because while they are also Abenaki, they are from the Arsigantegok subdivision and lived along the Saint Francis River in Quebec. That was quite a distance to travel at that time. Their principal village is Saint Francis which is also known as Odanak."

"Wait. Wasn't Mollyockett's family killed there?" gasped Fletcher.

"Indeed they were. It was an important place in her life, and she traveled there every year for confession at the Saint Francis Catholic Mission. She and her husband actually helped rebuild it after the Brits burned it down during the Revolutionary War."

Aldous closed his eyes and patted his forehead. "So essentially we have two tribes that are relevant to Mollyockett's life converging at exactly one place."

"Precisely," Von Piddle confirmed. "And if you remember, she was caught in the blizzard in the year 1810, fully fifty-five years after the killing of Jonathan Snow."

"Hardly a coincidence I would say," added Aldous.

"It would be hard to believe that she was just wandering around looking for *medical* patients that far from Bethel, especially since winter was approaching. She wasn't that dumb," said Woodrow, looking towards Fletcher. He recalled telling him the entire life story of Mollyockett while he was healing from the nasty incident at Buck's Ledge.

Alek ruffled his papers before continuing. "So, I decided to look into the incident for which the falls are so gloriously named: the massacre of Jonathan Snow in 1755. There's really not much in print, but I discovered an artifact in Augusta that may shine some light on her curse or whatever curse is floating around out there. In 1824, Elijah Hamlin in the very first issue of the *Oxford Observer* wrote about the events surrounding Snow's murder."

"Is he related to Hannibal Hamlin?" Fletcher asked.

"Older brother."

"So what did he write?" Aldous asked impatiently. "I've got an unpleasant conversation waiting for me."

Woodrow closed his eyes and shook his head in agreement.

"Very well. So, I guess that Hamlin had access to historical documents that are now lost to the ages. But what he wrote is quite alarming." Alek sniffled and cleared his throat. "Back then, the area around the falls was complete wilderness. Houses were being erected after the Revolutionary War when the mill was constructed. In 1755, Captain Snow and a man named James Stinchfield were hunting and trapping on the stream near the falls. Unbeknownst to them, the Saint Francis Indians were also in the area. When they *bumped* into each other, the large group of Native Americans attempted to take the two colonists prisoner. Stinchfield immediately surrendered, but Snow, well aware of the horrible sufferings of Indian prisoners, resisted. He grabbed his musket and went to the door and gave the sign of surrender to the lead Indian."

Fletcher held his breath. The monument at the falls told the ending to the encounter.

"Alek held a copy of a document and began to read:

> *Snow appeared at the door with his musket in his*
> *hand and made a demonstration of surrender; but he only*
> *did this to single out his victim. The Indian who covered*
> *the file in its approach was of ferocious appearance and*
> *uncommon stature. His head was adorned with plumage*
> *of the eagle taken entire, its wings depending over either*
> *shoulder, and talons and beak so arranged that it still*
> *seemed to have life and conscious of its kingly power. When*
> *within a few steps of Snow, and signifying request for*
> *quarter, now suddenly elevated the muzzle of his piece, and*
> *saying that he neither asked or gave quarter, discharged*
> *it into the bosom of the Indian Sachem, who rolled upon*
> *the ground in the mortal agonies of death. Before Snow*
> *could recover and make another movement of offense, he*
> *himself was slain and cut into pieces by the whole party,*
> *who furiously attacked him. They then betook themselves*
> *to lamentations and howling for the loss of their (beloved)*
> *chief. Now having performed all the funeral rites due to his*
> *rank, and significant of their consideration of his loss, they*
> *sank him in a neighboring bog and continued their march*
> *northward, taking Stinchfield along with them, calculating*
> *to offer him up as a sacrifice for the death of their chief.*

Alek sat down and removed his glasses. "What's interesting is that the mill at the top of the falls burned down exactly one hundred years to the day of Snow's death."

"You okay, Fletch?" Aldous asked, studying his son's face.

"That description you gave of the Sachem dressed like an eagle is exactly like one of the etchings on the wall behind the root cellar," Fletcher exclaimed with wide eyes. "Right down to him creeping up on a man holding a musket."

"You sure?" asked Woodrow.

"Positive, I'd never forget it."

"Unbelievable." Alek was stunned.

"Who's Sachem?" Aldous asked, looking down at Von Piddle's papers.

"The New England tribes called their kings sachems. It literally is the name of whoever is king of a tribe at the time."

"Jeez, I can see how they'd be peeved. No wonder why they cut Snow into pieces," Fletcher said, envisioning the etching on the wall of the cave where he encountered the Slaughter Makers.

"So, what ties all of this together?" Aldous queried while tapping his fingers on the table. "Why now?"

"No idea, but the incidents are happening over a wider area now and at a rapid pace. It's like they're in a hurry for some reason," said Alek. "If the pattern fits, I suspect there'll be an unfortunate incident at Odanak any day."

"But that's not in Maine," Fletcher stated.

Alek chuckled. "The travels of the Native Americans weren't confined to borders and boundaries established at a later date by the conquering Europeans. If I were a betting man, I'd—"

"Say that someone near Odanak is to meet his or her demise in the very near future," Woodrow exclaimed, finishing his sentence for him.

Aldous stood and faced them. "Obviously, the hysteria that's starting to grow in Oxford County will only get worse. We need to make a solemn promise right now that outside of the McKenzie family and Alek, none of this gets out. It'll only make the situation worse. Even the slightest comment by any of us could be totally misconstrued and reported to the authorities." His eyes pleaded for unanimity. "Okay?"

Everyone nodded in agreement.

"Here, here," said Alek.

Fletcher felt terrible. He wished he'd fought back harder against Tomhegan instead of fleeing Whole with his injured mother.

A knock at the door interrupted his thoughts.

Woodrow cautiously opened it.

"I know you didn't want to be disturbed, Woody, but Muriel is on the phone for Aldous. Something about Fletcher not showing up for detention," said an unknown voice from behind the door.

Aldous immediately shot Fletcher a confused look.

Woodrow looked as though he'd just swallowed a pine cone when he turned around. "Aldous, a call for you," he said, hunching his shoulders.

Red-faced, Fletcher stood up and silently followed his father towards the inn's lobby.

"Absolute adventurer that boy is. Reminds me of myself when I was his age," Alek uttered as Fletcher exited the room. There was elation etched in his wrinkly face. "Reminds me—"

"Alek, please!" Woodrow yelled, slightly stunning his longtime friend.

"What's gotten into you, Woody? Joining the Royal Club of Crabby Pants?"

Woodrow laughed loudly. "No, it's just the seriousness of what's in front of us right now." He picked up the house phone and told the staff to prepare the small house behind the inn for the arrival of Fletcher's parents and grandparents.

"What's your gut telling you, Alek? I don't think you've ever been wrong."

Alek shook his head.

"Well, there's a few things that are still confusing." He looked towards the door. "I didn't want to alarm the boy, but there's more than just bones under the falls. When I—"

"I thought we agreed to share everything," snapped Woodrow.

"We did, but not *when*," Alek responded casually. "A big difference."

"Semantics."

"Exactly. You know me too well. There's a proper time for everything. So, back to the bones. It was absolutely dreadful and I wished I'd stayed there longer for more clues. Someone has mysteriously laid the bones in various patterns that I'm quite positive tell a story. Always do. Looks as though it's a warning or curse of sorts." He paused, glancing at the door. "There are three skeletons with dried flesh in places. A woman, man, and child. Well, a boy to be more specific. That was clear by the clothing laid over the bones. I've seen things like this before in my travels. They may have been there to symbolize Fletcher, Muriel, and Aldous. That's what my gut is telling me."

Woodrow looked confused but now knew why this pertinent information had been withheld.

"I've studied bones my entire life, and I'm absolutely certain these are recently deceased individuals, unlike the others. I could tell by how white they were. Shockingly, an arrow was protruding from a charred hole in each of the three skulls. It's like they've been laid there as a message of sorts."

Woodrow's hopes of a quick fix immediately sank.

"So you think they expected us to visit that spot?"

"Clearly," answered Von Piddle. "As soon as I stepped behind the falls, the rocks holding it up, slowly opened as if inviting me in. Had I not known what you all told me about Whole, my intrepid heart would have given out on the spot."

"So that answers that question."

"What question?" Alek asked.

"Why the police investigating Croft's death didn't find your little cave with the bones. Or how it has remained undiscovered for centuries."

"Alek. We have two Native American tribes from two different regions that have converged at one spot at an important time in history," Woody continued. "Moreover, Mollyockett just *happens* to be wandering there during a blizzard many years after a Saint Francis king is killed there." He paused and wiped his forehead with a faded napkin. "And then there's Nimsy Cortland."

"Ah, let's not forget her," Alek blurted. "Innocent and loving Nimsy. Fearless and faithful adventurer she was."

Woodrow bit down on his lip. "Right. She's directly related to the Snow Family and devoted her entire life to taking down Muriel McKenzie. And finally, there's the float on Mollyockett Day the year after Fletcher saved his parents."

Alek frowned. "You lost me, old boy. Care to enlighten me?"

"Sorry, there's just so much. Well, the summer after Fletcher rescued Muriel, the theme of the parade was healthy living."

"So? Everyone dress up as baked beans and fiber, smelling up the entire town of Bethel during a hot day?"

Woodrow laughed loudly, slightly embarrassed. "No. The winning float was constructed exactly like Aldous and Fletcher said Whole looked like."

"And?"

"And, that first place float belonged to the Snow Family. How on earth did they know what Whole looked like? In fact, Chesley Snow accepted the first place trophy in front of the entire town. Fletcher and Aldous were beyond themselves."

Alek shivered. "Do you think Nimsy actually survived her unfortunate encounter with Fletcher?"

"We don't know that, but it looks like the Snow family has a little mole cozying up to someone who knows Whole very well."

Von Piddle nodded silently. "I don't even know how to describe what's going on right now, old boy. I feel like I've stumbled into a horrid dream that never ends. I mean, I literally keep pinching myself."

"Well, whatever it is, we need to tell Fletcher and Aldous what you've discovered. The boy's been through a lot and will be able to handle it. I'm positive of that."

"The old chap's tough as nails is he?" Alek asked crisply.

"Tougher."

Their conversation was interrupted by a commotion just outside the door. Without thought, Woodrow strode towards the noise and cautiously slid the chain lock open.

Alek clumsily fumbled with his papers, attempting to hide them from a possible intruder.

To their surprise, in stepped three individuals: Fletcher, Aldous, and Squire Susup.

CHAPTER 9

WILLAMETTE AND THE PATERA

THE SITUATION WAS URGENT.

"Stop! Please," said Pidianiski weakly, but Mollyockett ignored her cries. She was preoccupied with the task of concocting salves and other unique ailments to treat Pidianiski's broken and battered body.

"Just be glad you backed into Flow or you'd be dead right now."

"How'd you know I backed into Flow?"

"Merrimack."

"He was there?" Pidianiski asked. She grimaced sharply just as a thick white cream soaked through her skin.

"Any idea what happened?" Mollyockett asked, ignoring her question. She continued to slather the mushy concoction on her exposed back in between several large openings on her tattered rawhide dress.

"What's that?"

"What's what?"

"What are you putting on my back and leg. It tingles and burns."

"Zinc, copper, calcium, phosphorus, and silicon. You have more broken bones than I can count. In fact, a few of the bones are so badly broken, I'll have to mix some green vegetables, sardines, and salmon for your dinner. You'll be better than ever by nightfall. I promise. Nutrients, nutrients, nutrients. Thank your lucky stars you're in Whole right now."

"What about my burns?" she asked, studying several charred cuts on both her hands.

"Give me time," said Mollyockett patiently. "That brown lotion over there will heal them within minutes. It's loaded with antioxidant vitamins

A, C, E, the B-complex vitamins, and trace minerals such as magnesium, calcium, zinc, and selenium. I've topped it off with omega-3 fatty acids from salmon oil. I never had to mix so many concoctions in my life."

"Good. You've no idea how much everything hurts."

"Your hair is another issue, though?"

"What do you mean?" asked Pidianiski.

"It's singed up to your neck."

"You're kidding?"

"Nope. I'll make a tablet with vitamins C, B, E, biotin, niacin, and iron. It'll take a few days, but it'll be normal length again. What on earth! Looks like they got the better of you." Mollyockett stopped and blinked. She'd just spotted a large gash in Pidianski's scalp.

"That's an understatement," Pidianski admitted, shaking her head.

"Care to share?"

"We're in for an epic battle, Molly, and they're definitely one step ahead of us."

Mollyockett nodded. "Slaughter Makers?" she asked.

"You should see them. They're a formidable foe that's not to be under-estimated. Whoever created them has tapped into something quite evil."

Mollyockett chuckled deviously. "I've never underestimated Nukpana and Tygorge. Did you find anything?" she asked coolly, lifting the broken left leg to apply ointment.

"Well, the Ollantaytambo temple is definitely not vacant. The execution chamber is very much back in use, because—"

"Roll over, slowly," Mollyockett told her.

"Ouch, be careful," she pleaded. She carefully used her left hand to prop up her body. "My spine."

"Well, that's because it's broken in six places. Again, thank your lucky stars you're in Whole right now or you'd—"

"I know, I know, I know."

"You were saying."

"Huh? Oh, right. The entire death chamber was completely soaked in blood. Fresh blood."

"Any idea the source?" Mollyockett asked. "I wonder how they got so close to Whole's southern passage."

"None. But, what's interesting is that . . . Where's my knife?' She had expected to feel it when she turned over."

"It wasn't with you when I found you. You must've dropped it."

"I've had that knife for over two hundred years. How could I be so stupid," she said. "I'll have to go back. You know it's ability to—"

"I'll see if Machias can have Mado fetch it. I need you here."

"Why?"

Mollyockett hesitated. "Squire Susup was here this morning. They're moving faster than we thought. Apparently, they've marked not only my grave, Snow Falls, and Frenchman's Hole," she paused and watched Merrimack perch himself on a rose trellis overlooking the valley. "They've also raided Pequawket this—"

"Fryeburg!" Pidianiski exclaimed. She had expected a completely different answer from Mollyockett and was flabbergasted. "What happened?"

"According to Susup, it was more than six this time."

"So are Wells, Ogunquit, and Odanak up next?' she asked, feeling defeated.

"The pattern fits. I wish there was a way to warn—"

"Might as well hang a vacancy sign on Whole for all humanity to see," Pidianiski blurted.

"If you'd let me finish, I would've said that. What else did you find?"

Pidianiski rubbed her hand over her face. "The new Wabanaki Confederation is definitely showing it's hand quite boldly."

"What's that mean?" Mollyockett asked with a baffled look.

"Well, when I was in the death chamber, a mysterious voice demanded the code or they would kill me. It also referenced Chief Camaztoz."

Mollyockett closed her eyes and sighed deeply. "How about Uktena?" she asked.

"Nothing."

"We've most certainly lost the southern temple as well as the Quechuan Valley to them," she said, sounding deflated. "It's really only a matter of time before they access the passage down there. I really hope Machias comes through."

Pidianiski hesitated briefly, then nodded.

"You know what I find interesting about the Slaughter Makers?"

"What?"

"They're killers. I can attest to that. But they're unable to do the things that'll be pivotal if they invade Whole."

Mollyockett wrinkled here forehead. "Meaning?"

"Meaning, they can attack quite efficiently, but the source of the blast that knocked me unconscious came from an unknown person standing behind them. He was blurry and shimmering, like he was behind a moving mirror. It's one thing to be able to hide in a small enclosed area, quite another in the openness of Whole"

"Sounds like what Fletcher described to Susup."

"I know. I thought that too."

Molloyockett stopped slathering the thick cream on Pidianiski's legs and pondered the discovery. "Do you think their obsession with the code has anything to do with *that* or making the Slaughter Makers more efficient?"

"No idea, but they definitely cannot fight on their own in Whole."

"Hmm."

"What are you thinking?"

"I don't know, but I'm positive Machias will have a clue."

"That blue fog that was in Fletcher's room was also in the death chamber, by the way. It appeared right before they demanded the code and attacked me."

Mollyockett raised an eyebrow. "Well, that's interesting."

"I know."

"So this blue fog is doing the introductory talking for the Confederation, and the Slaughter Makers are its protector." She carefully lifted Pidianiski's burnt braids and rubbed cream on her neck. A small broken bone poked out from under her tanned skin. "And whoever the person was that blasted you, he was unable to step out from behind an invisible barrier, just like the Wabanaki Confederation when they summoned Fletcher."

"What's that means?"

"No idea, but it's quite possibly important. I wonder which one was able to infiltrate the area surrounding the southern passage?"

"It's gotta be Tomhegan. He's been there before and is very familiar with the everything that's there."

"Correct me if I'm wrong, Pidianiski. Didn't Fletcher *seal* it three years ago?"

"He did, and the star he removed was not on the symbol. I made sure before moving into the execution chamber."

Mollyockett gasped. "He was forced to surrender it to the Slaughter Makers that night in his root cellar."

"Oh, my God!" Pidianiski yelled. "It's all coming together."

"They're using him," Mollyockett said flatly. "I was wondering why he had joined them so prominently."

"Tomhegan?"

"Who else? He definitely held a respectable position while living in Oxford County, but not one equal to theirs. It all makes sense and I hope in the end he gets what he fully deserves when they no longer need him."

"I immediately noticed the star was missing from the symbol when I spotted it," Pidianiski repeated.

"Of course, it was. It's their key into Whole." Mollyockett swallowed hard. "It's not like they're going to put it back and walk away. We need to do whatever it takes to keep the staff, patera and *Whole Abounds,* as well as it's mysterious code, away from them."

"That still baffles me," Pidianiski said. She slowly sat up, analyzing her tattered dress.

"Don't worry, Mado and Ogbo went and got your things. I expect you're going to be here for quite some time."

Pidianiski turned and focused on the two light brown animals standing at the edge of a small stream, casually drinking. It always amazed her how these hog-like animals with short legs, fleshy snouts and big ears could continuously do the heavy lifting for Mollyockett.

"Thank you. I hope there'll be a time when I'm able to go back home."

Mollyockett didn't answer at once. She lowered her eyes and pondered their conversation. *The rules of Whole are changing,* she wondered. *How long before they perfect their techniques and overcome their deficiencies?*

"We need to protect Fletcher," she said tensely. "He's the one person who can access the powers of *Whole Abounds* and Vilcanota's Patera. And he can access Whole and the southern passage area. With him freely walking about, who knows what'll happen."

Pidianiski nodded. She, completely healed now, was standing over a small basket, changing into a crudely made dress.

"What's the history with that thing? Mollyockett asked.

"What? The patera?"

"Yes. You're the one who brought it here from the Whole's southern territory. It may help us."

Pidianiski nodded. She understood what was going on in Mollyockett's head.

"Well, as you know, I gave it to Fletcher before he saved Muriel from Tomhegan and Nimsy Cortland."

"I'm aware of that," said Mollyockett, impatiently. "I'm more interested in *where* it originally came from."

Pidianiski took a deep breath and shook her head. "Okay. During my time when I held the power of the passage." She paused. "Before you, Molly," she said. "I was studying Kozart's notes for translation into *Whole Abounds*. I believe it was the summer of 1707. Surprisingly, I stumbled on references he made about Ollantaytambo and it's almost extinct people. After studying his crude maps and notes, I made the decision to quickly travel there once I determined that they too had their own passage to Whole and needed to be protected from literally being wiped off the map. Much like the struggle of our people."

"That must have shocked you."

"More than you know. Our people always believed we were the sole protectors of Whole. So that summer, when it was time to visit this place, I applied what I learned in Kozart's notes and made my way to the temple at Ollantaytambo in the southern territory. It's truly one of the marvels of the universe."

"Where'd the name come from?"

"Name?"

"Vilcanota."

"Oh that. It's named after the river that flows just outside Ollantaytambo. Almost the same size as the one at Snow Falls and Frenchman's Hole. It—"

"I wonder if that's significant?" Mollyockett asked. "Three streams almost the same size."

"I'd guess no," answered Pidianiski. "The Saco is much larger as is the one up in Quebec."

Molloyockett nodded.

"So while in the temple, they clearly were expecting a future visitor from this side of Whole."

"Wait. You think they knew about us?"

"Must've. Because next to the patera were stone tablets inscribed with native symbols and expertly chiseled short stories, as well as directions marking the entrance to their passage. Not knowing what they were, I carefully gathered them and brought them home with me."

"Fletcher owns the patera. But who has all the other items?"

"I do. I've held on to them for safe keeping."

"You're positive they're still there, Pidianiski?" Mollyockett asked with concern. "There may be more there than you thought, especially since Camaztoz is now part of their ring of evil."

Pidianiski shot her a glance, swallowing hard.

"I'll check, but I'm almost positive they're still there. No one else even knows I have these treasures."

"Let's hope so. Machias may want to look at them to see if you've missed something."

"Missed something? I'm quite positive I overlooked nothing," Pidianiski huffed defensively.

"I'm not underestimating your abilities; it's just that sometimes people see things differently. Quite often, worlds apart. We need to consider everything."

"I understand. It just that I spent years deciphering them."

"I know. I don't think I could've done it. The very existence of Whole thanks you. Anything else?"

"There is. The better part of the tablets contained instructions on how to access the powers of Vilcanota's patera. You know, just like *Whole*

Abounds. As mentioned, that little oval rock Fletcher controls, allows him to tap into the powers of the six nutrients of the body. Greatly magnified of course."

Mollyockett looked befuddled. "I never really thought about it, but where do you think those powers come from?"

Pidianiski shook her head. "Never really thought about it. Just like you I've never questioned Whole. When I found the patera, I had no idea what I was looking at. Additionally, once I discovered its uniqueness and how to make it work, I had to wait for years to see if it could be transferred through my bloodline after I died."

"Well, thankfully, we now know the answer to that."

"I know."

"I think it would be best if I went with you to retrieve those tablets for Machias to look at."

"Why do you need to come?" Pidianiski protested. "I'm quite capable myself."

"Look what just happened to you," Mollyockett countered. "We can't take any chances given how important they are. And you as well. Especially given that Camaztoz is involved. It's obvious that the Mayan *death bat* is more than mythology. Machias mentioned they are associated with night, death, and sacrifice, all of which you just encountered."

Pidianiski crossed her arms in exasperation and closed her eyes. "You know how private I am with my camp. It's my whole life."

"Fine, have it your way. I just hope *that* camp is there after all this is over."

Silence reigned for a few uncomfortable minutes while Pidianiski's gaze followed a small cloud drifting slowly towards a row of pruned mango trees.

"You're right," she finally conceded. "When are you thinking of going?"

"Now. I'm sure Machias will be back soon."

NOW! NOW! NOW! Merrimack mimicked her happily, jerking his bright feathered head up and down while jumping upwards.

"Did I hear my name mentioned?"

Both ladies immediately pivoted towards the deep voice behind them. Machias slowly walked towards them. He was completely covered with black-and-white animal pelts. His signature horned buffalo mask covered his face. A large gathering of fireflies hovered slightly overhead, serving as guides as he exited the lush forest. Gold bracelets jangling from his leathery wrists sparkled brilliantly in the bright light. Four small lemurs bounded happily behind him, daring not to move ahead of his pace. As he strode on, they bounded forward, leaping and twisting and turning with each high jump.

"Hooey, Sebago, Casco, Mohegan, run along now, you hear?"

As if electrified, the four small monkeys jerked upward and headed towards Mado and Ogbo, who completely ignored them.

Machias raised his animal mask and nodded genuinely.

"My deepest apologies ladies, I honestly hadn't expected to be gone this long," he said, extricating himself from two, thick leather straps holding a wood basket on his back. "I'd say we're in for it." His solemn, deep voice was sobering.

Mollyockett immediately zeroed in on the dark circles under his eyes. *He's not stopped since I've last seen him.*

"I'm relieved to see my predictions about you being able to return to Ollantaytambo proved correct," he said to Pidianiski with an amused smirk, studying the torn and bloodied dress still laid out on the grassy surface. "Welcome back."

"Yeah, I'll have to do that again," she said coolly. "Absolute holiday."

To her annoyance, Molloyockett gave her an almost amused smile.

After a moment of silence Machias brought the conversation back full circle. "I fear we're in foreign territory with everything that's transpired over the past month or so ladies. Unfortunately for us, Whole's holding her cards close to her chest."

"How so?" Mollyockett asked bluntly.

He pulled out a small thin twig from his fur-covered pocket and inserted it in his mouth.

"It's as though the Wabanaki Confederation is rewriting the rules, and Whole is freely allowing it to happen," he replied.

"I can second that," Pidianiski called out while smoothing out a small glob of ointment on her left arm that had been overlooked. "Mollyockett has just mentioned the immediate need to protect Fletcher."

"Ah, good minds think alike. I've dispatched Squire Susup to do just that. He should be there by now."

Molloyockett nodded her head. "Good," she said.

"I'm moving the entire McKenzie family and some unknown compatriot of theirs to Whole's welcoming chamber."

They both gasped loudly.

"You're joking!"

"Impossible!"

"It may seem drastic, but I'm convinced there's a way."

"But why *all* of them. Why not just the boy?" Pidianiski replied.

Machias bit down on the twig. He turned towards Pidianski. "Need I remind you how loyal that family is to each other. Fletcher was almost killed three years ago when he risked everything to save his parents. The last thing we need right now is a bunch of pawns walking around Mahoosuc waiting for the Slaughter Makers to attack while we hold him hostage down here. They're waiting for us to figure out how to get them here."

Mollyockett turned flush. "I'm not second guessing you at all, Machias. In fact, I'll do whatever it takes. You know that. It's just that—"

"Just what?"

"It's just . . . well, you know as well as I the long-standing rules of Whole. It's one thing to tell Pidianiski that she's allowed to revisit Ollantaytambo but quite another to take those who don't precisely follow the bloodline into Whole. It's never been done."

Pidianiski cleared her throat, unable to wrap her mind around his plan.

"Ladies, calm down. Let me explain," he said, raising his voice slightly.

"I need to sit down for this," said Mollyockett, closing her eyes. Her favorite root chair immediately morphed into its distinctive shape.

"That's a wonderful idea," Pidianiski chimed in. "It'll help me from falling over."

"I'm all ears," stated Mollyockett, casually folding her hands on her lap.

"So am I."

Machias chuckled slightly. *I hope this works,* he thought. Taking a step toward Pidianiski, he lowered his head and looked directly at her.

"Remember when you transcribed Kozart's notes into *Whole* —"

"I think you're forgetting that *I* helped with that huge task," Mollyockett interrupted.

"Right, my apologies," Machias conceded while Pidianiski rolled her eyes sarcastically.

"So when you were *both* translating *Whole Abounds,*" Machias continued. "Do you remember what percentage of his notes you actually used to complete the book?"

Silence ensued as they both pondered his question.

"I'd guess about sixty percent," Pidianiski guessed.

"Why's that?"

"Why's what?"

"Why only sixty percent. Why didn't you translate all of his notes if *Whole Abounds* is so special?"

"Because, I focused on the nutritional part. Once I determined—"

Mollyockett shot her a death stare.

"I mean us," Pidianiski immediately corrected herself. "Once we determined a section had nothing to do with nutrition, we set it aside," said Pidianiski.

"What was the remaining forty percent that you decided not to use all about?"

"No idea, I, I mean we decided to move on once it was obvious a particular section of notes wasn't pertinent."

"Wasn't pertinent? Pidianiski, if your father took the time to document something about Whole, don't you think it'd be pertinent?"

"I see where this is going?" said Mollyockett, nodding her head. "Can't believe this has never come up before."

Pidianiski rapped her fingers on the arm of her chair with a rapid series of audible blows.

"Please tell me that you still have his notes," Machias pleaded, holding his breath.

"What'd you think I did with them? Start a fire? Of course I still have them."

"Where?"

"At my camp."

Machias exhaled deeply and genuinely smiled for the first time in a long time.

"It's a long shot, but I hope those lost notes will give us clues to other secrets Whole has to offer. I don't have to remind you both that Kozart was extremely meticulous and quite literally made provisions for every imaginable scenario.

"I feel like a total idiot that I would continue to overlook some of my father's notes," conceded Pidianiski.

"Well, given the task before you, I'd say you did a wonderful job," Mollyockett stated, surprising her. Have you seen those notes?" Mollyockett asked.

Machias shook his head. "No. Why?"

"Because there's a reason why Pidianiski ignored them once she, I mean we, determined that they weren't relevant to *Whole Abounds*. His writing is awful. Just reading them is torturous, yet alone deciphering them."

Pidianiski nodded her approval of the declaration. It definitely was the most excruciating thing she'd ever experienced.

"Well, if you both have a better suggestion, then I'm all ears."

Pidianiski smiled. "Mollyockett suggested we also study those stone tablets I brought home from the Quechuan temple when I found the patera. She's hoping they'll offer us more insight."

"Brilliant," replied Machias. "Splendid idea."

Pidianiski, caught between jubilation and dismay, sighed deeply.

"We'll definitely need a few of those strong coffee beans you keep hidden in your garden, Molly. I have a felling none of us will be sleeping any time soon." Machias laughed. He was thrilled to be in the presence of these two amazing women.

"We did mark off the sections we used for *Whole Abounds,* so at least that'll make it easier to review those notes we ignored."

"Thank God," said Mollyockett. "I still remember how massive everything was. I can't even imagine starting from scratch." She paused. "So what exactly will we be looking for?" she asked Machias.

"Anything."

"Anything?" The two ladies said together.

"Yes, anything that will allow us to circumvent the rules about who's allowed into Whole. Again, if I remember correctly, Kozart was very meticulous with his notes in his efforts to make provisions for every eventuality."

"That he was," said Pidianiski proudly. "I can't even begin to think how long it must have taken him to transcribe everything onto birch bark and tanned leather."

Mollyockett stood up. "Well, I say we get on with it given how precious time is right now. Fletcher's family is depending on us. Do you mind if I ask what Squire Susup is doing to protect Fletcher until we come through?"

"He's standing guard over the entrance to the passage in the root cellar. I told him to guard it with his life. He's also instructing the entire family to steer clear of any location associated with the Wabanaki nation, like Frenchman's Hole and Snow Falls. They're secretly staying at Woodrow's inn."

Mollyockett gulped hard as she thought about the wounds the two massive and savage Slaughter Makers had recently inflicted on Pidianiski. Saving someone in Whole was easy compared to healing them on the outside. "As Susup's mother, don't you think you should've consulted me?"

"No. Because you'd have said *yes* anyways," Machias answered her bluntly. "Besides we're all in this together."

"Who all are you planning on bringing to Whole if you don't mind me asking?" Pidianiski inquired, anxious to get started.

"Fletcher, Aldous, Muriel, Woodrow, Lucille, Edmond, and Alek Von Piddle."

"You *really* think we can make provisions for that many outsiders?" Mollyockett asked.

"Alek who?" Pidianiski added. "Is he a McKenzie relative? That's kind of important."

Machias raised his right palm.

"Ladies. I'm well aware how many people there are. And no, Mr.

Von Piddle is not related to the McKenzie family."

Mollyockett shivered.

"Unbelievable. I can see Kozart's notes possibly making provisions for someone related to the keeper of the keys to enter Whole under certain conditions, but a complete stranger? Impossible."

"Hasn't that been the bedrock of Whole?" asked Pidianiski. "Even my father couldn't have envisioned a time when that would have happened."

Machias silently nodded. "I understand," he said. "But does either one of you have a better plan?"

"Well, it's worth a shot," Pidianiski conceded. "Besides, there's a lot in those notes. There may be something just waiting to be discovered."

"A positive attitude will most definitely help speed up the process. Thank you," Machias offered. "Plus, remember, I said only the welcoming chamber of Whole. It's not like they'll be wandering around, unfettered. They can camp out in your garden. It'll be far safer than where they are right now."

Mollyockett closed her eyes, remembering the spectacular place where she first met Fletcher. *Alterations would need to be made to accommodate them if this works.*

"How do you want to get those notes and tablets? Right before you arrived, I told Pidianiski I didn't want her traveling alone, given what's happening."

"I wouldn't allow either of you near those items alone. I'm absolutely certain the Wabanaki Confederation and their little army have been on the hunt for them," Machias said, moving in the direction of Flow.

"What about your little friends over there?" Mollyockett laughed, pointing towards the small monkeys happily jumping from tree to tree at the edge of the stream.

"They'll be fine. I say we make a quick trip of it and set up shop here."

Without hesitating, the two women quickly fell in line and headed towards the humming blue rays awaiting them. Unbeknownst to them, at the exact same time, a small brown spot on Fletcher's hand was burning so badly, it literally knocked him unconscious.

Machias tapped his nose.

They'd been at it for hours. Kozart's notes were far more extensive than he'd ever imagined. Because Mollyockett and Pidianiski were familiar with his writings, he made the decision to study the centuries-old tablets found in the Quechuan temple.

"It's a travesty these amazing people were literally wiped off the map," Machias said, analyzing a long and broken series of unrecognizable symbols.

"It broke my heart when I traveled there. You should see the masterpieces they created," Pidianiski confided.

Mollyockett cleared her throat.

"Anything interesting?"

"Machias, just focus on those Ollantaytambo tablets, and I'll do my part with Kozart's writings."

Pidianiski chuckled.

He rubbed both his eyes, fully aware that before them was the potential to make all that was wrong, right. Their efforts could make or break the stunning world he'd called home for hundreds of years.

He scratched the bottom of his chin behind his beard. "I can honestly say these people were centuries ahead of their European conquerors. It's a downright shame they had no resistance to the diseases those criminals brought with them."

Mollyockett stopped reading and told him to be quiet. "Not to be disrespectful," she said. "But you're ruining my concentration."

Machias apologized and returned his attention to the tablets. She had been cantankerous for as long as he'd known her and in no way expected, or wanted, her to change.

"How are we to ask questions if we have them?"

Mollyockett rolled her eyes at him. "If you have something pertinent to what we're looking for, please ask away. Otherwise, please keep quiet."

"Well, this is interesting," Pidianiski blurted out, looking up. "Listen to this."

"What?" Mollyockett's face showed disbelief. "You find it?"

"I'm not sure. But it's clear my father was well aware issues would arise should the power of the passage transfer it to another bloodline." She looked at Mollyockett warmly, hoping she wouldn't be upset since she had decided to transfer power of the passage to a new bloodline after being controlled by the Pigwackets for centuries. She'd grown to love and respect the McKenzie family.

"Care to share your thoughts?' Machias stated, slightly impatiently.

"Well, he references a large field at the base of a small hill that for reasons unbeknownst to him can be used as a staging point of sorts if the bloodline of those who lost the power of the passage unite and fight."

Machias whistled.

Pidianiski continued, "And listen to this. He also says there is a small waterfall there that holds a dark chamber that'll protect anyone who moves against Whole."

"Protect them from what?" Mollyockett asked eagerly.

Pidianiski squinted as she studied the words on the rolled birch bark. "No idea. That part's missing."

Machias huffed. "I wonder what that means exactly."

Pidianiski tenderly unrolled the next bark scroll, exposing a crude map. Molloyockett immediately leaned in and studied it. "Good gracious!" she exclaimed.

"What?"

Her mouth gaped. "That's exactly where Snow Falls is located. I knew it." She was flabbergasted beyond belief. "I've been there!"

"It's right in the center of Wabanaki territory," Pidianiski said, her lips slightly quivering. "A little more than twenty miles from the McKenzie home."

"Anything that will help get us relocate the family to Whole?" Machias asked, feeling a sense of urgency more than ever.

"Wait! Didn't you say that Nimsy Cortland's family is from Snow Falls?" Pidianiski asked Mollyockett, ignoring his question.

"Unbelievable. Yes, her maiden name was *Snow.* "

"Well, that's definitely not a coincidence."

"So that little curse I put on the place was literally just the frosting on the cake? Little did I know I was walking right on top of the devil's playground that could help destroy what I'd worked so hard to protect."

"Curse?' Machias asked. "What curse?"

Mollyockett quickly retraced her steps that November day in western

Maine when she was caught in the early blizzard and sought protection from the elements.

Machias was convinced the events were not coincidental. "So, you *just* happened to be traveling through that point on a map in late November more than twenty miles from home?"

Mollyockett shook her head, saying nothing.

"And everyone turned you away? So you cursed the town? Why? You've never done that before."

"I did," said Mollyockett proudly.

"Can I ask what you were looking for?" Pidianiski asked softly.

Mollyockett remained stoically silent.

"Listen. We're not here to judge," said Machias. "Our only mission is to save Whole and to help protect the McKenzie family. I think that's a worthwhile endeavor."

"I was looking for Tomhegan, to kill him," she blurted out. "It may be hard to comprehend this, but I was determined to turn on *one of our* own, enough was enough. Too many good and innocent people had suffered at the hands of that vile man. I had heard he was living in the small town and went there to poison him before he could kill more settlers."

"Interesting. I knew you despised him, but I never knew you actually attempted to kill him," Machias said, lightly brushing her arm in solidarity.

"I'd had enough. He was terrorizing the locals, and I was afraid the McKenzie family would be next. Like I said, enough was enough."

"What's that mean?" Pidianiski asked.

"He was upping the ante so to speak. Each year, he became bolder and bolder. He was the chief of the Lake Umbegog area in Oxford County and would often raid the small villages I'd grown to love. It was a personal affront to me. Well, in 1781 he attacked Bethel, which was called Sudbury, Canada, back then. I'd aligned myself with the American colonists and he with the Tory loyalists who still pledged allegiance to the flag of Great Britain. Remember, they were reeling from the loss of the Revolutionary War. Tomhegan set out to kill Colonel Clark, a Boston trader and friend of other area

Indians. His entire plan was thwarted because I learned of the plot and warned them."

"Did he know you warned them?" Pidianiski asked.

Mollyockett nodded.

"How?"

"Apparently, Colonel Clark's circle of friends had been infiltrated. By whom, I've no idea. Not that it mattered. After that, Tomhegan moved silently throughout the county pillaging and murdering innocent people. As the years went on, it became too much for me to handle."

She closed her eyes and swallowed hard.

"I deeply feared for the lives of the McKenzie family and others close to me."

"Well, I'd have killed him too," Machias stated flatly.

"It went against everything I stood for, but I'd finally decided that enough was enough."

She hesitated.

"So, I mixed a powder out of poisonous roots and berries that could be harvested before the approaching winter and set out to find him. It was well known that Snow Falls was his favorite haunt. Clearly, he was well respected there, because not one person would give me refuge from the early and unexpected blizzard. I almost didn't make it."

She stopped speaking and held out her right index finger. The very tip was missing.

"Mollyockett," Pidianiski gasped. "I never knew."

Machias shook his head as he pondered her words.

"So the next logical question is why is Tomhegan spending all his time in the exact location that was referenced by Kozart literally hundreds of years earlier?"

"Exactly," said Pidianiski. "How on earth did he know about that spot? I'm positive not to get chummy with the Snow family. Were they Tory sympathizers?"

"They were. I'd learned that they actually led the resistance in Western Maine."

Mollyockett's insides churned. Even though it was two centuries later, she'd completely underestimated her old foe and felt totally hoodwinked. She feared that history was now repeating itself.

"Well, so much for our little theory about Tomhegan being used by the Confederation," Pidianiski admitted. "Clearly, he's far more important to them than we ever thought."

"Where'd the name come from?" asked Pidianiski.

"What name?" Mollyockett responded.

"Snow Falls. I'm assuming it was named after someone in the family."

"That's a story that'll make both of you furious."

"Care to enlighten us?" Machias asked softly, taking his eyes off the stone tablet in front of him.

Mollyockett's eyes blazed as she moved to face them both.

"When I was a young lady—"

"*Lady,* ha," Pidianiski chuckled.

Mollyockett shot her a playful look. "Do you want to hear the story or not?"

"Ladies, please. Can we focus on what we're doing?" Machias was getting annoyed.

"Very well. The year was 1755, and the Saint Francis Indians were visiting Fryeburg from Odanak. It was right when the French and Indian War was starting, and they wanted help securing their village on the southern shore of the Saint Lawrence River in Quebec. Of course, being part of the original Wabanaki Confederation we would do anything for them and they for us. Unlike the confederation that is now posing an immediate threat. Well, before they headed north with tools and warriors, they visited the falls where I placed that curse on its inhabitants years later."

"Just visiting?' Machias asked, not convinced.

"How would I know? I was busy with other things at that time."

"How far is that from Fryeburg? Pidianiski quizzed her.

"I'd say fifty miles or so, as the crow flies."

"Fifty miles!? Sounds like they were doing more than just visiting, given their mission and that their home was in the opposite direction. Personally, I'd have avoided that trip at all cost."

Machias scratched his beard in accord with Pidianiski.

"The falls at that time were called *Willamette,* which both of you know means running water."

"Well, for the sake of our sanity and respect for our people, let's call it that from now on," Pidianiski blurted out. "The fact that I've been using the word *Snow* is literally making me sick to my stomach."

"I've absolutely no problem with that. So, while they were at Snow—I mean Willamette—they encountered two men camping and fishing there. One of them was Captain Jonathan Snow. Not a very good person. He was inside his camp alone when our people stumbled on him. According to people who were there, he came to his door with his musket and gave the white man's sign of surrender. So the sachem approached to scout things out. He was wearing his traditional head-dress and gave the *peace* sign."

"Don't even tell me," Pidianiski stated, shaking her head.

Mollyockett nodded. "Right as the sachem neared the door, Mr. Snow lowered his musket and fired into his belly, killing him instantly. Not a very good decision."

"I can only imagine," said Machias.

"Before he could fire again, the scouting group ran towards him and viciously attacked him. Within minutes, he was cut to pieces."

Pidianiski huffed. "And he's *honored* by having the place named after him? Unbelievable."

"It's their world now," Machias reminded her. "Of course they'll honor the *poor* man." His words were tinged with sarcasm.

"But he was a Tory."

"I know, but remember, he was still a white man. Obviously, it didn't matter."

"I spat on the ground every time I walked through that village during my time on earth," said Mollyockett proudly. "Then I would say a prayer for the sachem on top of the falls. But, get this—"

"There's more?" Pidianiski asked incredulously.

"Squire Susup said that during the bicentennial celebration of the town of West Paris, which is just down the road, they triumphantly erected a monument to Mr. Snow. It literally proclaims him a hero and states that he was *massacred* by the Saint Francis Indians."

"Unbelievable," Pidianiski said sadly.

"Well, it sounds like he was, if what you say is true."

Mollyockett glared at him.

"Of course it's true. I spoke to the scouts when they returned to the banks of the Saco in Fryeburg. They were grief stricken and ready for all-out war."

"I'm not discounting your words, Molly. I'm just saying that he was massacred. You know as well as I that European settlers have a way of rewriting history. What I find absolutely fascinating is that Snow's descendants still live there. Especially after the entire town was abandoned by others. Why?"

She nodded in agreement.

"Unfortunately for our Saint Francis relatives, their village in Quebec was attacked four years later by Robert Rogers from Great Britain. At the time of the raid, there were mostly women, children, and elderly living there as the men were hunting in preparation for winter's arrival. The English slaughtered most of the tribe and were absolutely unapologetic about it."

"I've heard enough," Machias said sadly, returning his attention to a thin stone tablet in front of him. Deciphering the tiny symbols and characters was an arduous task.

Pidianiski remained silent and watched a small, white fluffy cloud form at the base of the tall waterfall in the valley below her.

"Willamette," she whispered. The conversation so disturbed her that she found it almost impossible to focus on her father's writings.

It was Machias who broke the silence roughly an hour later.

"Well, what do we have here?"

The two others looked at him, hoping for a helpful sign.

"Well, for starters, they were from the Inca tribe and not Mayan."

"Impossible!" Pidianiski protested. "I've studied them for years."

"Sorry to disillusion you, but these drawings are definitely Incan."

"Well, they're both the first two Mesoamerican civilizations, so I'd say they're very much alike."

"True, and they both, disturbingly, disappeared from the face of the earth in a very short time once the European conquerors arrived."

"I'm totally confused. Only the Maya practiced human sacrifices, and that's quite obvious everywhere in the temple."

"Perhaps they worked together," Machias suggested, agreeing with her.

"Impossible. Their hatred towards each other is legendary."

"That's well known. But look at it this way. If Martians attacked earth tomorrow, don't you think every nation on the planet would immediately come together to fight off the alien invader. Their national differences and ideologies would no longer matter."

Pidianiski pondered his words. "That's still a stretch," she said.

"There's a distinct possibility that the Mayans actually disappeared first and then the Incans took over their city. Think about it."

"Okay, you may have something there. I'll trust your judgement."

"And then they left the tablets to be discovered."

He stood and held up a tablet completely covered with drawings and strange markings. He quickly pointed to a long line of human figures standing over the crescent moon and star symbol that pointed towards Whole's entrance."

"That's also on the bottom of my grave, or at least was," Mollyockett said, leaning over the etching.

"If you notice, the figures standing behind the ones that are closest to the passage's entrance are not dressed like the others. They all moved in towards the small thin tablet and squinted at the tiny etchings. "And this one here," he said pointing to the man closest to the symbol. "He's holding the star in his right hand. Most likely, the same one that Fletcher recently gave to the Slaughter Makers."

Their eyes drifted to the second figure closest to the entrance. He too was holding a stone star. Mollyockett noticed that one star was missing from the crescent moon and star symbol marking the entrance to the passage. "Where'd the other star come from?" she asked.

Machias smiled. "From one of only a few places that a star could have come from."

"Good heavens!" Mollyockett exclaimed. "My grave marker."

"No," said Machias flatly after quick consideration. "These tablets were made long before your marker was created. There must have been additional ones out there."

Pidianiski's eyes widened. "So if I'm interpreting this tablet correctly, *either* star can be used to access the southern and northern passages as long as there are two stars?"

"And it appears that those not related to the bloodline but are with those who have both stars can enter as well." Mollyockett's eyes focused on the four human stick figures in the back of the line that were dressed noticeably different than the Incan leaders. It looked like they were standing near what appeared to be Frenchman's Hole. Mollyockett immediately recognized the distinctive rocks surrounding the cascading water and Mahoosuc mountain range etched on the tablet. A squiggly line pointing towards an eagles nest was etched in the upper right corner. It was too much of a coincidence to ignore. "That must have been a last dire attempt to save their people from becoming extinct by someone with knowledge that was similar to Kozart's skills. If only they knew how to get there."

Machias narrowed his eyes. "Maybe there just wasn't enough time."

They looked at each other solemnly, saying nothing.

Pidianiski handed Machias two tablets for confirmation.

Machias studied them intently. "Allowing others to enter may be possible. Apparently, only the northern star in Fletcher's root cellar can be inserted into the southern symbol to allow *strangers* to enter Whole, and only as long as there is a matching star. And I'm assuming vice versa. That's if I'm reading this correctly. Frenchman's Hole is clearly a starting point to enter the northern passage for them. This only makes sense. Why travel all that way with your very own passage literally a few yards away?"

"If only we had known. We could have helped them all enter Whole instead of being wiped out," said Piadianiski, scanning the horizon. "What a travesty."

"So sad," said Mollyockett, standing up. She too had used Frenchman's Hole as a beginning when she transferred the power of the passage to Jackson centuries ago. "I wish there was a way to travel back in time and help save them."

"Unbelievable!" Pidianiski blurted out. "I had no idea they knew about *us.*"

"Unfortunately, we now only have one star. This makes the McKenzie trip impossible," said Machia. He was deeply angry and annoyed at the loss of the southern star to the enemy.

The end of the long day was creeping over Mollyockett's garden. The trio had spent several hours silently studying the etched scene on the particular stone tablet, trying to decipher it's meaning and importance. They bandied about theory after theory, attempting to decipher the tablet's place in history. It was clear that some important member of the Ollantaytambo village, deep within the Quechuan valley, had spent a great amount of effort and time attempting to record Whole's secrets and make predictions of possible future events. Much like Kozart.

"Well," Machias said finally. He stroked his long beard and smiled while holding a tablet high over his head. "I say we find Squire Susup. This other tablet right here appears to be a backup of sorts to that second star requirement. It's quite possible that everyone can enter Whole through the southern passage with Fletcher's star from his basement and this wonderful tablet. That's if I'm reading it correctly."

Mollyockett almost tumbled backwards. "Do you think that's how they entered Fletcher's basement?"

Machias nodded quickly. "Not at that time. Remember, they needed the star from your grave plus the star from the southern passage to enter the northern passage in the root cellar. Which is possibly why they were behind that curtain Fletcher described. Plus, they *actually* never entered the passage. Strange."

"It's absolutely shocking they figured everything out," said Pidianiski. "How?"

"My God!" Mollyockett blurted out. The world she'd known and protected for hundreds of years could soon be dramatically upended if they were correct with their interpretation of the etched scenes. "The Wabanaki Confederation now has the ability to enter Whole from Fletcher's basement. But why create Slaughter Makers?"

"That's the most baffling thing," said Machias looking at the stone tablets with greater interest. "It's as though they are building an army of sorts. Alone, Nukpana and Tygorge can inflict enough damage to cripple everything around us."

Mollyockett gasped. "Perhaps to send a clear message that they are not to be messed with. From what Susup says, everyone is deeply horrified and completely terrified with what's happening right now.

"I'll never forgive myself," replied Pidianski now completely disappointed with herself for not taking the time to study the remaining tablets after discovering the powers of Vilcanota's patera etched into the tablets. *All of this could have possibly been avoided*, she thought.

Machias' eyes flashed. "It will be my turn to be as angry as you," he said. "But first I need to inform Susup of our findings. He has a stone in Fletcher's basement to chisel off, and I need to give him this tablet. The journey for all of them to South America will be long and emotional. I really hope they hold up."

Mollyockett was left speechless. There were no words left to express her complete horror of what was to come.

CHAPTER 10

STRANGE LANDS

LUCILLE STUMBLED BACKWARDS AND FELL ONTO A GRANITE BLOCK directly behind her. It was just too much to comprehend. Fortunately, the overstuffed backpack she was carrying cushioned her fall. She opened her eyes, taking in the stunning scene directly over her head. *What on earth is going on? God, please help me make sense of everything.*

"Luce, you ok?" Edmond wheezed as the others quickly surrounded her. His mind was in a fog.

Urgency was now paramount. Just as Mollyockett, Pidianiski and Machias were deciphering the Incan tablets and Kozart's writings, the confederation was building an army of Slaughter Makers. People in Maine as well as in neighboring New Hampshire and Massachusetts were in a frenzied panic. The multiple bizarre events were baffling and absolutely horrifying. It was too much of a coincidence with so many people now missing by similar circumstances.

Six lobstermen unloading the day's catch in scenic Perkin's Cove were the latest victims. The picturesque harbor, a small part of touristy Ogunquit, had been home to fleets of lobster boats for generations. Mollyockett knew the spot very well. The Pigwackets had camped there during the summer months, fishing, clamming, lobstering, and collecting shells before heading north to Fryeburg in the fall.

When dark clouds rapidly approached from a westerly direction, the men picked up the pace with the intention of unloading and securing the boat before the storm arrived. They quickly learned that intentions and reality quite often don't think alike. In an instant, a massive bolt of lightning rolled across the sky and instantly incinerated both the boat and pier. Dozens of tourists safely watched the horrific scene unfold from behind massive plate-glass windows in the dozen or so seafood restaurants and clam shacks lining the harbor. Panic-stricken rescuers from Ogunquit, Wells, York, and Kennebunkport searched the harbor for hours looking for survivors, or even corpses. Television stations from every corner of New England and around the country flooded the small town as the story grew. It totally defied logic that not a single fisherman's body could be found.

Muriel's main concern was for her aged parents. Both had to be sedated after being told of the McKenzie secret. In an instant the world they'd both known for nearly eighty years dissolved. Reality no longer made sense to either of them.

"We need to press on. Now!" Susup commanded, stealing a look towards the death chamber. He'd been informed of Pidianiski's encounter with the Slaughter Makers and couldn't avoid the massive amount of fresh blood in the temple, which immediately horrified everyone. Luckily, he spied Pidianiski's bent knife and silently stowed it in Fletcher's backpack for her. He knew of its unique abilities. He prayed that the interpretation of the stone tablet was correct as there was no turning back now. He'd gotten them into the massive temple by following the instructions given to him after being urgently summonsed back to Whole. Everyone's lives depended on the star they'd chiseled off the "carrot rock" in the root cellar and the Incan stone tablet opening the southern passage Fletcher had sealed off.

The trip from Portland, Maine, to South America had been a long, tense one. As instructed, they were all dressed like American tourists, except Von Piddle. He'd received severe looks when he arrived at the gathering point in Maine dressed as an outlandish African Safari Explorer. "No need to concern the locals once we arrive," Woodrow had told them after the escape plan had been laid out. It began with everyone begrudgingly leaving their cell phones at their respective homes. Clearly, they were a severe security threat with their GPS tracking once they were discovered missing. Susup was oblivious to the barrage of comments coming from amused airport travelers regarding his attire. He was still reeling from the loss of the feathers. Airport security in Maine deemed the adornments poking out of his top hat weapons and demanded he discard them or turn around. It didn't matter that they were traveling on a private jet chartered by Aldous. Woodrow quickly had them stowed in his luggage to lower Susup's anger. Surprisingly, the "authentic" Maine license Aldous secured for him went unnoticed both at the bustling Maine airport and at the small Peruvian airstrip where they had landed. Fortunately, he was allowed to carry the staff on board after claiming a back ailment. While on the flight, Fletcher told everyone that each time there was a deadly incident associated with the Slaughter Makers, the mark on his hand would severely burn. And it was burning again. This confirmed to them all that they had made the right decision to leave immediately. Susup had made the difficult decision to leave Lalia and Humeante in the root cellar to guard the northern passage. She was tough and tenacious, and he would join her soon.

Lucille sat down on the hard surface and began to whimper softly. Her aged muscles were giving out. The rush to leave and the long flight and trek to the lost village was taking its toll. Her stoic and hard demeanor was beginning to crumble. She recalled watching Fletcher remove the top star from the symbol in the root cellar and stow it in his backpack. While Muriel was missing in the Quetzal, she had taken over burying vegetables in the cool clay soil of the root cellar. One day, while unearthing carrots, she broke a nail on the mysterious stone hidden beneath the soil. From that point on, she referred to it as the carrot rock.

"Lucy, for the sake of us all, we need to move on." Edmond said, lightly stroking her white hair. His words reverberated off the sides of the majestic temple deep under the Peruvian jungle.

Alek was totally stunned. He and Muriel had *discovered* the lost village after she returned from her captivity, but he had no idea there was a massive and majestic temple hidden underneath it. It's splendor completely awed him. Carved patterns and scenes rose high above his head only to be swallowed by lush vines that were slowly invading the cavernous room. An elaborate mosaic depicting a public execution caught his eye. The macabre picture was the exact same one Fletcher and Pidianiski had looked at when they fought for their lives.

"Absolutely stunning," he said, stroking a small statute of an unrecognizable bird. "My mind is about to explode."

"Fletcher, help your grandmother?" Muriel said, moving towards Lucille. "Are you okay Mom?" she asked.

"Everyone, please hurry," Squire Susup exclaimed.

"Grans, it's okay. Here, take my arm. It'll be fine. Trust me."

She looked at Muriel and asked, "Is this where they held you captive? How on earth did you find—" Suddenly she could not hold back the tears.

"Why didn't you tell me?"

She wrapped her arms around her daughter and sobbed.

"Mom, it's okay. Seriously," whispered Muriel. "When you hear the entire story, you'll be very pleased I married Aldous."

"When did *you* find everything out honey?"

"Does that matter now?"

"For me, it does. I need to know."

Muriel hesitated. "When I was taken captive by Nimsy."

Lucille glared directly at Aldous. "How dare you."

Aldous quickly stepped behind Woodrow, not wanting to be part of the emotional conversation.

"Mom, trust me, it's okay. Fletcher's doing wonderful things which benefit everyone. Can we discuss this later? Please." There was urgency in her voice.

"Lucy, we need to go. You're risking our lives," said Edmond gently. "Squire Susup needs us to follow him right now."

Lucille raised her head, looking for Susup. She quickly thought back to the time they met on the Bethel common during the Mollyockett Day celebrations three years ago. *I can't believe he is involved too. How could I have been so naïve?*

Slowly, she stood and faced him.

"You're telling me Mollyockett is your mother?"

"Mrs. Blay, how is that important at this moment? You've no idea how much is at risk right now."

"Well given your past deceptions, I've no reason to believe what you're saying to me," Lucille said, feeling her strength returning.

"Why don't we have this little conversation when we arrive at our destination?" Von Piddle suggested timidly.

"She is, and she's a wonderful person," said Susup flatly, running out of patience. He tapped the staff on the ground and smiled. Then he stepped forward and grasped her hands. "If you want, I will personally introduce you to her. You both have a lot in common."

Lucille immediately backed away.

"I've known this most of my life and I still can't comprehend everything, Lucy," Woodrow finally told her. "Here, take my hand, and I'll personally tell you the complete truth. I promise."

"Here, here old chap," Von Piddle chimed in. "Well spoken."

Lucille stared at him, thought it over for a moment, and decided that she needed to regain her senses.

"Where's my purse?"

"I have it in my backpack," Edmond replied with a smile. "I'll hang onto it until we arrive. You definitely have no need of it right now."

A purse is useless where we're going, Susup thought.

"Arrive where? At some fantasyland park where roller coasters are made out of huge grapevines and have corn on the cob cars?"

"That's my girl," Woodrow chuckled. "Now, you'd be doing all of us a favor if you followed Squire Susup."

"Let's go!" she demanded. "Fletcher, follow me."

Edmond got up stiffly, took one last look at the ornate temple, and clutched his wife's hand. "Lucy, thank you."

Fully aware of the grave danger awaiting them, Susup immediately moved towards the back of the temple after herding them into pairs. Lucille with Edmond, Muriel with Aldous, Fletcher with Woodrow, and Von Piddle to his right.

"Entire place needs World Heritage protection," said Alek, completely mesmerized by his surroundings.

"A what?" Susup asked, giving him a baffled look. The honeymoon between the two of them had worn off while sharing a row on the small plane. Von Piddle's endless chattering and constant reminiscing had taken its toll. To shut him up, he agreed to let Von Piddle study his ornate mahogany gold-tipped staff. Von Piddle had silently rubbed the gold whole grain of wheat for hours. "What are you muttering about now?"

"Just saying this place needs protection. Don't want greedy developers coming in and converting it into luxury condominiums. Truth be told, though, I'd be first in line with a down payment. What a place to retire."

Susup ignored his babbling. His mind was elsewhere. He was thinking about what Machias had told him regarding the stone tablets from Ollantaytambo. He had made it very clear that what he deciphered from the etched scene on the tablets was only a hunch. If the star taken from the root cellar failed to open the passage, the gig was up.

"Fletcher, retrieve the star, will you?" Susup called out.

Fletcher nodded and stopped, causing a chain reaction by those behind him to come to a sudden stop. Silently, he lowered his backpack and quickly unzipped it.

Lucille and Edmond took in his every movement, wishing they were all back in the comfortable home they'd quickly abandoned the day before.

"Here it is," he said, fumbling with the bulging pack. "Now what?"

"You come with me, and Alek, you join Woodrow."

"Gents with gents," replied Von Piddle cheerfully as he eased beside Woodrow. "I'll call this chapter "Woody's Crew.""

"Assuming you'll survive to write anything," Susup said incredulously. "Besides, that wasn't part of the agreement."

Alek immediately back tracked. "Of course, so sorry. Scouts honor, kind sir." He timidly raised his right palm in front of him. "Always trust a scout."

Annoyed, Lucille scolded him with her eyes.

Susup turned and faced them all. "I'm going to be honest with you all," he said seriously. "What we're about to try right now may or may not work. Machias has informed me that this is our—"

"Machias, who?" Lucille snapped.

"Mom, let him finish," said Muriel. "He said he'd tell you everything when we get there."

"If we get there," Von Piddle chimed in.

"Good gracious," Woodrow huffed. "Shut up, man."

"Machias, Pidianiski, and Mollyockett have been looking for a way to get you all into Whole."

"*The* Mollyockett?" gasped Lucille. "You can't make this up," she whispered to Edmond.

Alek jovially clapped his hands. He was so excited to meet her that he completely forgot the imminent mortal danger they faced.

Susup sighed. "Yes as in *the* Mollyockett. Would you *please* let me finish and stop interrupting? They have been studying stone tablets taken from the Ollantaytambo village when Pidianiski visited this place centuries before Fletcher made his way here." He turned and smiled. "You're an absolute hero young man."

He stopped talking and waited for their reactions.

"Good, thank you for your attentiveness." He continued, "Control of the passage has been passed down from one generation of McKenzie to another after Mollyockett handed it over from her bloodline. Currently, Fletcher possesses that amazing power. You all know that."

Lucille cupped her mouth and whispered into Edmond's ear.

Squire Susup ignored her.

"Up until now," he said, pausing. "At least, I hope until now, the only person who has been allowed to enter Whole through the passage is that one person within the bloodline who controls the power of the passage." He nodded silently at Fletcher.

Von Piddle immediately backed up as though Fletcher were about to morph into a deadly reptile at any moment. "Eccentric fellow explorer you are young man. Must say you started a lot earlier than I did, Fletcher. I'm awed by your presence."

Fletcher smiled slightly.

"So, what's next?" Woodrow asked, bringing the conversation back towards Susup.

Von Piddle winked quickly at Fletcher in a show of solidarity.

"Fletch, insert the star into that spot," Susup commanded. He turned and pointed towards the ornate floor causing his blue feathers hanging inside his loopy earrings to sway outwards. He caught a quick glance at Woodrow.

He's witnessed this before. He thought.

Woodrow nodded knowingly.

Their silent interaction was not lost on Lucille who took in the entire scene unfolding before her with complete amazement. She tightly grasped her husband's hand.

Fletcher moved forward and stood beside Susup, his eyes blazing with nervous excitement. Silently, he bent over the crescent moon and surrounding stars. While holding onto the tablet Machias had given them, he carefully placed the stone star into the empty spot where he'd removed it's twin on his first visit to this very location. His heart raced and beads of sweat dripped from his soaked hair. The others watched silently in awe.

Susup touched Fletcher's right shoulder before stepping in front of him. He inserted the bottom tip of the staff into a round indentation located in the center of the crescent moon and chanted: "O our Mother the Earth, O our Father the sky, your children are we, and with tired backs, we bring you gifts." He removed his top hat and tilted his head backwards.

Alek closed his eyes. He'd recognized the words from his studies. "Wabanaki," he whispered to himself.

Lucille gasped and coughed. Edmond, completely mesmerized by the scene, tugged at her hand, willing her to be silent,.

The floor began to vibrate slightly. Aldous and Muriel instinctively took a step closer to Fletcher to protect him.

The room suddenly began to shake and shift, causing them all to lower themselves towards the floor. Muriel quickly looked over her shoulder to check on her mother who was now sitting in an upright position, both hands firmly planted on the moving floor. Edmond had pulled her head into his chest and wrapped his arms around her. Muriel smiled at him and nodded. Completely overwhelmed, he didn't respond.

Fletcher and Susup focused on the stone symbol waiting for it to turn into the familiar thick gray liquid doorway to Whole they were accustomed to. They exchanged alarmed looks as the rumbling increased, and the temple's massive stone blocks shifted above their heads.

Susup looked at Fletcher. Time seemed to stand still. *Machias was wrong,* he thought. *It's not going to open. We're doomed.* He was horrified as small pellets of rock and stone began to rain down on them. Lucille shrieked then curled into a ball.

They had barely time to cover their heads with their hands when the room began to spin and vibrate violently.

"Close your eyes!" said Fletcher, recovering his senses. He'd been here before.

Von Piddle hurtled himself towards the center of a growing mass of gray liquid matter. "Heavens to Betsy. What a wild ride!"

Lucille screeched loudly again and clawed at Edmond's hands that were still clutching her head.

The temple suddenly began to shift and spin. Aldous grabbed onto Fletcher and Muriel at the same time. His mouth dropped as he watched the entire stone floor begin to wave and roll as though it was made of water. Susup held tightly to his staff and reached for Lucille who had rolled towards him. She looked at him in horror as his hand moved through her body as though it was made of air. Edmond was aghast at the sight he'd just witnessed. Within seconds, they tumbled into total darkness, spiraling downward towards the unknown. Their arms flailed desperately in an attempt to grasp onto something, anything.

CHAPTER 11

ARRIVAL

"And who may you be?" Von Piddle asked nervously. He was sitting in the middle of the entire group and looking directly at Mollyockett. Deep inside, he knew the answer. How could he not. He'd studied her life for years. As he stood up, she took in his unique attire, a safari-style outfit worn by British officers who'd been stationed in Africa in the late nineteenth century. Khaki pants with a bush jacket that was crisp, drill cotton with large pockets and ivory buttons and a matching belt. On his head was a white Pith helmet. His engineered leather boots, with L.L. Bean stitched on the sides, were clearly Kenyan colonial style.

Pidianski and Machias were standing spellbound behind Mollyockett. The tablets were indeed spot on. They watched as the jumbled group gained their composure. Everyone had deferred to Von Piddle since he was the first one able to speak.

They were all sitting in the very center of a huge structure with brick walls at least two hundred feet tall that extended as far as Alek could see. Behind Pidianski and Machias was an arch constructed of thousands of honeycomb-shaped stained glass windows soaring to the ceiling. Each colorful pane—illuminated by an unknown light source—depicted a specific plant, fruit, vegetable, or animal.

The three brick walls contained numerous arched windows, each perfectly spaced between a pair of pink marble pillars shaped like giant Sequoia trees and adorned with tendrils, giving them a garden look. The windows held stained glass pieces in the shape of leaves depicted in the vibrant Autumn colors of Maine. It was the most brilliant display of foliage they'd ever seen. Every window looked like a masterpiece that belonged in the Louvre.

Mollyockett moved towards Alek with a concerned look. *Definitely the one who is not a McKenzie,* she thought. As she walked, her black knee-length dress swayed in the slight breeze. Both her dress and her bright red-and-black knitted socks that came to the tops of her knees were detailed with small white seashells dangling from delicate red beads. Her soft leather moccasins were highlighted with black, red, and blue stones. She wore silver looped earrings with small blue feathers dangling in the center. Her shiny black hair hung below her waist in two large braids. Surprisingly, she was wearing a black stovepipe style hat that was made of dark felt. Its wide brims curled up and over both of her ears. They all immediately thought of Abraham Lincoln whose portrait hung in the Bethel Library beside his first vice president, Hannibal Hamlin.

"I'm Mollyockett, and you are?" she asked. Lucille gasped and dug her nails into Edmond's right arm.

"Er, umm . . . I am," he pursed his lips and breathed out. *Impossible.* "Alek Von Piddle, ma'am. I'm sorry but I'm having difficulty—"

"You doubt me after what you've just witnessed? I find that truly hard to believe."

Fletcher finally gained his composure and stood. Muriel immediately grabbed his left hand, attempting to pull him back into the core of their group. Her mind was completely shot.

"We made it," he said.

"And that's a good thing. How are you my friend?"

He shook his head and smiled. "I never expected it would be like this."

She stared at him. "*We* never expected it, either." And that was an incontrovertible fact. He moved towards her and held out his right hand to shake hers. Although the entire floor was a deep mossy green that looked soft as silk, really it was hard as New Hampshire granite. Woodrow stood up and followed Fletcher after banging his knuckles. Off in the distance, he heard what sounded like a waterfall. Its cascade was slightly drowned by the harmonious chirping of birds. Woodrow looked up and studied the dark dome ceiling completely covered with a lush canopy of magnolia leaves. Intermingled among the fibrous leaves were countless flocks of birds in every color, shape, and size. He was shocked the floor was devoid of a single dropping.

"What's he doing?" Lucille whispered to Muriel. She had just spied Machias. "Is he good or bad?"

Muriel laughed and shook her head. "If he was a bad man, he wouldn't be sitting next to Mollyockett." She stood along with Aldous and joined Fletcher.

They held hands silently, everyone attempting to grasp the surreal moment.

"You must be Muriel?" Machias asked, taking a step towards them.

Muriel nodded silently and studied the furs hanging from his body.

"I'm sorry you had to experience everything you did when you were misled by your friend," he said sincerely. "I wish I could have helped sooner."

"It's hard to believe that things are far worse today," Mollyockett said.

"More than one can imagine," Pidianiski added. "We're really hoping time is on our side."

Machias stepped forward and shook Fletcher's hand.

Lucille buried her head into Edmond's chest, completely over-whelmed. "I feel like I'm in a terrible nightmare that won't end," she gabbled. "All I want to do is wake up."

Edmond patted her head lovingly and kissed it lightly. "Everyone's in this together, sweetie. Please do us all a favor and try to pull yourself together. I have a feeling this is just the start of things. Just be you. Please."

Machias nodded. "You're right about that. Fletcher, do us a favor and introduce everyone. Will you?"

Fletcher looked at him and chewed on his lower lip. "Okay. Is it possible for everyone to sit down first?"

"But we are sitting," called Von Piddle.

Mollyockett smiled and winked at him. She knew what he was thinking. "Please, if everyone could stand for a moment."

Von Piddle immediately followed her instructions and helped both Lucille and Edmond to their feet. "Just pretend we're on a safari in South Africa and about to watch a pride of lions. Just like that time I was in—"

"Oh, shut up, will you?" Lucille huffed and brushed off his arm. "Consider yourself lucky you're even here, you not being a McKenzie and all."

Von Piddle swallowed hard and moved towards Woodrow for support. Edmond chuckled and kissed Lucille's cheek. "It's good to have you out of that nightmare."

"I'm just so sick of him. I mean, how could one person do all of what he claims he's done. It's not possible."

"Here, here. Is she joking?" Von Piddle whispered into Woodrow's ear. "Please let her know—"

"I say we all make ourselves comfortable," Mollyockett said, taking control of the situation. She closed her eyes and began to hum loudly.

The entire group stepped back quickly and watched in absolute amazement as a cluster of brown roots rose out of the ground behind her and expertly wove themselves into her familiar egg-shaped chair.

"Good heavens!" Von Piddle and Lucille yelled in unison.

"We have a lot to accomplish, don't we?" Mollyockett nodded at Pidianiski and Machias and then let out a satisfied sigh as the roots finished conforming to her body. "Are you all going to just stand there? Why don't you join me?" She closed her eyes and breathed deeply.

"Exactly what does that mean?" Lucille asked and stepped towards the front of the group. "Are you going to make one of those for me too?"

Pidianiski laughed and moved towards Lucille. Lucille immediately studied her warm, delicate brown eyes. Her long jet-black hair was braided into two large strands elaborately woven into a bun. *Appears to be friendly,* she thought.

She told the entire group to think of the most comfortable chair they had. "And then what?" Snapped Lucille. "Just weave a chair for us? Impossible."

"Lucy, please listen and do what she said," Edmond said flatly. Surprisingly, he was losing patience.

There was a low rumble as the ground began to shake lightly. Von Piddle giggled and opened his eyes. "Reminds me of the time when I was in Italy. After the war—" He stopped talking and looked at Lucille. Immediately the small, wire-framed bifocals that were perched tightly on the end of his long, pointed nose began to bounce.

Mollyockett glanced quickly towards Pidianski and Machias and raised her left brow.

Within seconds, a large cluster of roots rose out of the ground and began to weave into chairs behind each one of them. Von Piddle thought of an ornate wood throne-style desk chair; Woodrow and Fletcher imagined the old chairs from the root cellar; Aldous created one exactly like the one in his office, while, surprisingly, Muriel had thought of the stone bench in her garden. Lucille and Edmond quickly glanced behind them and gasped at the exact replica of the wing-backed chairs located in their bedroom now awaiting their bodies.

Von Piddle turned and lightly rubbed his index finger over the words *M.I.T.* carved expertly into the back of his wood chair. "I'm at a loss for words."

"Well, that's a first," Lucille retorted. "Never thought I'd see the day." The entire group laughed.

Fletcher remained standing while everyone sat down after cautiously testing the sturdiness of their chairs. He cleared his thoughts.

"Everyone, this is Mollyockett."

Von Piddled giggled as he wiggled backwards in his chair. Fletcher ignored the interruption.

"And this is Machias and Pidianiski. The entire group remained silent and studied the three individuals now sitting in front of them.

Fletcher rotated towards Machias and continued "You all remember my father."

"Always good to see you, Aldous," Mollyockett said with a smile.

"It's good to be back, especially with everything that's going on right now." Aldous replied solemnly.

Fletcher nodded at Mollyockett and his father. "This is my mother, Muriel; my grandparents, Lucille and Edmond; my uncle Woodrow; and finally, Alek Von Piddle. He's a good friend of our family."

Mollyockett, Machias, and Pidianiski took particular interest in Alek and his attire.

"The one that's not a McKenzie," Pidianiski said loudly after studying his odd hat.

"Good heavens, you sound like I'm a deadly virus or something," Von Piddle said with wide eyes. He looked around, confused.

"Sorry to worry you, good man," Machias interjected while walking towards him. Alek immediately shielded his face fully expecting to be blasted back to Maine at any second. "It's just that having someone here who is not blood related is completely alien for all of us. It's never happened."

Alek swallowed hard and then relaxed. "Can I do something to change that? The blood related part," he replied weakly. Machias ignored the comical question.

"Thank you, Fletcher." Machias moved back to his chair and stood behind it. He waited for Lucille to finish studying the ornate pattern on the arms of her chair.

"Ahem." Edmond cleared his throat to get her attention. "Lucille, please."

Lucille immediately looked up and blushed. "My apologies," she said. "It's just this chair. I'm really so confused and a little flabbergasted right now."

Machias nodded at her. No apologies needed Lucille. I'd be thinking the same thing right now if I were in your shoes. This is a lot to take in." His words were soft and compassionate. "Unfortunately," he continued. "We need to bring everyone up to speed. As I speak, Squire Susup has headed back to the root cellar to check on Lalia." He paused and took in their reactions. "Time is of the essence, and we need to formulate a plan very quickly."

Aldous bit his lower lip. He knew Machias well and his grave tone spoke volumes. He desperately did not want his entire family to be involved.

For a few seconds, Muriel was distracted. She was looking past Machias and up at the ornate ceiling. Massive gold chandeliers in the shape of upside-down willow trees with bright, golden pear-shaped lights illuminated Whole. Each light was attached to the branches by strings of rubies that cast a reddish hue. Her mind was on her last visit to Whole where she was held hostage by Tomhegan and Nimsy Cortland. *How can a place so beautiful as this allow such evil to thrive near its walls?*

"So, what I'll do is go over everything with you all," Machias said, snapping Muriel back to the discussion. "I'll hold nothing back. You all need to know the impending danger that's facing us all as well as Whole itself."

Von Piddle raised his hand.

"Yes."

"Umm, I hate to sound dense, but what *exactly* are you expecting us to do? I've been quite fortunate to have experienced the wildest of expeditions in my life, but this is quite out of the ordinary. Literally tops them all. I must say."

Pidianiski gave him a long hard look. "There could be blood," she warned.

Muriel and Lucille gasped and stood up in protest.

"You don't have to worry. You're all safe at the moment, and we'll do our best to protect you," Mollyockett interjected quickly. She shot Pidianski a look to shut her up. Machias nodded in agreement.

Lucille raised her hand and looked directly at Machias. "Exactly how long do you plan to keep us here?" She gazed towards the jumbled pile of backpacks and shook her head. "As nice as it is are you expecting me to actually live in this chair?"

This was getting worse by the second, Mollyockett thought. For years she had been the protector of Whole. She knew its secrets and what to do in any situation. Now, she wasn't so sure. The feeling was completely alien. "I've had individual huts constructed in my garden for each of you. You'll see they're all quite comfortable and stocked with all the necessities." Muriel and Lucille sat down. "I know it's not home with all the comforts you're accustomed to, but we've done our best." There was finality in her words.

Fletcher stood and faced them all. "We've no choice but to listen to Machias. Clearly, this is the best place for all of us given what's happened to everyone that's been turned into a Slaughter Maker." He paused and looked directly at his grandmother. "I was there in our basement and witnessed what they can do. Trust me. It's not a pretty sight. The last thing I would want is for anyone of you to be their next victim."

Von Piddle stood and clapped loudly. "Well said, young man. If I ever have a son, I would want him to be exactly like you, Fletcher."

Woodrow laughed. " At your age Alek? Whole may be magical, but even that is stretching it."

"Given what we've just experienced, Woody, I wouldn't rule anything out. Last month I would have agreed with you. But now I believe anything is possible."

Machias motioned with his index finger for Von Piddle to come forward. His bottom lip trembled as he stood and timidly walked towards the fur-covered man.

"I really could use your help right now," said Machias.

Von Piddle's chin trembled. "I'll do anything you ask."

"Squire Susup tells me that you have a doctorate in both survey engineering and Native American studies. He said you're considered an expert in locating ancient burial sites and important archeological treasures."

"That would be one hundred percent correct. He's left out the part that I enjoy deciphering symbols and ancient drawings. I've also been most fortunate to have recently visited the site under Snow Falls right after that most dreadful incident. Reminds me of the time that—"

"I had no idea," replied Machias, cutting him off. "Then I really need you to listen to me. You will definitely be able to assist us in formulating a plan."

Von Piddle swallowed hard as Machias patted him on the back. "You can return to your seat. You're definitely an asset, my good man."

Mollyockett nodded and gestured towards his empty seat. Von Piddle immediately jolted forward almost tripping over Woodrow's leg on the way.

Machias returned to his customary spot beside Mollyockett and closed his eyes. After a moment of charged silence he could feel them all poised in their seats, waiting for his next words. "Actually, it may be prudent to start with the very spot Alek just mentioned: Snow Falls, which our people called *Willamette*, which translates into "running water."

"Lovely name but quite the dreadful place if you ask me," said Von Piddle. "Had I known there'd be so many bones and dead bodies, I'd have avoided the entire area completely."

Machias pursed his lips together then raised his eyebrows. "Would you mind sharing with us all what you saw?"

Alek stood up and removed his glasses. "Where do you want me to start?" He aimed his question at Pidianiski. He sensed she had unique abilities quite similar to his and wanted to learn more.

"I'm assuming that you got wet. That may be the best place to start." Mollyockett quickly leaned forward to hear him better. She knew the place extremely well and had been to Willamette dozens of times. She never expected anything to be under the falls.

Von Piddle began to wildly twirl his glasses in his left hand. "Well, it was clear that most of the rocks around the falls had recently been displaced, and quite violently. Normal erosion would not have created the shiny spikes that were glittering in the sunlight. So, the only normal thing to do was to investigate further. I approached a large black spot under Snow Falls . . . err, I mean Willamette. It appeared to be an entrance of sorts. I dove under the water and towards that location." He paused and put his glasses back on. "When I stuck my head out of the water, I was in a cave of sorts. The first thing I smelled was the putrid odor of extremely bad breath. It was the worst thing I'd ever smelled in my life. Even worse than Amos McCarthy, and that's saying something."

"Please, just the facts, Mr. Von Piddle. We're pressed for time," Machias interrupted.

"Well, I almost fainted. It was that bad. I could also feel the warmth of the putridness on my face. As my eyes adjusted to the light, the first thing I noticed was human remains. Hundreds of them."

"Where do you think the light in the cavern was coming from to allow you to see?" Mollyockett asked.

"That was the weirdest thing. The walls in the front of the cave were glowing a lime green color, which surprisingly helped my vision."

Fletcher immediately thought back to the night he'd been forced to visit the cave under his basement and encountered the two Slaughter Makers. "I smelled the same thing the night that Croft and Walton destroyed that pig."

"Hmm. That must have been what was in the back of the death chamber," Von Piddle said with a quiver. "As I looked closer, it was clear that many of the bones had clothing on or around them. Most looked like attire from the seventeenth and eighteenth century. Clearly, many of them were Revolutionary War soldiers who had fought against the British." He paused and looked towards Woodrow. "As I was about to leave, I noticed the bones of a man, woman, and child. It was obvious they hadn't been there for nearly as long as the others. The clothing on the child was that of a male."

"What are your thoughts on this?" Mollyockett asked.

"It was as though they were expecting one of us to visit the site. But that's just a hunch." He paused and swallowed hard. "From what we know now, I have a feeling that a curse of sorts had been placed on Aldous, Muriel, and Fletcher. I've had extensive experience with Native American rituals."

Lucille shrieked and stood up. "When will this nightmare end?"

Everyone looked at one another, but not one disputed the old man's words."

"Thank you," said Machias. "You've been invaluable," he said. "What do you know about this?" he asked Mollyockett, who had turned ghastly white. "You're the only one here that placed a curse on Willamette."

The entire group was on the edge of their seats. The story of Mollyockett's curse on Willamette was legendary.

Good heavens, is this really happening? Woodrow thought to himself. His mind took him back to the time Fletcher was recovering from the rockslide at Hamlin State Park. He was the one who had told Fletcher the story of Mollyockett getting caught in the blizzard and her saving Hannibal Hamlin as an infant.

Mollyockett stood to address the group. Everyone was on pins and needles. Rarely had she ever discussed the curse she'd placed on the thriving village at Willamette. "Who here hasn't heard the story of my curse?" she asked. Silence from the entire group. "Well, why I was there isn't important. What is important is what Von Piddle said about the three individuals who apparently had recently died . . . I mean, been murdered." She swallowed hard and looked directly at Fletcher. "This is shocking and extremely relevant to what is happening at this very moment." She quickly pulled out her stone pipe Fletcher had given her and lit it.

Von Piddle leaned forward to get a closer glimpse of the pipe. He'd recognized it immediately as belonging to the Inca people from long ago. *Absolute treasure that is. Belongs in a museum. I wonder if she'll trade for my timepiece.* he thought.

Mollyockett continued, "When I placed the curse on Willamette, I had to make sure there was a way to remove the curse. You see, there always has to be a way for a curse to be removed by the cursed. I was taught that as a young girl. It also has to be relevant to why you placed the curse in the first place. Rules of the game so to speak. In this case, the curse and way to remove it related to the residents of Willamette and their cozy relationship with that beastly Tomhegan. He was furious that I had transferred the power of the passage to someone outside the Wabanaki bloodline. He started pillaging and pilfering the entire area, including shamelessly slaughtering many innocent people. I had received word that the residents of Snow Falls, I mean Willamette, were harboring Tomhegan, who by then had a bounty on his head. And rightfully so. After the war, the village was somewhat of an outcast given they had sided with the British during the Revolutionary War."

"We're all familiar with the curse," Machias interrupted. "You mentioned something about a way for the curse to be removed."

It was painful for Mollyockett to relive the nightmare. She could hear the screaming of the father, mother, and son whose bones were viewed by Von Piddle under Willamette. She winced at the memory of being stranded in the blizzard with no place to seek shelter. She knew the small town and its inhabitants well from past experiences.

"Well," she said. "I had learned this type of curse from my mother when I was a child. It was one of the more difficult curses. It took several weeks for me to understand it fully. I spent an entire summer thinking of a way to mask how it could be removed or even prevent it from being removed at all."

Everyone was sitting on the edge of their seats completely spellbound by her words. Mollyockett was obviously feeling uncomfortable telling the story.

"Please continue," encourage Machias.

"As mentioned, the curse had to be relevant to the events surrounding the purpose for the curse. The most obvious place to start was Tomhegan. He was livid that I had transferred the power of the passage to the McKenzie family. Therefore, the most efficient and powerful way to place the curse was to associate it with that. To all of you," she said slowly. "I did it to protect you."

"We believe you," Lucille said warmly.

Mollyockett nodded in appreciation and continued, "So, I decided to give the curse two layers of protection. First, it can be ended only during the year when certain rare events coincide."

"What events?" Von Piddle said cautiously.

"Machias will tell you. Let me continue." Mollyockett did not appreciate the interruption.

"The first layer of protection had to do with the Moon of Falling leaves since that's when it happened."

Lucille raised her hand high over her head. "What is the Moon of Falling Leaves?" she asked.

Mollyockett smiled. "It's the full moon in October," she explained. "When it is almost time to stow the tools and put the garden to bed for the winter. When the trees lose their leaves, and you can see the nests of the summer."

Muriel nodded. Having worked in her garden her entire life she understood well about putting it to bed. *Oh, how I wish I were there right now.*

"So the curse could only be removed during this one particular time. To make it impact the residents of Willamette even harder and to hit them where it hurts, I added a second layer of protection for removing the curse. There needed to be a sacrifice of a person in their village. In this case, a member of the Snow family who was similar in age and stature to whoever in the McKenzie family held the power of the passage. The person had to be sacrificed on the exact date of the Moon of Falling Leaves."

Mollyockett stood up, looked down at everyone for a considerable moment, then walked towards Fletcher. "I never imagined that the power of the passage would be held by someone so young. Which, I suppose, is why that poor boy and his parents were murdered." Her fingers closed tightly around Fletcher left hand.

The entire group gasped loudly.

"It's quite clear that there are three members of the Snow family that are no longer alive," Pidianski said sadly.

"Now," Woodrow drew in a deep breath, "I know why Chelsey Snow was present on that exact night at Snow Falls, I mean Willamette, when Croft was turned into a Slaughter Maker."

"Absolute beast!" Von Piddle shouted. "And the way they were grotesquely laid out."

"Meaning?" Mollyockett asked curiously.

Von Piddle stood up, clearly disturbed by the images in his mind. "The young boy was lying on top of his parents clutching the necks of both his father and mother."

A shadow fell over the entire group as images of death played in their minds.

Mollyockett shook her head.

Lucille pulled out a cloth handkerchief and patted her eyes. "How on earth?" She muttered to herself. "That poor boy."

"What do you think that means? I mean—." Fletcher hesitated because he didn't want his family to hear the answer. "Why make it look that way?"

Machias stood and moved in the direction of Fletcher and Mollyockett. "We promised that there would be no secrets." He drew back a bit, looking directly at Mollyockett.

She glanced around, then held up her hands as though to prepare them for her next words. "Tomhegan. We were both taught how to create a curse that makes someone unwillingly kill their immediate family. The bodies of innocent participants had to be placed at very specific locations in exact positions. I never imagined placing this type of curse. It involved killing good and innocent people." She paused. "Apparently, he added a more sinister layer to counter my original curse."

Aldous gasped. Muriel and Lucille looked at each other in horror.

"I would never!" Fletcher yelled. The whole idea was preposterous. He stepped around Mollyockett and hugged both Aldous and Muriel.

Lucille, who was sitting directly behind them, was sobbing. It was just too much.

Machias and Mollyockett turned and walked towards Pidianiski.

"I never expected that," he growled. "Is there more?"

Mollyockett nodded slightly.

"And?"

"That particular curse is one of the most powerful ones in Tomhegan's arsenal. It's literally unbreakable and time doesn't wait for it."

Machias stopped walking. His mouth fell open. "Let's hope Whole gives Fletcher some immunity. I can't even begin to imagine."

"The three of us should meet before we move on," Mollyockett whispered. "Let's bring them to the huts and let them rest." Thinking back to her mother's class on the banks of the Saco River she thought, *It's right before our eyes. I fear the release code is the reunification of the five nations of the Wabanaki Confederacy. Something I thought would never happen. How can they not know what has already been set in motion?* Mollyockett fell back into her chair and reached for the stone pipe.

CHAPTER 12

WABANAKI CONFEDERATION MOVES

"Who do you think will be their next target?" Lalia asked Squire Susup while petting Humeante's back. Her small frame had plenty of room in the leather chair in which she was sitting. As she spoke, she surveyed the stone wall supporting the north end of the house.

"More than likely it'll be Odanak in Quebec. It's the only major site that was important to Mollyockett in her lifetime that's not been attacked," Susup replied, holding Onion tightly by his collar. The short-haired white dog was growling at the black cat sitting comfortably on Lalia's lap. Beside him was his black stovepipe hat with its three large blue feathers. His well-manicured fingernails matched hers.

"If I'm counting them correctly, the Slaughter Makers number about two dozen," she continued. "It looks like everything may be coming together for them."

"Unfortunately, yes. I really wonder how much they know," he said softly, and his penetrating look made her realize, for the first time, how deeply concerned he was. "We both have unique powers, Lalia, but as the tea leaves are telling me even those may be limited."

She nodded slightly. Her eyes focused on two long chiseled lines in the center of a large boulder. The lines had been made to prevent thick ropes from slipping when it was moved into place hundreds of years ago by a team of oxen. She breathed deeply. Nothing would ever compare to the invigorating scent of vegetables placed in a root cellar in the autumn after harvesting. "So Lucille was the most difficult one to take the journey, "Lalia remarked crisply. "That really surprises me from what I'd heard about her."

"I'd take Lucille any day over that dastardly Von Piddle. No wonder he lives alone. His constant talking and exaggerated stories would drive even a dead tree crazy."

Onion suddenly stopped growling and faced the stone wall at the far end of the root cellar. He became silent and focused on a small crack between two large rectangular boulders. Lalia grimaced as Humeante dug his claws into her legs and stood up, arching his back high into the air. His yellow eyes zeroed in on the same spot.

Susup moved from his chair silently and methodically. "Somethings happening," he whispered. He crept slowly towards the wall. By the time he reached it, he knew something was wrong. "Shh."

Lalia quietly stood, leaving Humeante on the chair. "What is it?" She whispered, moving towards him.

He looked at her strangely.

"What?"

"There's the most putrid smell emanating from between those two stones."

"Putrid, how?"

"Like the worst smell I've ever encountered." He paused and backed up a few feet. "And it's warm."

She shook her head. "What do you think it is?" She knew the answer but asked anyway.

Onion's growls changed to a whimper as he backed away from the wall. He always had quick and accurate instincts.

Squire could feel the warm air change to a cool breeze in a matter of seconds as a light fog rolled from the small stone crack.

Susup was fighting. Fighting the smell, fighting the cool air, and most of all fighting the light fog that crushed his chest and sealed his throat. He bucked, straining with every ounce of energy, then was forced back violently against the chair he'd been sitting in just a few seconds ago. He touched his mouth. His eyes were blinking rapidly and watering. He looked at Lalia in an effort to get his bearings. There were unrecognizable sounds that sounded like voices in the fog that continued to surround him and move towards her. A trail of thick mist slid across the dark soil and over his right foot as he reached for his hat. He gulped the air outside the wet droplets then closed his mouth. The hot air caused large beads of perspiration to form on his forehead. Grunting and puffing, he moved towards Lalia, who was now holding Humeante tightly and moving behind her chair for protection.

"It appears I was dreadfully wrong. Odanak is not the next place to be attacked."

They exchanged glances as Susup pursed his lips and squinted. He was calculating his next move. *Fight or flee?*

Susup solemnly raised his index finger and pursed it to his lips. He quietly grabbed Onion's collar to get him to stop whimpering.

Just then, a deafening roar emanating from the small space between the two stones filled the room. The fog was now like a mirage, floating in a layer of mist above the entire surface of the root cellar.

This is it, he thought. His palms were sweating; he rubbed them on his long tail black tuxedo, causing his loopy silver earrings with small blue feathers to bang against his neck.

"Run," he muttered to Lalia, who was now standing still near the door, transfixed by the sight unfolding before her.

Suddenly a brilliant blue beam of light flew through the air causing the door to slam shut. The unmistakable sound of slow scraping rocks quickly followed. Lalia, holding Humeante tightly, turned and looked at Susup.

"What now!?" She screamed and pulled tightly on the copper door handle. "Ow!" she yelled and rubbed her hands on her chest. The handle was as hot as a lit stove. "It's locked!"

In unison, four large boulders on the far wall rolled backwards into the dark void behind them. A loud crash reverberated towards them as the top three boulders crashed onto the solid granite floor surrounding the clay soil, causing them to split into smaller pieces. Immediately, the fog coiled into a large ball and slowly swept the floor as it moved towards the newly created opening.

"Move and you die," a raspy voice called out. "Don't doubt us."

A large tunnel of sorts appeared in the darkness that was slowly illuminated by an unknown light source.

As Susup took a cautious step forward, the floor joists above his head began to creak and splinter as if caught in an unrelenting tornado. The sound soon became deafening as small pieces of plaster and dust rained down on their heads. A small rusty nail struck Lalia in the forehead. She quickly moved forward and stood beside Susup.

"What now!?" She screamed again, bewildered by the action. A small streak of blood appearing between her eyebrows.

His fingers twitched, remembering that he had powers that may help. So did she.

"Let's," he began, and then stopped. The swirl of careless thoughts disappeared like water down the drain.

The entire house over their heads began to move and sway in every direction as long floorboards separated from each other and splintered into hundreds of pieces. Onion barked loudly and ran towards the wood table between two of the leather chairs.

Just then, the three other stone walls moved in unison, closing in on the root cellar, creating a prison cell of sorts. Slowly, the walls of the large room enclosed just the dirt section that covered Muriel's recently buried vegetables. In an instant, the lights flickered then went out as the massive house exploded. Their eardrums ruptured as small bits of wood, metal, rug, clothing, glass, and stone rained down on the entire basement. Instinctively, they ran towards the dirt area that was now protected by the stone walls. It was like a fortress in the middle of mayhem. Onion quickly ran forward as he was violently struck by a piece of rusty nail-studded roofing. Lalia shifted position to get a better fix on the opening in the back of the root cellar. As she did, a large piece of granite kitchen countertop crashed into Susup's body. He fell onto Onion in a heap. Lalia quickly crawled beneath the countertop and felt Susup's left wrist for a pulse. Nothing. Susup and Onion lay motionless on the cold dirt floor. One of his blue feathers from his hat had impaled his leg so deep blood was pooling around his right side. A small carrot that Muriel had recently buried poked upwards directly over his head.

"Lalia, stop!" A deep voice roared from the dark area. Lalia pulled Humeante close to her and blinked. How? It knew who she was? An army of Slaughter Makers vomited a ghastly roar at her immediately entombing her in a fog of breath so vile it caused the vegetables buried below her to wither and rot. She remained silent.

"You're going to die for someone who is already dead?" The voice screamed.

It was now or never. Lalia closed her eyes and began to recite words quietly as she hugged Humeante. She rolled onto her side, and quickly began to morph into an unrecognizable shape in front of the advancing Slaughter Makers. A ripping and clawing noise surrounded the entire army of dragon like creatures and the group of men standing behind them. Lalia's eyes bulged then shut as her chest ripped open before her eyes. Humeante clawed at the exposed ribs still protecting the beating heart. Lalia's first seven pairs of ribs opened wide exposing her vital organs. Humeante meowed happily and knowingly fell behind the protruding ribs. The cat's actions showed no impact on Lalia's now life-less body. An enormous flash of light seized the back of Humeante's head and pushed him into the cavity next to Lalia's heart, which had stopped. The pulsating light surrounded the fleshy opening and began to mend the incision as if nothing had happened. Silence filled the room. Lalia suddenly jerked upward and spat out blood. She reached for her chest and yelled, *"Avonaco!"* She had no time to think. There was a deafening, screeching roar again, and the army of Slaughter Makers packed them-selves tightly into a single line and advanced towards the middle of the root cellar. As the pain from the surgical incision subsided, Lalia's fingers splayed open and began to vibrate. The blue jets of light that had healed her shot past her chest and encircled her ten fingers and then vanished. She knew what was next.

"Have it your way!" The deep voice screamed in delight. *"Ayawamat!"*

Lalia glanced towards the direction of the voice and held her breath. At least thirty enormous moose-like creators stood, reared up on their hind legs and advanced slowly. She could smell their hot putrid breath from across the room. The transition interrupted her thoughts. Deep scars began to appear on both her hands and moved upwards towards her painted black nails. She meowed haphazardly as each nail jerked outwards then fell into the soil. Slowly, under her murmured whispers, small protractible claws grew from where her fingernails had been. Her ears grew a special fur for sensing and protection as they quickly pointed upwards. This allowed for her feline body to move in one direction and point her ears in another direction. Immediately, she growled and hissed then turned her ears back. She honed-in on the direction of the army of intruders. Her now yellow eyes shone on the pile of flesh and skin that had been Susup and Onion only a few minutes ago. *"Ngadozig!"* she cried out.

A buzzing sound slowly filled the totally wrecked basement then grew louder. Thousands of black flies entered the root cellar tomb and swarmed the mangled bodies of Onion and Susup. Within seconds, they flew off through the small hole in the ceiling from which they entered. As quickly as they left, thousands of small white maggots appeared and happily munched on the decaying flesh of Onion and Susup. The blue light returned and engulfed the shattered bodies. It swirled around as small bits of flesh, skin, sinew and bone reattached and reformed into the bodies of Susup and Onion once again. The large pool of coagulated blood hissed then warmed as it slowly seeped into the porous small holes that remained on both their bodies. For a brief moment, they were barely recognizable.

Susup lay face down, listening to the growling Slaughter Makers. *They're attacking.* Onion growled and crawled in front of him. They both lay in the bright blue light that was now moving towards the back of the root cellar and the door that was now blocked by rocks and debris from the destroyed home. Nobody seemed to notice the small fire that had started and began to grow in the front half of the basement.

He sat up and surveyed his body. He appeared to be unscathed. He patted Onion and smiled. "Thank you," said Susup. "I owe you."

"I thought you and Onion were dead for sure." Still watching the Slaughter Makers with her yellow cat eyes, Lalia backed towards Susup. "We need to move quickly."

In one quick, fluid motion, the army of Slaughter Makers screeched in delight and lowered their heads as they advanced with their spiked horns." Lalia could not hear Susup over the roar of the oncoming savage creatures.

Chaos reigned as Slaughter Makers slung the enormous boulders sideways creating an even larger opening for the army to advance through. The clatter of racks of horns grew louder and louder. Lalia covered her nose then vomited from the smell. Her eyes grew wide. More and more Slaughter Makers were coming into sight as the front row stomped at rocks still blocking the entrance of the root cellar. Annoyed, they lowered their block shaped heads even further and flung the stones towards Susup, Lalia, and Onion.

"It's now or never!" Shrieked Lalia. She dug deep, channeling her powerful lion like strength and pounced upwards, kicking the thousand-pound granite counter towards the enemy. Susup stood up and moved beside Lalia as a unified pair. He quickly surveyed Lalia's new appearance, saying nothing. Onion barked loudly then growled as he scratched the dirt with his front right paw. The attack had commenced. The very survival of Whole was at stake.

CHAPTER 13

MACHIAS AND VON PIDDLE

THE SHORT JOURNEY FROM WHOLE'S WELCOMING CHAMBER TO Mollyockett's garden was awe inspiring. It momentarily took everyone's minds off what they had just learned. Mesmerized, they all followed Pidianiski, Machias, Merrimack, and Mollyockett up the staircase with its gleaming gold bannister.

"Must be worth a fortune," Von Piddle muttered under his breath as he ascended the stairs. "I'd love to snap a few selfies standing on this."

When they reached the sparkling bridge constructed totally of purple amethyst, the entire group stopped and gasped.

"Is it safe to cross?" Lucille asked.

Mollyockett searched for the right words to reassure the nervous woman. "As safe as those seal looking pancakes you make at 42 Sangar Drive."

Edmond and Fletcher laughed loudly as Lucille smiled and stepped onto the bridge, leading the group. Halfway across, she stopped. She'd spied an enormous entrance made of pink marble and carved into the shape of a Venus flytrap. Her eyes focused on the massive needle-sharp leaves of the stone plant.

"Grans, they're harmless," said Fletcher. He moved forward and grasped her hand. "I promise."

"Well, I would hope so," said Lucille, smiling at him. "How'd she know about my seal shaped pancake by the way?"

"I've no idea." He smiled at her, knowingly.

"I still can't believe this place exists and you've been here several times."

Fletcher smiled. "Grans, sometimes . . . actually, quite often, I feel the same way."

"Well, I'll be glad when this is all over. And I pray that its soon."

Aldous and Muriel froze, staring at Mollyockett's surreal garden.

"What on earth?" Muriel gasped.

"What?" said Lucille loudly.

"Would you look at that!" Von Piddle yelled, moving past the Venus flytrap that he had been tenderly caressing.

Machias and Mollyockett looked at each other with relief that the group seemed comfortable in the garden.

"You live here?" Von Piddle asked

"For a very long time," said Mollyockett, smiling around at them all. "I've just never had this many visitors at one time."

Fletcher let go of Lucille's hand and lead them further into the garden. The cluster of small huts caught him off guard. He wrinkled his forehead and looked at Mollyockett. She smiled and nodded, saying nothing.

"What a beautiful place," Muriel said brightly, taking Aldous' hand as she entered the garden.

"Absolutely stunning. Kind of reminds me of the time when I has in Brazil and about to start that trek into the Amazon when I was—"

Von Piddle's splutter was interrupted by Woodrow who had moved past the cabins. "Alek, just let us absorb the beauty, will you?"

Everyone ignored the activity taking place on the tip of Von Piddle's nose with his glasses.

The unbelievable lush garden stretched as far as the eye could see. Thousands of fruit trees hung low with ripe apples, oranges, pears, tangerines, bananas, plums and hundreds of other fruits. Their fragrance filled the air with the most sensuous smell. In the distance flowed a majestic waterfall, its mist creating a slight fog.

"Look at that!" Woodrow cried out when he spotted the gigantic swarms of fireflies hovering over the spectacular orchard, their bodies glowing like that of a brilliant star. Their vibrating wings created a gentle, relaxing hum.

"This has always been my favorite place in Whole," Mollyockett announced as soon as everyone was huddled together.

"There's more?" Lucille gasped. "How can that be?"

"A lot more," Machias pointed out. "For now, though, this is your final destination. I hope you like it."

Everyone looked at him then glanced back at the glimmering waterfall.

Muriel beamed at him.

"It's wonderful. I'm glad we're here. I—"

She broke off. Two enormous animals with everyone's backpacks on their backs slowly trotted into the garden.

"Tapirs," Mollyockett said, continuing the conversation. "You'll usually find them in tropical America or Asia. The darker one's name is Madockawando. The other one's Ogbomosho." Both animals stopped and lifted their heads then glanced towards Mollyockett at the mention of their names. "I call them Mado and Ogbo for short. You'll soon find out that they're wonderful for doing the heavy work. They're both harmless and love to be petted. She nodded as they both headed towards the huts with their cargo.

Mollyockett motioned for Lucille to come closer. She picked up a clay pot sitting on a tree stump. It emitted a trail of steam through the tiny hole in its lid. As she poured hot tea into several stone mugs, Merrimack landed on her right shoulder, jerking his head up and down happily.

"You'll love this," Mollyockett said to Lucille. Lucille turned and looked at Muriel and Aldous for reassurance. They didn't hesitate to join her. "Please, you'll be pleasantly surprised. I promise."

Lucille picked up one of the mugs and smelled its contents. "My goodness. Do you have any cream and sugar?"

Mollyockett was delighted. "I'm sorry, I don't. But you'll not need any of those here. Especially the sugar, you'll be up for weeks."

Confused, Lucille took a small sip. The thousands of tastebuds on her tongue immediately snapped to attention, analyzing the alien sensation. Then it registered in her mind. The taste was mind boggling. Dazzling balls of light bounced around her brain, causing her to smile wide.

Waves of orange and green rays soon took over and cascaded throughout the four hemispheres of her brain beginning with the frontal lobe then weaving through the parietal, temporal and occipital lobes. Lucille had never ever felt anything so wonderful.

"What is this?" Her smile was wide.

"Tea, Whole-style," Pidianiski responded. "Drink as much as you want. The quantity's unlimited here."

Lucille closed her eyes and sat on the stump that had held the mugs.

The silence swallowed them as Machias and Pidianiski gave everyone a mug.

"Mollyockett," said Lucille, standing to attention. "Is this some type of illegal drug?" Her mind was racing between elation and common sense.

"Oh hush, it's nothing but common tea. Hot water poured over the fresh leaves of Camellia sinensis, the same as in your world. It just impacts you a little differently here."

"I only meant . . . please forgive me for asking." Lucille felt a mixture of embarrassment and euphoria at the same time. Mollyockett let the issue go.

Machias moved to the front of the group and announced himself to the excited and happy travelers. Von Piddle was sipping the tea and dancing as though he hadn't a worry in the world. Shockingly, Woodrow and Aldous broke into an ancient Irish stepdance and loudly yelled out *Yes!* Their arms clinging tight to their hips.

Machias immediately realized what had just transpired. He'd need time for the tea to wear off if he was to have a serious conversation with them about formulating a plan. The danger was too close, the potential for violence, enormous. He nodded towards Pidianiski and Mollyockett who immediately lead the happy revelers to their prospective huts.

"Ah, Alek!" Machias said to Von Piddle after five hours had passed. "How'd you sleep?"

"Sleep!" Von Piddle giggled loudly. "I was dancing with myself the entire time. Wonderful place you have here. Over-the-top spectacular."

"Good, you're all here." Machias spoke to the others who were emerging from their huts at the sound of Von Piddle's voice. Wide smiles on their faces.

"Let's get right to it," Machias announced as Mollyockett, Merrimack, and Pidianiski joined him. "Time is of the essence. Think of your favorite chair and please get settled."

Fletcher sensed the enormity of the situation. Without asking, he moved towards Mollyockett and stood between her and Machias. The brown mark on his hand was burning, its intensity increasing by the second. *Something is happening.* Knowingly, Aldous nodded his approval towards his son.

Machias cleared his throat. He had not expected Fletcher to join him but immediately thought it was for the better. If his plan played out as he hoped, Fletcher would be a major player.

"Please, everyone, take a seat and give me your attention. This meeting is why you're all here."

Everyone came to attention. Lucille and Edmond exchanged looks. "I don't like the fact that Fletcher is up there with them" she said quietly. "My gut is telling me that something very bad is going to be shared with us."

"Lucy, we're not here for a family vacation. Now shush and let's pay attention," Edmond whispered.

Machias stood with his back to the waterfall and began. At his feet was the patera, the staff, *Whole Abounds,* and dozens of ancient stone tablets stacked on top of each other.

Von Piddle was transfixed by their presence.

"Let me start with what is absolute," he said, clearing his voice. "As Mollyockett mentioned earlier with respect to her curse, certain events have had to collide to actually lead us to this very spot where we are right now." He scanned the group looking for anyone not paying attention. "I'm telling you this to give you the complete picture of what's happening. This year, one of the rarest eclipses took place. You can rarely see Venus when it passes in front of the sun because its orbit is inclined at 3.3 degrees to the plane of Earth's orbit. The—"

"It's inclined at 3.4 degrees," Von Piddle announced quickly, cutting Machias off.

"What?" Machias snorted as he stared at the thin man.

"It's 3.4 not 3.3."

Perplexed, Machias looked to Pidianiski.

"He's right. It's 3.4," she affirmed.

"Who really cares?" Lucille interjected. "It's not relevant to the situation at hand."

"By the end of this conversation, you'll all care," Machias said sternly and nodded towards Von Piddle. "I stand corrected Alek," he said. "Thank you. Rarely do the sun, Venus, and Earth line up like it did just a short time ago. Just as important to the Native Americans, this eclipse coincided with the Moon of Falling Leaves and on the first frost of the winter. It's a very rare collision that will not happen again for hundreds of years. This very year is unique because it was a type of invitation, to say it lightly, for a group of villainous accomplices to use these events to come together, build an army of sorts, and make their murderous move. It's also the exact date Mollyockett choose with respect to her curse she placed on Willamette. The one we talked about earlier."

"Accomplices from here or where we're from?" Von Piddle asked.

"Both," Pidianiski replied, staring him down.

"Are we in danger right now?" Lucille asked, hands firmly placed on her hips. "If so, stop holding out and tell me right now. We have a right to know." She had a "Don't mess with me" tone.

Machias was already exhausted.

"I'll never get through this," he muttered under his breath. "Yes, yes you are," he said, leveling with her.

Lucille's hand jerked upward to cover her mouth. "How?" she asked softly.

There was a brief silence in the garden as the impact of Machias' words registered in their minds. Aldous was glaring at Muriel; Edmond reached out and reassured Lucille, whose hands were still cupped over her mouth; Woodrow and Von Piddle stared directly at Machias, wishing him to continue. Finally Woodrow blurted out, "She's right. We have a right to know. Especially if our lives hang in the balance and if we're going to actually live here for the rest of our lives."

Muriel and Edmond gasped in unison. Lucille lightly sobbed and began to shiver. "I can't handle the thought of not being able to return to. . ." she cried uncontrollably into Edmond's chest.

"Let him finish," Fletcher said as he moved closer to Machias in a show of solidarity. "We're all here for a reason and time is not on our side. Pull it together."

Lucille stopped crying and focused on her grandson. *Where has my sweet little boy gone?* Her mind was racing all over the place. It was totally spent.

Fletcher continued, "I've no idea if any of us are ever going back to Maine. What I do know is that we need to work together and listen to Machias, Mollyockett, and Pidianiski. I know them and they'll pull no punches."

The group shook off the thought of staying in Whole forever and forced themselves to accept what Fletcher was saying.

Machias patted Fletcher on the head, cleared his voice, and said, "Thank you, young man."

Mollyockett stepped forward with a suggestion. "A few years ago Fletcher had an assignment of sorts here in Whole. He needed to learn volumes of information in a very short time. Very much like today. Here in Whole, nutrients work at an exponentially quicker and more intense level than where you're from. Much like that delicious tea you recently drank."

"I still don't know what to think about that!" Lucille offered. She'd never even come close to experiencing the multitude of sensations the tea had caused. It had wreaked havoc with her mind at first but eventually turned to euphoria.

"I apologize," Mollyockett said calmly. I should have given you all some sort of warning. With that said," she paused. "We gave Fletcher ginko biloba by having him rub the twig's oily leaves. Ginko biloba is native to Asia in your world. It's used to improve one's memory and is quite common. Here, however, it will immediately enhance your memory to a level that's incomprehensible to most of you."

Von Piddle's glasses began to bounce on the tip of his nose even though he was silent. He loved an adventure. Mollyockett ignored him. "I am giving you all the option to experience the same thing. Machias has a tremendous amount of information he needs to share, and it has to be taken in without interruption. As we mentioned, we have very little time left to decide what we're going to do."

"I'm in," Woodrow said without hesitating.

"Please let me finish. With your minds greatly enhanced, you will be able to remember everything, so you should listen without interruption and save all your questions for later. It's our only option." There was finality in her words.

Machias smiled his appreciation towards Mollyockett.

Pidianiski opened the largest of Mollyockett's baskets and retrieved a clay pot holding the ginko biloba and passed it around. They all followed Fletcher's lead and smelled the plant's pungent odor before rubbing the oily leaves and yellow berries between their thumbs and index fingers. As soon as they started rubbing, their minds exploded in vivid flashes of bight blues and whites, reminiscent of a wobbly star exploding in the galaxy. Small electrical currents sparked and zapped in every area of their brains jerking them to attention. Loud gasps filled the lush garden.

"Ahh! I wish I had this in college," said Von Piddle sharply and gave a grunt of pleasure. "I'd have finished in one week instead of four years!"

Lucille giggled as treasured memories from her childhood vividly cascaded throughout her mind.

Machias looked down at the stone tablets sitting as his feet and waited for a few seconds. "Thank you," he said. "Now remember, no interruptions." He ignored Von Piddle's hand waiving wildly over his head.

"If those are what I think they are, Machias, I may be able to assist you," Von Piddle interrupted. "Inca and Mayan cultures were a large part of my studies in Boston. In fact, I recognize many of those letters and symbols on that top tablet. May I?" He stood up and waited. His entire studies flashed into his memory as if it were yesterday.

Machias didn't know if he was deeply annoyed or enormously elated. He knew that Von Piddle would be now be able to recall everything he'd learned while in undergraduate and graduate school with his greatly enhanced memory.

Pidianski gazed approvingly at Alek.

Machias moved his head up and down and smiled ever so little. As everybody look at him, Von Piddle moved towards the stone tablets in an exuberant manner. The moment, surreal. These lost treasures matched those displayed in the world's foremost museums.

Machias asked for Mollyockett and Pidianiski to be seated. Focus was paramount. It was clear Alek's moment had arrived. "Thank you for your undivided attention," he said. With your enhanced memories, you will definitely be able to retain everything I." He paused. "I mean, we tell you."

Lucille threw a concerned look at both of them. Her gut told her that Fletcher, by having the power of the passage, would soon be setting out a dangerous adventure. Fletcher, meanwhile, still had dozens of questions to ask. As protector of the passage, he knew his role would be central.

"Let's start with the enemy," said Machias gravely. "Their names are Slaughter Makers, Nukpana, Camaztoz, Uktena, Tygorge, and Tomhegan. Most of you are quite familiar with the last name." He paused. "For the sake of it, let's throw in Chelsea Snow and his entire family."

Lucille gasped. So did everyone else. Muriel closed her eyes as images of Nimsy Cortland flooded her mind. The betrayal was too deep and severe for her to ever fully recover from.

Machias ignored them and continued. "As all of you know, there have been many incidents in Maine and beyond where good and respected individuals have fallen victim to these murderers. As mentioned earlier, we are now in a time of the rarest eclipses." He nodded at Von Piddle, who was listening intently. "What most people from Maine and beyond don't know is that those innocent victims have been turned into an army of violent Slaughter Makers who are now ready to wage war on Whole in an attempt to gain control over it." He paused and gathered his thoughts. "Fletcher *met* a few of them in the back of the root cellar. I'll let him describe what they look like."

Fletcher eyed him with a mixture of shock and horror. He hadn't expected this. Especially in front of his family. He'd let them in on that night but not in detail.

He rose and turned towards everyone. "Machias did say he would hold nothing back." He paused. "Those individuals at Willamette, Mollyockett's grave and—" Von Piddle giggled slightly while looking at Mollyockett.

Machias returned the gesture with a severe look. "Continue on, will you?"

"Ogunquit, Fryeburg, Frenchman's Hole, and others were all at places important to Mollyockett when she lived where we are from. After they are murdered by what appears to be lighting, they are turned into an army of Slaughter Makers. These monsters are enormous moose-like creatures that stand on their hind legs. Their hairy bodies are extremely muscular and strong. Long limbs with razor-like claws give them enormous power. In addition, their blocked shaped heads are lined with rows of shark-like teeth. Tall antlers with many points stand on their heads and are massive weapons on their own." He swallowed hard and continued. "Finally, they have bat-like ears and eyes that glow red. But it's their horrible breath that has the longest impact. You'll never forget that smell."

"Thank you, Fletcher," said Machias. "This is the army they're building with the intent of destroying us."

"You're joking!" shrieked Lucille.

"You're not serious," said Muriel "like their namesake, they'll destroy us."

Machias ignored the interruption.

"They've made it very clear that if we don't turn over these items," he stopped and looked at the artifacts at his feet. "That you'll all be killed."

"Then give them to them if that is all they want," said Lucille while driving her nails into Edmond's wrists.

Mollyockett snorted loudly and rose. "If we do, we might as well kill ourselves. That'll be far quicker and much less painful."

"So, who are these other characters you mentioned, Machias?" Woodrow asked in an attempt to lower the tension.

"The first is—"

"Does anyone know of a piece of cloth that relates to actual transfer of the power of the passage?" Von Piddle asked. He was gently holding one of the stone tablets,

"My scarf Pidianiski made for me," said Fletcher, slightly elated.

Machias turned to Mollyockett.

"How could we have been so stupid?" he said flatly.

"It's in my backpack. I'll get it," Fletcher called out and ran towards his hut. Quickly he unfolded the silk scarf and extended it for everyone to see. It was decorated with scenes featuring various animals and plants, much like the one Aldous had been given when he was transferred the power of the passage. Both told a story unique to each of them.

Mollyockett focused on the central scene that contained three different symbols. Von Piddle had zeroed in on them too and asked about them.

"I put them there at the direction of Kozart's notes," Pidianiski muttered. "Every transfer had a different prophecy that was related to the alignment of the planets that particular year."

"May I?" Von Piddle asked Fletcher, stepping towards him. "There's a very good chance they may hold the clue to all of this."

Silence reigned as Alek dropped to his knees and intently studied the three symbols. Surprisingly, his glasses remained motionless. "This black butterfly here has deep meaning in the Native American community," he said. They all followed his boney fingers as they traced that square shaped insect. "Butterflies symbolize transformation. However, the color of the butterfly provides further important information. In this case, black signifies violence and bad news."

"Please, take a closer look!" yelled Lucille. "You've made a mistake."

"It's *not* a mistake," said Alek angrily. "I've spent my entire life studying this stuff."

"Continue on, please," Machias said with warm eyes.

The next image was that of a unique animal with a confusing maze drawn on its body.

"This here is a coyote. Coyotes are holy creatures with many tribes. Unfortunately, they symbolize a trickster deity. This spirit is mischievous, selfish, greedy, and deceitful." He paused. "It's not a good sign to be here with a black butterfly."

Out of fear of another lashing by Von Piddle, everyone remained deadly silent.

"This last symbol here," he pointed towards three curves attached to each other. "It represents the return of a warrior. There have been many ceremonies and homecoming dances held whenever a warrior returns home." Fletcher and Mollyockett immediately thought of Tomhegan and his new gang of friends.

Machias bent down and studied the images. Von Piddle, without thinking, brushed his bushy beard off the scarf.

"Is there a reason why these three images were placed on Fletcher's scarf?" he asked Pidianiski since she had created it. Alek continued on without waiting for an answer. "It's one of the worst signs possible for Native Americans," he said in a hoarse voice. "It's a warning of violent and permanent change. And it'll happen tomorrow as predicted with certain planets being aligned." His enhanced mind was vivid as ever.

Pidianiski hunched her shoulders. She was out of answers.

"Good heavens," Lucille called out in a quivering voice, "and when I didn't think it could get any worse."

Mollyockett stood. "Is there a reason why all of these individuals and the Slaughter Makers have come together? At this very moment? Seems like an odd group?"

Machias nodded. "If what Alek says is true, we don't have much time. First, there is Uktena who is the horned serpent of the Cherokee nation. He is not Mayan as I first believed."

"He also appears in the mythologies of many Native American tribes," said Von Piddle, correcting him. "Details vary among tribes, with many attributing the horned serpent to rain, lightning, and thunder."

Machias stood up and continued. "Then there is Tygorge and Nukpana, who have surprisingly reunited with each other as leaders of the five principal nations of the Wabanaki Confederacy. Mollyockett has a good hunch this is the actual *release code* they keep demanding. Apparently, they have no idea that they have already set it in motion. Pidianiski found quite a few references to the reunification after studying Kozart's notes in greater detail. He predicted this would happen. Not a good sign at all if Uktena is involved. Tomhegan appears to be their guide to whatever is happening at Willamette." Machias went silent and studied it all. "They're all using each other to obtain victory. If that's obtained, and I hope it never is, they'll definitely turn on each other afterwards. They all know they need each other right at this very moment."

Everyone went silent and pondered his words.

"Why is Snow Falls, I mean, Willamette so important to them?" Edmond asked.

"I'll explain the importance of Willamette in a minute. Finally, there is Comazotz. In Inca mythology, this means—"

"He's Mayan *not* Incan," said Alek anxiously. It was all adding up.

"Mayan," Machias muttered to the others. "It means the *death bat* in the K'iche' language. It has always been associated with night, death, and sacrifice."

"What a truly terrifyingly odd group," Lucille, who was still being consoled by Edmond, said flatly. "And *they* were all in our basement recently?"

Von Piddle continued to study the scarf as there was a slight commotion as everyone tried to calm Lucille. He pointed his wrinkled forefinger at a flat field with a circular indentation. "Any idea what this is?" he asked.

"It's called Sixth Day," Mollyockett offered. "It's where the transfer of the power of the passage took place with respect to Fletcher and all the others before him."

Machias opened his mouth wide and looked gravely at Fletcher.

"That must be it," Pidianiski told Mollyockett. "It's where they intend to wage their battle if they are to control Whole. I'm positive."

Mollyockett's eyes stayed focused on the scarf and remained silent.

"Well, well, well," Machias said quietly. "It makes all the sense in the world."

"But how are they going to get there?" Aldous asked. He understood Whole and its many secrets.

Pidianiski and Mollyockett moved closer to Machias and Von Piddle.

Mollyockett thought of the star removed from the bottom of her gravestone and the southern star Fletcher had been forced to give them during his encounter with the Slaughter Makers. "They have the tools to make it happen," she said gravely. "I just hope Squire Susup and Lalia will be able to hold them off. I wish they were able to have reinforcements." She ran her right hand through her hair in exacerbation.

"And where are they?" Aldous pleaded.

The garden went very still. Machias' eyes moved from Von Piddle to Fletcher. "In the root cellar on Sangar Drive."

Lucille went blue in the face; she looked like a young girl who had just stuck her finger in a live light socket for the first time. Again, she buried her face in her arms.

Mollyockett raised her hand. "The importance of Willamette is now no longer relevant to this conversation. Those days have long passed. It's clear as day what's about to happen." The garden gradually fell silent again. "Will everyone return to your huts?" she requested. "Will you four stay behind? she asked, nodding at Fletcher, Machias, Von Piddle, and Pidianski. We'll need to study these tablets a little further and decide what we're going to do. We've literally run out of time. And options."

She caught Aldous' eye who was silently pleading for any hope. Amidst anxious protests, he took charge of Woodrow, Lucille, Muriel, and Edmond and lead them to their respective huts.

Mollyockett waited for everyone to be out of earshot before she began. Fletcher sat in his root chair turning the patera in his hands.

Von Piddle was perfectly still, listening, waiting. Never in a million years had he expected to be part of something so dangerous and surreal.

"Do you think they made it past Susup and Lalia?" Mollyockett asked, taking a long drag on her stone pipe. A cloud of smoke immediately engulfed her face as she exhaled.

"If I still had power, I would have joined them. Do you honestly think they will be able to hold off *that* murderous coalition?" Machias wondered.

"No," Pidianiski said. "What if—"

"We'll have none of that," Mollyockett snapped. "I've known Susup since the day he was born. His drive and tenacity alone will outwit the enemy."

Von Piddle removed the top stone tablet and studied the one beneath it.

"I'll be right back. I'd like my backpack," Fletcher announced quietly.

"This tablet is just dreadful," Von Piddle said bleakly.

The others quickly bent down and listened to Alek describe the scenes etched into the tablet centuries ago.

"Fletcher!" Muriel shrieked.

Aldous opened his mouth to scream, but before he could Fletcher had wrapped his hands tightly around his father's neck.

Muriel yelled again and fell against the back wall of the hut. A tiny stream of blood oozed out of her mouth and onto her shirt.

Machias was the first to bolt towards the sound. The others were close on his tail.

"Fletcher!" Mollyockett cried. "Fletcher!" She threw down her pipe and pushed past Machias. She was well aware of what was happening. *The curse. Tomhegan's dreadful curse.*

CHAPTER 14

TWO STARS AND THE CONFEDERATION

SUSUP AND LALIA STOOD IN HORROR. IN FRONT OF THEM A HUGE cluster of blazing, hate-filled eyes stared them down ready for attack.

Lalia was unable to hold a stoic look with her feline face. The overwhelming pungent smell caused her to wrinkle her nose and gasp for air. Behind the army of Slaughter Makers stood five individuals in a single line. Pure elation etched on their faces. Their time had come. Susup immediately recognized Tomhegan. His long, dark hair was hung in two braids behind him. His black eyes were focused on Lalia and her new look. He assessed her feline claws.

Lalia reared up and angrily hissed at them.

"TOMHEGAN!" Susup bellowed. Lalia was so shocked she reared backwards. "YOU DON'T HAVE ANY CHANCE! WE KNOW YOUR PLAN."

The front row of Slaughter Makers rose and growled visciously sending a plume of deadly green gasses in their direction. Susup and Lalia immediately covered their noses. Onion howled then barked at the odorous gasses now enveloping his entire body.

"WE'VE BEEN WAITING FOR THIS FOR A VERY LONG TIME, SQUIRE SUSUP. NEVER IN A MILLION YEARS! ITS YOU TWO WHO NEED TO SURRENDER. YOUR CHANCE OF SURVIVAL BY OUR CALCULATIONS IS ZERO!"

There was complete silence in the root cellar.

In one swift motion the Slaughter Makers jumped forward and

quickly advanced through the large stone hole in the back wall of the destroyed cellar.

The flash of red eyes flickered over the roar of the oncoming army of moose-like creatures advancing into the root cellar.

Susup patted Onion on the back and protectively stepped in front of him while Lalia turned her head and focused her cat-like ears in the direction of Tomhegan. She moved towards the creatures. Her unexpected actions caused the Slaughter Makers to slow their advance just as Susup jumped onto a boulder that had once been part of the back wall.

Lalia leaped onto a boulder directly to her right. Her deadly claws now extended more than six inches from her paws.

The Slaughter Makers stopped dead, waiting for the next command from behind them.

Tygorge stepped forward from the others, his long brown stick with large white feathers in his leathery hands. The glow of the Slaughter Maker's eyes bounced off the quartz and amethyst stones that decorated its tip. Without hesitation, he aimed the wand at the back row of Slaughter Makers. Instantly, the killer army jumped up and towards the root cellar.

As before, Nukpana laughed loudly and casually folded his hands in front of him. The horrific sound skin and fur being ripped and bones crunching reverberated off the rock walls and remnants of the destroyed home. The attack was on.

Lalia immediately sprung backwards after witnessing Onion being mauled by the first row of Slaughter Makers. Blood was everywhere and large chunks of fur and bone were strewn throughout the small section of the root cellar that still existed. Susup could only watch in horror from atop the large stone that was protected by parts of the floor that had recently collapsed.

Nukpana slowly nodded at Tygorge who was now pointing his wand directly at the space between Lalia and Susup.

"*Manaba!*"

A brilliant flash of white light filled the entire root cellar. Lalia violently flew backwards into a jagged pile of debris from the collapsed house. A broken leg from what was once a kitchen chair plunged into her feline back. She crashed down into the clay soil, slid on the remnants of metal roofing, dug her claws into the dirt and then hissed loudly.

Susup quickly pulled the chair leg out of Lalia's back and swept her into the fold of his right arm, nearly crushing her front paws, and leaped into a small space behind the stone kitchen counter.

"Aaaah! Aaaah!" Lalia hissed as she gulped the dusty air.

There was no time to assess the injuries. Susup reached into his right pocket and pulled out a silver metal tin. Mollyockett had given it to him just weeks before. Instinctively, he rubbed a dark green mixture directly onto the opening in Lalia's back. He jerked his hand backwards when she shrieked as his forefinger touched a broken and exposed rib.

"Hold still! It'll work faster." He quickly picked up a rock, blew black powder on it and hurled directly at a Slaughter Maker that was fast upon them. It was a direct hit. The vicious creature stumbled backwards, unable to comprehend the gash in his forehead. It glanced down just as clumps of bloody matter hit the floor. In a thud, it went down, temporarily blocking the path of other Slaughter Makers.

Lalia was up. It had worked. She hissed angrily and extended her claws for battle.

"Thank you," she said under her breath as she sprung upwards and beside him while examining her razor-sharp claws.

Nukpana and Tygorge angrily stepped forward and towards the downed animal with Tomhegan on their heels.

Nukpana, stopped and quickly turned towards him.

"I thought you said—"

Tomhegan cautiously stepped backwards and shook his head. "I've no idea how."

"Speak!" Nukpana demanded.

Tomhegan swallowed hard and removed the wicker basket on his back. "Just get me into the root cellar. All I need is a few seconds to make it work."

"You better be right. Soon, we'll have no use for you."

Tomhegan took a deep breath. "Okay. Just get me there. Everything is according to plan. Trust me."

Nukpana didn't bother responding.

The distrust and irritation in both Nukpana's and Tygorge's eyes spoke volumes. None of them noticed Susup pulling Onion's destroyed body into the small cave that was protecting he and Lalia from an imminent onslaught.

The front line of Slaughter Makers slowly moved forward until they were directly under the opening of the back wall in the root cellar. The smell emanating from them was now hot and stifling.

"This is not a case of if you will win, Susup. It's how you will die," yelled Nukpana.

Susup poked his head out slightly and spat towards the growing army. It was then when he spotted a second line of Native American men advancing with Tomhegan, Nukpana and Tygorge. *The Wabanaki Confederation. So it's done*, he thought.

Susup poured some of the black powder into Lalia's open hands. "On one," he whispered. His words were interrupted by a slight whimper from Onion whose mangled body was crumpled at their feet. They stood up, raised their hands, and threw the powder directly at the front line of Slaughter Makers who were now directly in front of them ready to attack.

The entire front line was lifted upwards and into the remaining jagged boulders with a massive crunch and shattering of bone. They then smashed onto the dirt floor in a massive heap.

"I've seen enough!" Nukpana said to Tygorge.

Susup blinked and Lalia screamed because for a moment it appeared that the closest Slaughter Maker was about to land directly on them.

"Move back!" Susup yelled, pulling Onion backwards with him. The creature that had once been attacking seconds ago now landed with a loud thud in the clay soil in front of them. Lalia cried out as the monster's massive antlers pierced her right arm. A small trickle of water cascaded over them from firefighters who were now on the scene after numerous reports of an explosion at 42 Sangar Drive had been called in. Mayhem reigned throughout the peaceful neighborhood. A gentle breeze ruffled the clothes that Lucille had hung on the line only recently. Horror stricken neighbors filled the street as a desperate and frenzied search for the McKenzie family played out.

They had no idea of the horrific battle taking place below the smoke and flames.

"IKTOMI!" Nukpana yelled. The word means *trickster spirit* in his language, and he was calling Uktena, the horned Cherokee serpent. Tomhegan let out a terrible scream and froze.

A strong, swirling wind quickly passed high over the huge army and directly at Susup and Lalia. A brilliant white flashed then exploded throughout the root cellar. The dirt immediately blew away exposing the stone entrance to the passage.

Lalia and Susup desperately struggled against the raging tornado that surrounded them. Susup cursed under his breath and fell onto Onion. A movement outside the whirling vortex caught Lalia's eyes. A Slaughter Maker had lowered his head and was charging directly at them. His pointed antlers ready for the kill.

"Susup!" Lalia thundered. "Look out!" She took a step back and then another. The moose-like creature was fast on his feet. They both backed away quickly as the longest points from the antlers pierced their bodies. Susup felt a pillar of fire and smoke as the sand swirled like a tornado in Kansas.

The ferocious Slaughter Maker vomited a thick green substance at them then clawed them into the wreckage that had only recently been a majestic and elegant home. Lalia was thrust backwards. Slowly, life ebbed from her body as Susup landed on her, pinning her against wood that had once been the headboard for Aldous and Muriel's bed.

Without hesitation or remorse, Tygorge, Nukpana, Tomhegan and a dozen other men stepped around the still warm bodies of the few Slaughter Makers that did not survive the battle.

"Now, show us what you have," Nukpana snapped at Tomhegan.

Tomhegan smiled villainously and gently removed the two stone stars from the wicker basket after instructing Nukpana to insert the tip of his staff into a small indentation. Nukpana and Tygorge stared at him as he bent forward and expertly placed the stars into position. He closed his eyes and whispered a chant only he could hear.

The tattered room suddenly began to shift, causing the Slaughter Makers to move backwards while growling angrily. Nukpana's mouth sneered upwards as he watched the huge stone turn into a thick grey liquid that quickly grew into an opening large enough to accommodate the army of Slaughter Makers. Tygorge, thrown off balance by the overwhelming whirling sensation, backed into a huge boulder. His eyes widened as he watched the action continue. Suddenly, the hole grew larger, outgrowing the root cellar. Massive boulders cracked then split under pressure from the expanding hole.

Nukpana's black eyes were slits. The Slaughter Makers were huddled behind him and ready to charge.

Tygorge gave a delighted laugh as they followed Nukpana into the black passage. Joyous chaos reigned. The charging Slaughter Makers were falling over each other as they violently stepped into the passage. Tomhegan smiled then hissed as he stayed in step with the army. They had waited centuries for this exact moment to come. They were in.

CHAPTER 15

TIME TO MOVE

UNCLE WOODROW WAS THE FIRST TO ENTER MURIEL'S HUT. WHAT HE saw took his breath away. A horror-stricken Muriel was backed into a side wall of the small structure. She glanced at Woodrow and then towards the large bed where Fletcher was straddling his father. His strong hands were wrapped around Aldous' neck. Woodrow moved in slow motion; he saw Mollyockett, Machias, and Pidianiski enter the hut and towards Fletcher.

"Stay there!" Mollyockett yelled at Von Piddle, Edmond, and Lucille who were approaching the hut.

"Fletcher!" Screamed Machias, attempting to pull him backwards.

Fletcher did not answer. He continued to drain the life from his father with a totally blank stare on his face.

Mollyockett knew what was happening and what needed to be done, if there was time. Her mind focused on the spell she'd learned from her mother at an early age. Every second mattered. Fletcher had secretively taken the patera and accessed its powers. Something only he could do.

Fletcher turned, spotting Mollyockett chanting silently to herself. He increased the grip on Aldous' neck in a desperate race for time. It was a surreal moment for everyone witnessing the horror. His father was no longer moving. Fletcher leaned forward and delivered one final push on his windpipe. His face twisted with fury as he moved his attention towards his stricken mother.

Muriel's eyes were wide.

"Fletcher! I command you to stop!" Mollyockett yelled and continued to chant unrecognizable words that soared high into the air then directly at the bed.

"Try to stop me," Fletcher chortled as he slid off the bed. In seconds, Machias was on him, pinning him to the floor. His long beard blinded Fletcher as he reared up, thrusting Machias into the air.

Then, as quickly as it began, it was over. Fletcher fell back to the floor in a thud.

"I'll help Aldous!" Mollyockett shouted and frantically began to work on him. She reached into her pocket and quickly slathered a white substance on his throat.

"Machias, can you check on Fletcher?" She boomed.

Fletcher was now sobbing into his right arm. It took perhaps a full minute for him to fully realize what had happened. "Mom, I'm so sorry. Oh my god!" The pain in his head was so severe he couldn't stand up. At that moment he realized that both he and his father were deadly pawns in the enemy's quest to control Whole. It was completely overwhelming.

Lucille rushed into the hut and fainted on the spot. The image of her traumatized daughter and Mollyockett giving Aldous CPR was the final straw.

"They took control of my mind," said Fletcher, sobbing. Muriel rushed to his side and hugged him tight. "I know. We were warned. I'm so sorry you have to live through this." She kissed Fletcher's head then looked up at Mollyockett and Aldous.

Aldous jerked slightly then began to breathe slowly. Von Piddle began to clap loudly with relief. Aldous' eyes widened as his mind flooded with clarity of what had just transpired. He coughed uncontrollably as Mollyockett stroked his head then focused on Lucille who had been propped up against Fletcher's bed.

"What just happened?" Edmond demanded after placing a cold cloth on his wife's forehead.

Machias looked to Mollyockett for some sort of direction.

After a short pause Mollyockett said, "It was the curse we recently discussed. The one with the three victims under Willamette. I've no idea how they managed—"

"Good heavens!" Edmond shouted directly at her. "Get us out of here right now. You have no right to make us stay." There was furry in his blurry eyes. "Lady, look what is happening to my family."

"I wish it was that simple, Edmond. I really do," she quickly replied with deep empathy. She was still winded from helping Aldous. "Our options right now are extremely limited. Unfortunately, that is not one of them. Please trust me."

"How dare you!" Lucille yelled loudly after regaining consciousness while moving towards Muriel. "What other surprises do you three have in your big bag of tricks?"

After another short pause Pidianiski said, "we don't have much time. I know this may sound callous after what just happened, but we really need to take action immediately if any of us is to survive."

Lucille snapped. "I'd rather die right now then follow the lead from any one of you. Get away from me."

Fletcher closed his eyes and considered his involvement. He had just assaulted his mother and tried to kill his father. *I need to push on. For them*, he thought. He had great difficulty getting to his feet as everyone refocused their attention on the shell-shocked boy.

There was complete silence in the room.

He could not comprehend the magnitude of his actions and emotionally broke down.

"Mom, Dad," he sobbed. "I'm so sorry. I truly am."

Muriel began to cry too and gently rubbed his head. "We know sweetie," she said.

"Let's head to my garden," Mollyockett commanded loudly. "I hate to say this, but we don't have much time. We really don't." She looked Lucille directly in the eye. "Trust me. Please."

"Do as you please," said Lucille simply. "This isn't my world. Thankfully."

Mollyockett did not respond. She quickly looked away and exited the tent.

The soothing fall of water filled the air as everyone silently headed back to their root chairs in the garden.

Surprisingly, Von Piddle took the lead as soon as they were seated. "Before *that* happened—"

"Let's not talk about *that* ever again!" Lucille commanded, cutting him off.

He nodded and gulped a deep breath. "We were studying Fletcher's scarf and the second and third tablets Pidianiski rescued from the temple at Ollantaytambo. They—"

"Where?" Lucille demanded. She would no longer stay silent.

"My apologies, Lucy. The temple that you traveled through to get here."

"Thank you for clarifying. Continue."

Machias remained silent and let Alek continue speaking. "

"Like you all, I can't believe I'm *actually* here. But I am. If what Mollyockett says is true about limited time, and I do believe her, we desperately need to hurry and formulate a plan that will allow us to return home."

Pidianiski and Mollyockett stole a glance at each other.

"It appears that whatever is about to happen was forecasted by both Kozart and the lost Quechuan people. The ones," he stopped and looked directly at Lucille who was now glaring at him. "The people who built and lived in that magnificent temple in Ollantaytambo. And from what we now know, if the enemy is to be successful, they must make their move at this very moment. Clearly, it's their only window of opportunity. If we sit idly by, they'll be victorious."

"Well, isn't that just dandy," Lucille huffed. "I guess that's just too bad for us." Everyone left her to her thoughts, knowing she was teetering on the edge.

Machias cleared his throat. "Their plan was to eliminate both Fletcher and Aldous, knowing they both had or have control over the power of the passage." He stopped and nodded. "I'm sorry Lucille, but everyone needs to know exactly what is going on."

"I'm listening," she replied coldly after crossing her arms over her chest. "Get on with it."

"Pidianiski made Fletcher's scarf for us to place over his head at Sixth Day when Mollyockett and I transferred the power of the passage from Aldous to Fletcher." He paused. "It's always been required as part of the transfer ritual."

Aldous smiled then winked lovingly at his son, trying to forget the recent attack.

"So it is very clear that Sixth Day is the exact place where they plan on staging their assault. We need to foil their plot by keeping one step ahead of them."

"Meaning?" Woodrow asked. "Why not just stay here and let them wander into an empty Sixth Day?"

"Here, here," Lucille affirmed quickly. "Let's just all stay here."

"I wish it were that simple. If it were possible, we would," Machias said then stepped backwards towards Mollyockett, Pidianiski, and Fletcher. "I will tell you this. Most of you will be staying here. Whole holds many secrets, but we know for a fact that she has no plans for some of you to travel to Sixth Day. You'll be of no use and quite frankly, in the way."

Lucille and Muriel were on their feet.

"Who *exactly* is going!" Lucille yelled. "If you're taking Fletcher, you're taking me. End of discussion," she huffed folding her arms over her chest while glaring at them.

"We do have one advantage," Mollyockett said, ignoring Lucille's comment.

"To get here, you had to travel through the southern passage, which took quite some time. They, on the other hand, will enter through the northern passage before arriving at the southern temple. That's because of the power of the southern star they stole from Fletcher. Apparently, it works the same as the root cellar star that delivered you here but in reverse. From there, they will need to traverse some rugged and dangerous territory if they are to make it to Sixth Day. Their army is quite large, and it will take some extra time. That actually may close their window of opportunity. Hopefully."

"Umbegog Gulch?" Aldous asked curiously.

Mollyockett shook her head. "No," she said. "Whenever there is pending danger, Umbegog Gulch rises over its banks. It's never been wrong. Aldous, right now, it's at a record level. It's impassable for even us, which says a lot." She turned towards Fletcher then faced the group. "Hopefully that's bought us time."

"Wait. Didn't you say Lalia and Squire Susup were guarding the passage in Muriel's root cellar?" Lucille asked loudly. "Good heavens! Have you lost faith in them?"

Mollyockett was quick to respond. "I have all the faith in the world in my son and Lalia. We can't, however, be derelict and not formulate some type of backup plan. As it stands, some of this is only a hunch."

Lucille's eyes widened. *Hunch?*

"So what's the plan?" Woodrow interjected.

Von Piddle smiled wide and picked up the top stone tablet.

Lucille stood up and raised her hand. "One last question, I promise. Sorry, Alek."

Machias shook his head. He was having a hard time keeping his temper in check.

"Someone mentioned something about Sixth Day and the need for Aldous and Fletcher to not be around anymore in order for them to take power of the passage. So if they're still here, how can that happen? Isn't this all for nothing now?"

Machias turned to Mollyockett and said, "Care to give it a stab?"

Mollyockett felt a great rush of affection for Lucille. It was clear her family meant the world to her and she would protect them in any way she saw fit. "Lucille, great question. I wish I had thought to bring it up before you did. We've no idea," she replied sadly. "I've been living in Whole ever since I departed your world. She has her own rules that can change drastically over time. Clearly we're dealing with heartless murderers." She paused. "And to tell you the truth, I am worried about Squire Susup and Lalia like any doting mother would be. He is my son, and I worry about him all the time. Especially at this very moment. I know he is talented and a grown man, but I still worry. I always will."

A hush fell over the garden. No one had expected this usually stoic woman to show such emotion.

Lucille swallowed hard and dabbed her eyes. "Thank you," she said softly. "I truly appreciate everything you all are doing."

Von Piddle looked around, unsure if he should continue. Machias nodded for him to press on.

"As mentioned, it is clear from Fletcher's scarf that Sixth Day is the only place where any type of battle can take place. Additionally, these tablets are resolute that we can't just sit around and wait for them. We might just as well waive the white flag of surrender." He reached down, took the top tablet, and held it high in the air for everyone to see. "If you notice these etched figures, it's almost definite the Quechuan people knew their time as keepers of the southern passage was about to come to an end."

Everyone leaned forward to get a better glimpse of the tiny ancient writings. He continued, "They clearly wanted to protect it and subsequently, Whole. Apparently, they too used Sixth Day to transfer the power of the passage to others in their tribe when such a transfer needed to take place."

He gently handed the stone tablet to Pidianski and picked up the next one. "They attempted to address every scenario possible." Completely immersed in the moment, he turned the tablet outwards for everyone to get a glimpse of what he was telling them.

"After consulting with Machias, it's obvious this huge circular indentation etched here is the very center of Sixth Day," Von Piddle said, pointing to the center of the tablet. "And the exact location where every transfer of power over each passage has taken place." He looked down at the etchings for a few more seconds, then nodded knowingly. Everyone was on the edge of their seats.

"Expecting intruders to somehow learn about the transfer of the power of the passage, they spent an incredible amount of time rebuilding the circular indentation, also known as the bowl, to serve as a type of trap where any intruders would subsequently become trapped then annihilated when the very bottom failed."

Mollyockett's jaw dropped. "Never in a million years would I—"

"They were very intelligent," Von Piddle interrupted, having been caught off guard by her reaction. "But, and this is amazing. When lined up in the correct order, all of these tablets give an exact map on how to make this happen."

Pidianiski grunted then looked away. She'd had these tablets for centuries and was never able to fully decipher their meaning.

"The very fact that you created Fletcher's scarf after deciphering

Kozart's words, Pidianiski, led me to this realization. So, thank you. I could not have figured it without you," said Alek gently. "Your knowledge is extremely admirable."

"With that," Mollyockett said gravely as Von Piddle began to line the tablets in proper order, "it's still important that we have a plan and stay unified. Not for one second can we underestimate them. If we do, it could cost us our lives."

Aldous patted Fletcher on the head. Machias and Pidianiski knelt beside Alek. Lucille was watching them all closely. She now had a deep admiration for Mollyockett and at that point, made the decision to let things play out. She had no other choice.

Mollyockett was now focused on Merrimack. He was now soaring high above the garden. With wings wide and flying in a particular zig-zag pattern, she knew the news from the root cellar was not good.

CHAPTER 16

SIXTH DAY CONFRONTATION

"How dare you look at me like that," Refinna boomed at Odella in the reception area of Cygnus. "I'm quite positive you value your job."

"Yes," she said sharply, "Why?"

Winola and Serena were slouched on a leather couch directly behind their sister, glaring hatefully at Aldous' trusted assistant.

Odella was horrified that these three ladies showed little emotion with respect to the sad and horrific situation at hand.

"I told you, Refinna, you are all *persona non grata* here now. Aldous was very clear that if anything—"

"How dare you curse at us. And don't take that tone with me, Odella," shrieked Refinna, causing her double chin to bounce.

"Someone has to run this place and the McKenzie Inn now, and I can assure you it's not going to be you!" Refinna paused and sized up the immaculately dressed and poised assistant. "And do tell me again. What's your last name? Hmm? It's surely *not* McKenzie."

Odella's and Refinna's eyes met. Refinna was shocked that things were not going as planned. Odella had flatly refused to turn over the keys to the office at Cygnus. Even though it had been only a day since the destruction of 42 Sangar Drive, the three portly sisters immediately tried to take control of the situation. It looked hopeless that anyone had survived the "gas explosion" at the McKenzie residence. Surprisingly, the only body recovered in the rubble was that of a deceased man with painted black fingernails. His identity was unknown.

"I've read that you three have started your own food company. How's that working out?"

"None of your business, Missy," replied Refinna. She hadn't expected this normally timid person to resist. She quickly and loudly snapped her fingers.

"The keys, right now!"

Odella's eyes drifted towards the secret safe behind the portrait of Margaret Chase Smith, the Maine woman who became the first female to serve in both houses of Congress in Washington. Her blue eyes then sadly looked at Aldous' locked office. *I don't care how much they hurt me. I will not give in.*

Odella spontaneously laughed when she saw Winola and Serena salivating deliriously as they looked out the window at a large white truck backing into the distribution center across the street. It was the exact truck that had once distributed fat-laden, sweet treats when they were in charge of Cygnus a few years ago. It used to deliver products that were no longer part of the portfolio of the healthy company. It took two years of wrangling with lawyers, but Aldous had managed to bring the company back to its core values: healthy foods. Odella eyes moved to the large flag pole in front of the company's headquarters. Both the American and State of Maine flags were flying at half-staff. She had made the decision early this morning upon arriving at work. She knew her presence at the company today would be mandatory for the very reason now confronting her. She had to keep it together for the sake of the McKenzie family.

There was a brief silence in the room as Refinna contemplated her next words.

"What's the matter, Riffy? The cat got your tongue?"

Serena's hand jerked upward and covered her mouth. She knew what was to follow.

"How dare you!" Refinna boomed and raised her large, green crocodile skin purse high over her head. Surprisingly, Odella rolled her eyes and remained stoic. None of them had seen her press the black button under the lip of her desk to alert security a minute earlier.

"Refinna, stop!" Winola squeaked in an excited voice. "She'll have you arrested."

Odella quickly moved two steps to her left just as the massive purse came crashing down on a side table. As usual, Refinna's aim was hopeless.

An ornate white lamp crashed off the table and landed on the floor in a thud. Sparks flew briefly as its light bulb shattered.

Odella remained still and bravely crossed her arms in front of her chest.

Refinna looked stunned and outraged.

"Do we have a problem here?"

Their attention turned to a tall security guard that had rushed into the room. Winded, he focused on the broken lamp on the floor. "Everything alright, Odella?" Widemouthed, Serena and Winola pushed themselves further into the couch, which creaked precipitously from their combined weight.

"Jeffrey, actually yes," replied Odella casually. "Would you please escort these fine ladies off the premises and call the authorities. Additionally, have them issue an order prohibiting them from visiting us again. Please let them know that if they try, they'll be immediately arrested." She paused and looked over at Serena and Winola. "When you come back, I'll make a copy of the instructions Aldous left in case something happened." Next she focused on Refinna. "And these instructions include the McKenzie Inn."

"Liar!" Refinna shouted. "Uncle Woodrow would never—"

"Oh, yes, he certainly did. It appears he knows you three quite well," Odella retorted cutting her off. "I have no idea what is going on, but I'm quite confident we will be seeing everyone again in the very near future."

Confused, Refinna wrinkled her forehead and narrowed her eyes. "Exactly, what does that mean?"

Odella ignored her. "I believe I've instructed Jeffrey to immediately escort you off the property."

"This isn't the last you'll hear from me, you pathetic human being!" Refinna yelled just as Jeffrey firmly grabbed her arm.

Odella casually watched the trio disappear down the hallway then collapsed into her chair. She covered her eyes with shaking hands and began to weep. Her thoughts lingered on the now missing McKenzie family and Alek Von Piddle. *What on earth is going on?* Four generations of respected McKenzie men looked down on her pain, each painted in front of the original Birch Bread factory.

After an hour of loud protests and heated discussion, Machias placed two of his fingers into his mouth and loudly whistled everyone to attention. "I'm sorry, but Aldous, Muriel, Woodrow, Alek, Lucille, and Edmond will have to stay here. End of discussion."

"Even me?" Aldous asked. "I'm quite familiar with Whole."

Machias nodded. "Even you, Aldous. You no longer hold the power of the passage and will be of no use. I'm sorry."

"I understand," his said with resignation. "I'll take care of every-thing here."

Mollyockett was seated in her root chair off to the side, smoking the stone pipe. Merrimack sat idly on her left shoulder. Her thoughts wandered to the early winter of 1810 when she traveled to Willamette seeking out Tomhegan. She'd never expected the raging blizzard that took its toll on her seventy-year-old body as she aimlessly wandering in whiteout conditions, searching for the one person she hated most. The time had come. Her mind was confused quite often and there were many days when she couldn't even get out of bed back then. She was often unable to recite curses, remember medical cures, or recognize trusted neighbors and friends in Maine. She knew she had little time left and wanted to rid the county of Tomhegan and his murderous deeds. She contemplated the situation she was in at this very moment. Little had she expected that her actions from that fateful day had now come full circle as Tomhegan and the vicious confederation he was a part of now hunted her and all she loved.

She took a long drag on the pipe, closed her eyes, and then patted Merrimack on the head before sending him off to scout Sixth Day.

Mollyockett, Fletcher, Machias, and Pidianiski rounded a corner and took a break. Off in the distance Hooey, Sebago, Casco, and Monhegan jumped in delight as a cluster of bright butterflies fluttered over their heads. The winged insects immediately located a patch of white cactus flowers and began to land on them. After much thought, Machias had made the decision to bring the lemurs in case a distraction was needed. Something they were all well suited for, especially Hooey.

The journey around Umbegog Gulch had taken much longer than expected due to the rising river. As they rested, Pidianiski sharpened her knife, the one she'd accidentally left in the temple at Ollantaytambo. It had taken hours to straighten her beloved prize then sharpen it.

As they conversed about their plan, a twig snapped, bringing the conversation to an immediate halt. Ahead on the path stood a figure half feline, half human. Onion sat directly in front of it.

Mollyockett immediately knew. It was a feeling only mothers could experience when one of their children is no longer there.

"*Susup,*" she whispered then lowered her head.

Lalia cautiously walked towards them, well aware of the significance of her presence with Onion.

The four lemurs continued to play, ignoring Lalia and the panting dog as they approached.

Lalia headed straight for the group.

"I'm sorry," she whispered while extending her cat-like claws for relief. "It's been a long and lonely journey."

"You don't need to tell me anything," said Mollyockett sadly. "My gut sensed it right before we left."

Lalia arched her feline spine then knelt before her. Mollyockett immediately spotted the recently healed scars. She glanced over at Onion, tracing his massive scar lines on his body with her eyes.

"We're here because of him."

"I can see that," whispered Mollyockett. "Was it quick?"

Onion barked loudly, then growled.

Lalia nodded. "He fought so bravely, but it was just too much. We never expected what they had in store for us."

The group listened intently as Lalia recounted the action in the root cellar and what they could expect at Sixth Day. She told about the moment the Slaughter Makers charged and Nukpana unleashed a storm of immense magnitude that quickly led to the demise of Susup. She retraced the exact steps Tomhegan took when he expertly placed the two stars onto the rock that had been buried in the root cellar.

Machias rested his bearded chin on his left palm then swallowed hard avoiding eye contact with Mollyockett.

Lalia reached her claw into the leather bag she'd been carrying and pulled out a crumpled blue feather. Mollyockett recognized it as one that had until recently poked out of the top of Squire Susup's stove-pipe hat.

Without saying a word, she twirled the feather in her forefingers then looked directly at Lalia. "Thank you," she paused and refocused on her fresh scars. "So it works."

Lalia nodded sadly and patted Onion's head while applying an ointment Mollyockett had handed to her for both their injuries. Within seconds, any trace of the deep scars had vanished. "He was worse than me. Far worse. His injuries were too severe even for your lifesaving ointment. I've no idea how Susup could have ... Mollyockett, I'm quite positive he'd want you to take care of Onion for him."

Mollyockett didn't hear Lalia , as she was lost in grief.

"You've been through a lot Lalia. I'll have Casco and Monhegan help you back to the others," said Machias, refocusing the conversation.

Lalia immediately narrowed her yellow eyes. "I came here to fight. Trust me, we're going to need all the help we can get. Their army is one for the ages."

"What are our chances?" Mollyockett asked. She pulled on a clump of grass and began tearing them apart. "Are they that formidable?"

Lalia hesitated. Her front left claw dug deep into the dirt, exposing a giant earthworm. She extended a single claw, pierced its body and then quickly swallowed it. "The number of Slaughter Makers is roughly ninety from what I could count. They've been well trained and will pounce at the slightest provocation. It's the powers of Nukpana, however, that we need to be concerned with."

"And the house?" Fletcher asked.

Lalia quickly looked towards the four lemurs innocently jumping on a large rock. "The condition of 42 Sangar Drive is irrelevant now."

Fletcher didn't press her any further.

"Nukpana's powers, tell us about them," said Mollyockett, sounding suddenly irritated. The immense loss was settling in. To get through the sadness and anger, she had to focus on the moment.

Machias quickly brought Lalia up to speed on Von Piddle's interpretation of the events to take place.

"We'll need to meet them head on," Mollyockett said flatly. "Right in the middle of Sixth Day. If Von Piddle is—"

Pidianiski gasped. "That's wide open. They'll slaughter us all"

Mollyockett noticed Merrimack flying high over their heads. Intently, she watched him soar in patterns only she could understand. "We need to move now," said Mollyockett. "Merrimack has just signaled that they've arrived at Sixth Day and are planning on moving this way if they find nothing. I'm stunned they were able to make it so fast. Completely stunned."

Fletcher stood and shielded his eyes searching for Merrimack. "We now all know that Sixth Day is the only place we can defeat them. Let's not let them leave."

"So it's on," blared Machias. In one swift motion he grabbed the wicker basket holding *Whole Abounds,* the staff, and Vilcanota's patera. "Let's go. For Whole and for Squire Susup," he called out.

They all stood up and quickly followed Machias' towards the ridge and Sixth Day.

After a while, they heard the distant sound of pounding drums and came to an immediate stop. Pidianiski, Mollyockett, and Machias immediately recognized the sounds of war. As they slowly approached Sixth Day, everyone heard the ancient Native American war cries. Mollyockett stopped and listened intently while again watching Merrimack high over their heads.

Machias bent down and spoke some unrecognizable words to the four lemurs. In a flash, they were off.

"I'd like the patera back if you don't mind," said Fletcher.

"Of course," said Machias. "You know it better than anyone."

He quickly handed Vilcanota's patera to Fletcher. "Okay, here's what we've got to do if we're to lure them into the circular indentation," he whispered urgently. "We need to work together and follow Mollyockett's instructions that are relayed to her by Merrimack."

Fletcher listened intently, briefly thinking back to his encounter with Tomhegan when he'd rescued his mother several years ago. A sense of *déjà vu* flooded his mind. It was Merrimack who turned the tide, enabling him to overpower Tomhegan. He looked up at the small speck soaring high over the army of Slaughter Makers and the Wabanaki Confederation. Mollyockett had consumed beta-carotene while in her garden to greatly improve her eyesight before leaving. She could make out every feather and spot on Merrimack. He was now soaring so high, even Lalia with her tremendous cat eyesight could no longer see him.

"They've spotted Hooey, Sebago, Monhegan, and Casco," Mollyockett called softly. "They're sending a dozen or so Slaughter Makers to investigate."

"That's our cue," she said smoothly. "Let's go."

"It's wide open out there!" Pidianiski protested quietly. "We don't stand a chance." Silently, she was thinking of Squire Susup.

Mollyockett estimated they were roughly two hundred yards from the front line of Slaughter Makers. She kept her eyes peeled on every move Merrimack was making. "If you have a better plan, I'm all ears," she responded coldly. Her eyes were fixated on Merrimack and her mind on her son.

Machias nodded towards Pidianiski and then stepped in line with Mollyockett. In solidarity, Fletcher and Lalia quickly joined them as did Pidianiski. Lalia turned her head and aimed her pointed feline ears in the direction of the massive field that made up Sixth Day. She listened intently to a conversation taking place between Tomhegan, Nukpana, and Tygorge. She raised her right paw indicating for everyone to remain still.

"They're about to head this way," she called.

Mollyockett nodded. "Merrimack is indicating the same thing," she said.

"Let's just meet them here instead of the open field," Fletcher offered up. "It may be to our advantage." He turned the patera knowingly in his left hand, causing protein to flow throughout his body and into his muscles.

Without a word Mollyockett advanced towards the enemy. "If Von Piddle knows what he's talking about, we need to lure them into the middle of Sixth Day, not away," she said.

"I agree," whispered Machias as he followed her.

A violent squeal broke the tension as Hooey was attacked by a

Slaughter Maker. The shriek was deafening even from their location, even reverberating off Entreat Point that soared high over the action.

Fletcher took off running behind Machias, his heart pounding in his chest. They moved out of the woods and onto the path at the edge of Sixth Day.

They'd been spotted.

The left flank of Slaughter Makers reared up angrily at the sight of Fletcher, Machias, and Pidianiski. Mollyockett, Onion, and Lalia crept to the right while still in the thick forest. They were trying to outflank the Slaughter Maker army in an attempt to outmaneuver them.

Machias' heart sank as Hooey's cries for help subsided.

Surprisingly, it was Fletcher who first stepped onto the battlefield.

Nukpana's eyes blazed with hatred at the sight of the McKenzie boy. Fletcher rubbed the etchings representing the amino acids of proteins on the stone in his pocket a second time for additional strength. He then rubbed the etching representing omega-3 oil, prompting his muscles to balloon to the point where tiny tears in his plaid shirt appeared.

Three Slaughter Makers growled and howled in delight as they charged him with their antlers pointed low to the ground. For a brief second, he thought of the boar that was decimated behind the root cellar.

"Not this time!" he yelled as two more Slaughter Makers appeared from behind the first row.

Fletcher jumped up just as the first Slaughter Maker attempted to spike his body with its pointed antlers. With everything the patera had given him, his mind and body felt weirdly disconnected now. He reacted without consciously thinking. The beast fell forward and towards two large trees directly behind Fletcher and in front of Machias and Pidianiski.

Pidianiski immediately jumped around the tree and drove her knife directly into the right temple of the vicious creature. The beast howled angrily before crashing forward into a granite boulder with a thud.

Fletcher quickly jumped backwards.

"Nice job, Fletch!" Machias yelled as he too stepped onto the field.

None of them moved. They were waiting for the expected onslaught of five Slaughter Makers who had stopped advancing at the sight of their downed comrade.

"Offensive!" yelled Pidianiski as she ran forward directly at the five beasts who were all panting uncontrollably.

In an instant, they were on her. Fletcher spun around and picked up a handful of rocks. Without hesitation, he quickly threw them at the pack of animals. Each one hit directly in the center of their block shaped skulls. The sound of crushing bone reminding him of the boar that was quickly and violently dismantled behind the root cellar.

Fully taking advantage of the stunned Slaughter Makers, Pidianiski backflipped over one of the monster's horn racks and delivered a fatal blow with her long knife. The beast howled in agony.

Machias moved towards the left and crouched behind a large boulder on the edge of the forest. His focused on the circular stone indentation that was so important to both sides. He opened his wicker basket and removed a large slingshot from a protective cloth pocket. Breathing hard, he stood up and focused on the center of the large antlers on the next line of Slaughter Makers that were advancing on Fletcher and Pidianiski. "Die, you filthy beast!" he yelled as he released a large rock from his sling. The animal roared then rose up. It flailed its long limbs and razor-like claws before crashing forward.

Pidianiski delivered the final blow with her knife, once again, to be totally sure.

They continued this distract and attack numerous times with a new line of Slaughter Makers immediately stepping forward after the others fell at the hands of Machias, Fletcher, and Pidianiski. Machias expertly shot at skull after skull with direct hits every time.

One animal, however, crashed directly onto Fletcher after being hit by Machias' stone. Pidianiski, once again, delivered a mortal stab before pulling Fletcher out from under the Slaughter Maker.

Nukpana had seen enough. More than half of their army now lay lifeless on the ground next to the forest. With no time to spare as the next line of killer beasts advanced, he yelled out commands only recognizable to the Slaughter Makers. The cluster of animals immediately broke rank in the center, charging outwards with Nukpana and Tygorge.

Merrimack, watching from high above, changed his flight path and began to soar in circular patterns. Mollyockett now knew what to expect..

A flash of light and fiery explosion catapulted Fletcher, Machias, and Pidianiski backwards and into the edge of the forest.

A large broken branch pierced Fletcher's lower back, pinning him against the trunk of the massive tree. Winded and unable to move, he looked towards the others for any help they could give.

"That must be what Lalia was talking about," said Machias as he tugged Fletcher off the bloody branch. Immediately, he applied an ointment given to him by Mollyockett for this very purpose.

Pidianiski whirled around, wiped off her knife on her deerskin dress, and ducked behind a tree, the image of retreating Slaughter Makers happily etched in her mind.

Machias turned and caught a glimpse of Mollyockett and Lalia directly behind Nukpana and his diminished army. In an absolute rage, he raised his staff and aimed it at two animals who were in full retreat. A second brilliant flash and loud boom emanated from the staff, and the Slaughter Makers instantly dissolved for everyone to see.

Nukpana, completely enraged, threw another lightning bolt directly at Machias, knocking him unconscious. The flash of light was so severe a plume of flame and smoke enveloped several trees, alighting them.

Fletcher and Pidianiski lay winded on the ground. They could only watch as the entire army lurched out of the stone crater and towards them.

It was the moment Mollyockett and Lalia had been waiting for. Unnoticed, they devised a plan for Lalia and Onion to move into the center of the stone crater now that it was vacant. Von Piddle's plan was in play.

Lalia immediately left her position beside Mollyockett and pounced into the stone crater. In her right paw, she gripped Susup's staff tightly. The circular bowl, which was larger than she had expected, had a perfectly round dark stone in its very center.

"Lodestone, just as Alek had predicted," she whispered, scraping the black stone with her two front paws as a test.

Mollyockett quickly moved into position and instructed Onion to bark loudly. The ruse worked perfectly.

Just as Nukpana, Tomhegan, Tygorge, and a new front line of Slaughter Makers were about to attack Fletcher, Machias, and Pidianiski, Onion's loud barking caught the immediate attention of Nukpana. Lalia raised her paws, claws extended, opened her mouth, and yowled as loud as she could in unison with Onion.

Nukpana and Tygorge, looking like deranged madmen, turned in the opposite direction of their attack.

Nukpana hit Onion with his staff as he slid down into the stone bowl, leading a new and more frantic charge. But it was too late. With the help of Casco, Lalia clasped the staff with her sharp claws and quickly inserted its bottom into a small indentation in the very center of the loadstone. A trickle of smoke and fire gently rose out of the rock just as the entire army cascaded over the lip of the bowl and towards Lalia.

Mollyockett felt herself move involuntarily as the ground shook. Von Piddle was absolutely correct.

Distracted by the sudden movement of earth, Lalia and Onion managed to escape the lodestone just as the bottom of the bowl burst opened in a fiery explosion.

That is when it hit Mollyockett. The stone bowl she'd been visiting for years was actually the top of an ancient active volcano. She was flabbergasted that the lost Quechuan tribe was intelligent enough to engineer such a masterful wonder. *They did plan for this,* she thought to herself as Onion and Lalia joined her to watch the finale. Merrimack continued to fly in circles around the volcanic disruption, making sure no one or nothing escaped the fiery inferno, which was growing larger by the second.

The Slaughter Makers howled and screeched in horrific pain as they were roasted alive on the blazing hot stone. Tomhegan, Nukpana, Tygorge, and the others were instantly incinerated as the lodestone collapsed into itself and fell into the boiling magma below with a heavy splash. Large globs of billowing magma shot upwards high into the sky. Three massive lightening bolts hit the crater's rim in rapid succession. The eruption was exceptionally large and created its own weather system.

After the massive explosion and collapsing stone, a quiet calm reigned throughout Sixth Day as everyone slowly comprehended that it was over much quicker than they ever expected.

Mollyockett, Onion, and Lalia carefully walked around the lip of the volcano and towards the others. In the distance, Casco, Monhegan, and Sebago leaped triumphantly towards Machias.

Fletcher and Mollyockett stood side by side watching a river of lava spill over the banks of the fiery volcano and towards the forest as the others headed back. They had no idea how long the event would last and didn't care. They had a garden full of individuals that needed to go home. Whole would heal itself; it always did.

CHAPTER 17

A TRIBUTE TO SUSUP AND HOOEY

THE JOURNEY BACK TO THE DESTROYED ROOT CELLAR HAD BEEN FAR easier than expected. After the battle at Sixth Day, they all enjoyed a huge meal in Mollyockett's garden. Mollyockett and Von Piddle studied Kozart's writings that hadn't yet been deciphered by Pidianiski. Apparently, the past protectors of the northern passage had been just as diligent as their southern cousins. Anticipating that there was a possibility that individuals with no power of the passage might be able to travel to Whole during troubled times, they left very specific instructions for exactly how to return. Once the feast was complete, Machias took *Whole Abounds* and the staff and placed them on a flat rock at the very top of the waterfall Mollyockett had admired for years. Immediately after moving these items into place on the rock, the water flow stopped and exposed a huge tunnel directly underneath. The trip was quick and uneventful, just as Lucille had wished. Lalia had warned them beforehand of the condition of the house so there were no surprises there.

Woodrow, Von Piddle, Fletcher, and Fletcher's parents and grandparents all stood in front of the new home which had been rebuilt exactly like the one that had been destroyed in the *horrific gas explosion*. The story they told everyone about being away on a last minute vacation in the mountains of Arizona was somewhat believable. The beloved family was known to be adventurous. Everyone was thrilled beyond description that they were all alive. They feigned ignorance regarding the poor soul found in the rubble of their home. Nevertheless, Aldous diligently lead the effort to make sure this *stranger* had a proper burial. The gravesite selected was *randomly* fifty feet from Mollyockett's final resting place. Lucille admired her front porch and the exact replica Adirondack chairs. They'd invited Von Piddle and Woodrow over for a house-warming dinner and some private conversation.

The town, county, and state were slowly recovering from the unexplained disasters that had caused the deaths of so many respected and loved individuals. A state inquiry commissioned by the governor of the State of Maine came up empty handed even though the frightful incidents were beyond coincidental.

"Here, let me show you this," said a delighted Aldous as he walked towards Muriel's rebuilt rose garden. In the very center a gray canvas covering something roughly four feet high.

"Gather round, you'll love this," a jubilant yet reserved Muriel said as she slowly pulled the canvas off a sculpture of a top hat with three feathers poking out of its top. Beside it stood a smiling lemur that had both paws on one feather as if ready to cause a ruckus.

Fletcher closed his eyes and thought back to the first time he met Squire Susup. It was during a packed Mollyockett Day festival years ago. Never would he have imagined that Susup would eventually give his life to save his family.

Slowly, he stepped forward and lovingly rubbed the top of the sculpture. Lucille wiped her eyes then tightly held her grandson's hand with the brown spot. She too remembered that exact day and regretted how severe she had been to the Squire during their first conversation.

A much smaller replica of the statute has been commissioned by Aldous and Woodrow. Fletcher would take it with him on his next trip to Whole and present it to Mollyockett and Machias.

Muriel grasped Fletcher's and Aldous' hands and tugged them towards the new kitchen. "Let's eat," she said, "Mollyockett helped Lucille quickly create a new cookbook that included recipes based on all that was good in Whole with ingredients that could be obtained on earth.

Everyone laughed as Von Piddle picked up the pace. "That reminds me of the time I was in Seville. It was the most wonderful meal."

ABOUT THE BOOK

THIS BOOK IS ONE OF MAGIC. IN 2015, GARY SAVAGE BEGAN TO VOLUN-teer weekly at Farwell Elementary School in Lewiston, Maine as part of the Library's Author Studies Program. The central topic of the weekly elective for grades third through sixth was *Fletcher McKenzie and the Passage to Whole*. Soon, the sequel, *Fletcher McKenzie and the Curse of Snow Falls* was added to the curriculum. Roughly eighty students participated every Thursday. In addition to reading *Fletcher McKenzie and the Passage to Whole* as a class, participants would compete in essay writing, skits involving characters in the book, artwork competition, and a year end presentation during an all-school assembly. Additionally, every year, four students were selected to win the prestigious Barbara Bush Author Studies Award for excellence in the program. In 2018 and 2019, United States Senator Susan Collins announced the winners of this award in front of an all-school assembly that included parents and press. Every

year, dozens of residents and local business leaders volunteered to judge the year end competition and mentor students throughout the year.

In 2018, as part of the library's year end competition, sixteen small groups of students vied for L.L. Bean certificates by creating a major character for this very book. As a result, Lalia and her cat, Humeante, were born. You'll find a brief appearance of both in *Fletcher McKenzie and the Passage to Whole*. They are both pivotal characters in the quest to protect Whole and the McKenzie family. Miriam LeMay, Wyatt Tarr, Rebecca Jacques, Audrey Bilodeau, and Annora Johnson were members of the winning group. They have all since graduated from Farwell Elementary School.

In the photo above, students are traveling throughout Western Maine as they retrace the lives of nonfictional characters and locations that are central to both books. Characters and places that include: Locations important to Mollyockett, Hannibal Hamlin's residence and museum (Abraham Lincoln's first vice president), Snow Falls, Mollyockett's grave in Andover, Maine, and The Bethel Historical Society.

The entire Author Studies Program changed dramatically in March of 2020. As a result of the Covid19 pandemic, the school was forced to close and all classes went virtual. The year end competition and annual field trip were canceled as well as all weekly meetings in the school's library.

After much deliberation, the school's Librarian, Kathy Martin, made the decision to continue Author Studies online with Gary Savage and a few volunteers. The original manuscript for *Fletcher McKenzie and the Passage to Whole* became the new assignment. The task was to convert the original manuscript into the year 2020 and make the pandemic a central theme.

Each week, seven students were assigned two chapters of the manuscript and vied for monetary awards by rewriting entire sections of the manuscript with Covid19 and the pandemic in mind. It was a gargantuan task and took seven months to ready the re-edited manuscript for the publisher. *Fletcher McKenzie and the Passage to Whole* is a journey throughout Maine and the fantastic world of Whole. These revisions made by elementary school students give readers exactly what they crave

— excitement, vivid characters, fantastic journeys, historical lessons, healthy eating and nutrition, Covid19 exhaustion, magical experiences, deadly suspense, grave danger, and closure.

We truly hope you enjoy these student inspired books.

Gary Savage, Author. Gary is the author of several health and fitness books as well as *Fletcher McKenzie and the Passage to Whole*. He is a graduate of Dean College and Boston College. He holds a doctorate from Suffolk University. In 2019, Gary was voted *Best Artist* in Portland. He resides in Portland, Maine.

Kathy Martin, Librarian. Ms. Martin has been the Librarian at Farwell Elementary School for fifteen years. She, with the assistance of Gary Savage, has given the Author Study Program solid footing since 2015. At Farwell, Ms. Martin is best known for her wacky stories, silly voices, and fun-filled library. Most students consider the library program their favorite subject. She is very proud of every student who has participated in the Author Study Program and is elated with the many lessons they experience. Kathy is an avid reader and is definitely the captain of our ship.

Carol A. "Grammie" Christopoulo, lead volunteer and mentor. Carol is a retired elementary school teacher. In 2013, she joined the Senior Corps "Penquis Foster Grandparent Program," and became a volunteer at Farwell Elementary School. During her time as a volunteer, she met Gary Savage and has been a vital part of the Author Studies Program. She is thrilled by the growth she has witnessed with every student in the program.

Annora Johnson, Contributing Author. Lalia's cat, Humeante, is a touching tribute to Annora's cat, Smokey, which passed away in 2015. *Humeante* is Spanish for *Smokey*. A perfect tribute. Currently, she is a sophomore at Lewiston High School. She has participated in dance class since kindergarten and is now dancing contemporary, jazz and tap. She is also enrolled in Teble Choir and Latin classes. Active in Girl Scouts, she enjoys hanging out with her friends, reading, and watching movies. Stephen King is her favorite author and Mac and cheese is her favorite food.

Rebecca Jacques, Contributing Author. Rebecca is now in the 10th grade at Lewiston High School. While creating Lalia and Humeante, her focus was on creating the type of character that she "would have respected" as a child. Rebecca has a cat named Linda and loves music.

Wyatt Tarr, Contributing Author. Wyatt has been homeschooled since kindergarten. He enjoys reading and being creative. Music is his true passion. Wyatt spends the majority of his time studying music. He plays drums, bass, acoustic and electric guitars, as well as piano. He also enjoys creating videos with his friends for their YouTube channel, Fast Discomfort. It was while Wyatt was taking itinerant classes such as gym, music, and library at his neighborhood public school when he met Ms. Martin in the library. Soon, he was heavily involved in the Author Studies Program. He is excited to read the new book and discover how his characters, Lalia and Humeante, have evolved.

Audrey Bilodeau, Contributing Author. Audrey is currently a sophomore at Lewiston High School. She has three sisters and three guinea pigs. She is a cheerleader, participates in soccer, and plays the guitar. She is "is very active" and enjoys baking at home.